Wayfarer

Janalyn Voigt

WayFarer

The author is represented by and this book is published in association with the literary agency of WordServe Literary Group, Ltd., www.wordserveliterary.com.

Contact Information: titleadmin@pelicanbookgroup.com

Cover Art by Nicola Martinez

Harbourlight Books, a division of Pelican Ventures, LLC
www.pelicanbookgroup.com PO Box 1738 *Aztec, NM * 87410

Harbourlight Books sail and mast logo is a trademark of Pelican Ventures, LLC

Publishing History
First Harbourlight Edition, 2013
Paperback Edition ISBN 978-1-61116-292-9
Electronic Edition ISBN 978-1-61116-291-2
Published in the United States of America

Dedication

To the memory of my father, Carl Thomas Weise.

Praise for DawnSinger

Janalyn Voigt is a fresh voice in the realm of fantasy. Her writing is crisp, her verbs muscular, and it's all wrapped up in a lyrical style. Blending action and romance, DawnSinger is a journey through fear, failure, and faith, and I look forward to its sequel. Eric Wilson, NY Times bestselling author of Valley of Bones and One Step Away

In DawnSinger, Janalyn Voigt has penned a novel full of surprises. With adventure, mystery, and an unlikely romance, this beautiful, epic fantasy debut will leave you scrambling for the next book in the trilogy. Jill Williamson, Christy Award-winning author of By Darkness Hid

DawnSinger is a delightful fantasy spun with bardic prose and threaded with danger and intrigue. Linda Windsor, author of Healer, Thief and Rebel, Brides of Alba Historical Trilogy

Janalyn Voigt builds an exciting world, tranquil on the surface but filled with danger, ancient enemies, and a prophecy yet to be fulfilled. DawnSinger leads you into a land only imagined in dreams. I can't wait to read the second book in the Tales of Faeraven trilogy. Lisa Grace, bestselling author of the Angel in the Shadows series.

Acknowledgements

Nicola Martinez, Harbourlight Editor-in-Chief, has given me the rare gift of caring about me as a person first and an author second. Nicola also perfectly captured the mood of my writing in her stunning cover designs. I am grateful for the patience and wisdom of Lisa McCaskill, Fay Lamb, and the other Pelican Book Group editors who assisted with this book. My critique partners at Northwest Christian Writers Association also deserve a mention. *WayFarer* is a better story because of you.

Lisa Dawn, and now Pamela S. Thibodeaux, continue to back up my marketing efforts.

Barbara Scott and Greg Johnson of Wordserve Literary stepped in to help negotiate my contract just when I most needed help. Thanks for making life easier for a new novelist.

My husband, John Voigt, and my children have selflessly supported me as a writer in more ways than I can name. I so appreciate and return their respect.

I rely upon the High One's guidance and inspiration when writing and must here express my thanks to Him.

A glossary is located in the back of book.
Author's Website
http://fantasy-worlds.janalynvoigt.com

DawnSinger: Book One
Synopsis

Kai, personal guardian of the dying lof raelein (high queen) of Faeraven, delivers a summons to Shae of Whellein, a princess he is sworn to protect. Shae believes herself his sister, but Kai knows that she is only bound to him by secrets. At Torindan, high hold of Faeraven, Shae discovers her true identity as Lof Raelein Maeven's daughter and her calling as DawnSinger of prophecy. Her mother kept her hidden to protect her from an unknown contender who took her father's life. Maeven asks Shae to sing the ceremonial death song at her funeral. After Shae agrees to do so, she learns such an honor belongs by tradition to Freaer, first musician of Torindan. Freaer both fascinates and frightens Shae because of the intense emotions he arouses in her.

Shae experiences the almost-physical touch of a dark soul. A second, gentler soul touches hers as well. She keeps these encounters and the unexpected visions that visit her quiet, unable to explain to others what she herself doesn't understand.

Maeven's health improves, and she seems ready to recover when she is poisoned by Shae's servant, Chaeldra. Shae also drank the same poison that took Maeven's life, but she survives because of the knowledge of a tracker, Dorann. Chaeldra has disappeared.

Kai, second son of the royal house of Whellein and voluntary servant to Maeven, must choose whom he will serve after her death. He can pledge his service to Maeven's son, Elcon, or in the absence of his missing older brother, rule and reign in Whellein. Despite pressure from his parents to come home, Kai makes the difficult choice to pledge fealty to Elcon.

Freaer and three shraens (kings) who break alliance with Faeraven challenge Elcon for the throne at his coronation. Freaer states that Maeven gave him claim to Shae in exchange for the right to sing her death song. When Elcon rejects his words, Freaer and his followers attack and attempt to kidnap Shae. Kai defends Elcon and falls to the sword. Shae cries out to the High One and is able to tap an inner source of light that flares out to lash Freaer. Shae's kidnappers drop her and flee. Freaer and the three shraens escape.

The DayStar appears in the sky, a sign that the time of prophecy has come. Before it completes its arc of the sky, Shae must travel to the Well of Light and sing a song that will release the DawnKing into Elderland to save it. When Shae asks what song to sing, no one can tell her. Elcon directs Kai to protect Shae on her quest. Wingabeasts (winged horses) carry Shae, Kai, and a small band of protectors through twisting canyon lands where they dodge giant raptors. Large, spidery waevens almost defeat them at a ruined stronghold. In the ruins of Pilaer, an ancient place of defeat for their people, they face their own dark regrets. Goblin—like garns attack them in a dark forest. In a lost wasteland, privation and hardship test them. Through these trials, the company of protectors dwindles.

Kai's love for Shae changes in nature, and her growing attachment to him creates conflict for them both. Shae rejects her feelings for Kai until they become separated in the Lost Plains and she believes him dead. Grieving and alone, Shae enters the Cavern of Death in a desperate bid to fulfill prophecy, if it is not too late.

When her lamp burns out, what seems at first the specter of Kai approaches. After a sweet reunion in which they declare their love, Kai's spirit sword, Whyst, lights the way to the ancient stairway that winds upward through the rotting heart of the Cavern of Death.

When Kai loses his footing and drops Whyst, Shae has to go on without him, for there is no time to spare and she is able to see by an inner light. At the top of the crumbling stairway, a natural bridge spans the chasm known as the Well of Light. But the bridge terminates at a blank wall of stone rather than at the Gate of Life she expects.

Freaer rides a giant raptor to enter through a breach in the mountain. He tempts Shae to escape with him but can't approach her while she stands on the bridge because he fears the flames of virtue burning in the chasm. The Gate of Life appears in the rock wall at the end of the bridge. A youth waits within. He identifies himself as the DawnKing and calls for her to come through the gate so that he can enter Elderland in her place. Freaer warns Shae that if she does so, she will never return. Shae wavers, but then cries of the perishing within Elderland carry to her from the Well, and she knows, at last, the song she must sing.

Shae sings her own death song as she steps through the Gate of Life, changing places with the DawnKing. The gateway closes, shutting Shae behind it. As it carries on the wind throughout Elderland, the DawnSinger's song brings healings.

Emmerich, the youth who calls himself the DawnKing, accompanies Kai and the band of protectors back to Torindan.

RAVENS WITH NAMES OF SHRAENS AND RAELEINS

Whellein—Shraen Eberhardt and Raelein Aeleanor
Chaeradon—Shraen Ferran and Raelein Annora
Tallyrand—Shraen Garreth and (raelein not named)
Glindenn—Shraen Veraedel and (raelein not named)
Morgorad—Shraen Lenhardt and (raelein not named)
Braeth—Shraen Raemwold and Raelein Reyanna (last shraen and raelein of Braeth)
Daeramor—Shraen Lammert (raelein not named)
Merboth—Shraen Aelfred and Raelein Ilse
Graelinn—Shraen Enric and Raelein Katera
Selfred—Shraen Taelerat and (raelein not named)
Rivenn—High Hold, Lof Shraen Elcon

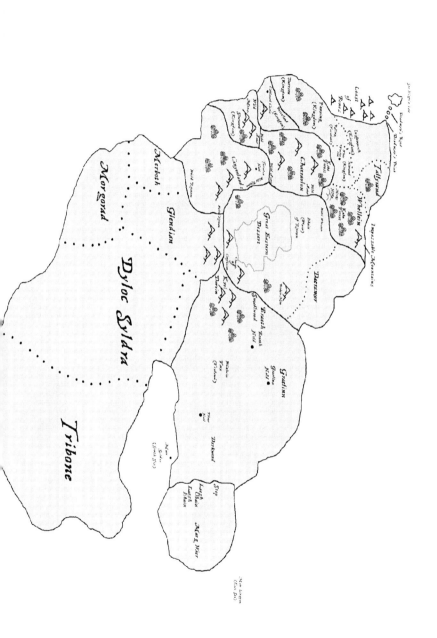

Part One: The Bridegroom

1

Return to Torindan

An indrawn breath alerted Kai. Unsheathing his sword, he peered into the shadows beneath a weilo tree's curling tresses.

Nothing stirred.

"Show yourself!" His challenge rang through the vale.

No response.

He stepped closer.

Kai. His name sighed in a sudden wind that ruffled the waters of the weild. Morning mists eddied above the river, but the leafy canopy over his head remained still and silent.

Impossible! And yet he knew that voice. "Shae?" With his heart beating in his throat, he pressed forward.

Beneath the weilo a many-hued light shimmered, swirled, and took shape. Shae stood before him, her eyes closed as if in prayer. Her unbound hair cascaded in burnished curls to her waist. Beneath her scarlet cloak, she clutched something at the end of the fine chain encircling her neck. The glint of silverstone between her fingers told him she wore his locket. She opened her eyes and smiled at him. "Kai."

But he backed away. "Are you some dryad come to enchant me?"

"Please." She held out her hands imploringly. "Stay."

"Why should I trust you?"

"You have nothing to fear. It's me—Shae."

He shook his head. "I saw you vanish from this world. Do you return by another gateway than *Gilead Riann*?"

"Gilead Riann is the only Gate of Life, but there are soft places like this one where I can look into Elderland, if only for a time. When I saw you near, I called to you over and over."

Even as a spark of hope flared, he hesitated. "I heard your voice once only, borne on the wind."

She clasped her arms about herself and smiled, although tears glistened in her eyes. "And yet you answered my call."

"I love you, Shae."

"No. Release yourself." Her voice broke on the whispered words.

The longing to take her into his arms left him weak. "You ask more than I can give."

"I can't bear to see you suffer."

"Then you must not look."

Shae's image shimmered like a reflection in wind-stirred waters. "I release you."

"Wait!" As he rushed toward her, she dissolved into glimmering light that melted into shadow…

Jerking heavy lids open, Kai blinked against the weak light tilting through swishing weilo leaves. His dream had seemed so real. A moan sprang to his lips but died behind gritted teeth. Short, swift breaths relieved the tightness in his chest. His mind, however, knew no ease.

He turned his head and met a pair of dark, rounded Elder eyes. He let his lids close to shield himself from their penetrating gaze.

"Kai."

Emmerich's murmur called him back from the edge of thought. He rolled onto his side and pushed to a sitting position. His companions, their shapes little more than shadows in the gathering mists of morning, bent over their bedrolls. Behind them the canyon walls of Doreinn Ravein rose into obscurity.

At the expression of pity on Emmerich's face, Kai balled his hands into fists and rode out a surge of heat. Shae might stand beside him now, but for Emmerich.

As soon as the unworthy thought came, he pushed it away and forced his hands to unclench. Shae had willingly traded places with Emmerich at Gilead Riann. She'd sung her own death song by choice. And he, to his joy and sorrow, had urged her on.

He glanced sideways at Emmerich. "Sometimes, when the wind blows, I think I hear her calling."

Emmerich's eyes gleamed. "Perhaps she does."

Kai waited until he could trust himself to speak again. "She comes to me in the land of dreams."

Emmerich tilted his head, and a lock of dark hair fell across his brow. "Does she speak to you?"

Without answering, Kai bent and rolled up his bedding.

Emmerich waited.

Kai sighed and looked away. "She tells me to wait for her no more."

"I see. And will you heed her?"

He dusted off his hands, lingering over the task, and then glanced sideways at Emmerich. "At odd moments I expect to see her, to hear her voice. I can't stop hoping for a sight of her—looking for her return." The words wrenched from him in a rush. "I can't release myself from loving her. I don't know how."

"Patience does not spring from sorrow with ease."

All at once, Kai laughed. "You have both wisdom *and* youth—a fearsome combination."

"Those with ready ears often hear wisdom, even from a youth."

৵৵৵

"Steady, Fletch." Kai touched the neck of the winged horse beneath him and looked out over the frothing weild, which fell to rapids here. Sudden memory caught at him. He could almost see Shae combing her hair on the flat-topped rock at water's edge.

At a restive movement from the other wingabeasts, Fletch shuddered in sympathy. Kai turned away from the wraith of memory and gathered his wits before facing his companions. "Thank you for your faithful service. Each of you went beyond duty. Although we–" He heaved a breath. "Although we return without Shae, our quest succeeded. In that we can give thanks to Lof Yuel, the High One, who has kept us in His care."

He signaled Fletch, and wings rose to enfold him like a feathered curtain. As the great wings lowered and they lifted on invisible currents to the top of the canyon walls, draughts rippled across him. At this height the mists thinned but would still hide their movements from any stragglers from Freaer's forces retreating from the siege of Torindan.

How would Lof Shraen Elcon, Faeraven's new high king, react when Kai returned without Shae? He put the thought from him and focused, instead, on navigating the twists and turns of the canyons. They emerged into a flat land as the horizon blushed and the shadows lengthened to stain the eastern desert purple.

The ground folded and rose beneath them, and then crested a rise. In the distance, past the broken peak of Maeg Streihcan, swelled the hills that Kai's people, the Kindren, called Maegren Syld. The Elder nation knew them as the Hills of Mist. To the west, the kaba forest stretched to meet sandy shores where the tides of Maer Ibris ebbed and flowed.

Torindan, fortress of Rivenn, perched on an arm of rock thrusting into Weild Aenor, the wild river of legend. Kai caught his breath at the sight. How long ago it seemed since they had left.

❧◦❦

Raena Arillia stepped toward Elcon in the dance, jewels and eyes aglitter. Her figure had softened since he'd seen her last, and the luster of her golden hair echoed the glow of her skin. He captured her by the hand and waist and turned her toward him. When she smiled at him, he forgot everything but her beauty.

He clapped his hands in tempo, and Arillia swayed in a circle that brought her back to him. Dainty, light on her feet, and quick to smile, she reminded him of Shae.

Shae.

Elcon's hands stilled, and his smile died. He'd tried and failed to reach his sister with the shil shael, the hereditary soul touch they shared. He could only hope she still lived.

Arillia's smile faltered. "Are you well?"

Without replying, he offered his arm to her. She took it without hesitation, and he guided her out of the crush of dancers toward the leaping fire in the nearest of the great hall's three large hearths.

Arillia's parents smiled down upon them from the dais at the end of the long chamber. Shraen Ferran and Raelein Annora had conspired with Elcon's mother to thrust Arillia and Elcon into one another's company all of their lives. No formal marriage pact existed, but he and Arillia knew they were expected to wed. As children, they'd laughed at the notion many times.

With a tug on his arm, Arillia brought him up short. "What ails you?" Such trusting eyes she turned on him, eyes of palest gray. She knew him well, but he thought she did not guess he used her company as a balm. In her presence, he found ease for the worries that tormented his rest.

Her gaze probed his, but he glanced away, out the tall window behind her to the fieldstone paths that cut through the lush sward to the inner garden.

Ah, the garden. They'd often whiled away entire afternoons gathering the roses that nodded beneath twisting strongwood branches. Side by side, they'd dropped bright petals into the silken waters of the pool and watched the water cascade in glinting ribbons from the tiered fountain.

Elcon pushed away his memories and looked

down into Arillia's troubled face. "Naught but shadows."

Her expression registered her disbelief, but he offered nothing more. For Shae's safety, he couldn't claim her as his sister. And how could he explain to Arillia the feeling of doom that weighted him?

And yet, when he looked into the cool depths of her eyes, he could almost persuade himself she understood. The thought should draw him to her, but it only made him uneasy. Perhaps he and Arillia shouldn't spend so much time together.

"As you please, Elcon." Irritation edged her voice. "It's clear you mean to keep your thoughts private." Arillia stepped closer to the fire and gazed into its depths as silence stretched between them. "But I still wish—"

Elcon took her by the elbow. "Forgive me. I must return you to your parents."

Her eyes widened, but as he pushed her through the crowd toward the dais, she didn't resist. His perfunctory bow to her parents included Arillia. He caught the glint of tears trembling on her lashes and hesitated, but then hurried across the great hall. Arillia, and all the confusing emotions surrounding her, would have to wait.

By the time he reached the main archway, Weilton, the second guardian of Rivenn, had joined him. In Kai's absence, Weilton had assumed his duties as Elcon's personal guard. Elcon answered the question in Weilton's light gray eyes. "I saw from the window a company of wingabeasts approaching from the south. Kai and Shae return."

இ௸

Kai sent Flecht into a spiral and touched down beside his companions on the arched bridge outside Torindan's barbican. Although they could have flown into Torindan, protocol and good sense called for the guardians to land their wingabeasts outside all strongholds, even their own, and obtain entrance in the usual manner.

"Who goes there?" A guard called from the parapet above the barbican.

"Kai of Whellein and a company of weary travelers, all friends of Torindan."

With a rasp and screech of metal, the drawbridge lowered over the moat's dark waters and the barbican's timbered metal doors swung open.

As they passed beneath the iron fangs of the portcullis, Aerlic drew his silver wingabeast, Argalent, abreast of Kai. Just behind, Emmerich rode Ruescht while Guaron and Dorann brought up the rear. They had barely passed through when the doors thudded shut and the bar clanged back into its rests. Chains clanked, and the portcullis dropped with a squeal and a thump, sealing them into the treacherous "walls of death."

Fletch's hooves clattered on the wooden floorboards and rang when they found trapdoors above pits. As Kai guided his wingabeast onward, bars of light penetrating through arrow slits in the outer walls fell over him. With much clanking and screeching, a second portcullis gave way, and they emerged before the inner gatehouse.

Kai, blinking in the sudden light, answered another round of salutations. A small drawbridge lowered across a second channel of the moat. More doors opened, and they passed beneath twin turrets into a short corridor.

Footsteps, light and fleet, approached from the outer bailey. With his eyes adjusting again to dimness, Kai halted Fletch and his companions gathered around him. Two figures entered by the archway from the outer bailey. "Kai. You return."

Kai's vision cleared, but he'd already recognized Elcon's voice.

One of the guardroom doors along the corridor flung open and Craelin, First Guardian of Rivenn, stepped out, the lines around his eyes crinkling from the force of his smile. Beside him strode Eathnor, dressed in the green and gold of the high guard.

Kai dismounted and bowed before Elcon. "I've returned, but without Shae."

"Rise."

Kai obeyed.

Elcon looked him over. "You're too thin, and I'll warrant, weary. You look like a strong wind would knock you over. Still, I'm glad to see you. Has Shae stayed behind with her sister in Graelinn?"

Kai swallowed his surprise at Elcon's response. "Forgive me, but I should explain in private."

"Tell me where she is."

Kai flinched. "She remains within the gateway of Gilead Riann."

Elcon's eyes narrowed. "What madness is this?"

"Only the truth, I promise. Shae went through the gateway of her own will."

"Why would she do such a thing?"

"So that Shraen Brael could enter Elderland."

"The DawnKing of prophecy has entered Elderland? But *where* is Shae?"

Craelin stepped forward. "If I may suggest, whatever news Kai brings might better be given in private, Lof Shraen."

Elcon opened his mouth as if to speak but closed it again. "Yes. Yes, of course." His glance slid past Kai and landed on Emmerich, just dismounting. "Tell me, Kai, why you ride with this Elder. Has he strayed from his path so far it brings him among the Kindren?"

Emmerich lifted his head. "I know well my path, Elcon, Shraen of Rivenn, Lof Shraen of Faeraven. I follow it to you."

"I don't understand."

"That is the simple truth."

Elcon paced before Emmerich, his gaze a challenge. "Who are you?"

Emmerich stood without flinching. "Are you certain you wish to know?"

Elcon stared at him, but then looked to Kai. "Bring him to my meeting chamber, and we'll discuss these matters at length." At the archway to the outer bailey, Elcon shot a final piercing glance at Emmerich. "I look forward to that conversation."

Elcon went through the archway with Weilton behind him. In the small silence that followed his departure, Kai drew his hands into fists at his side. After all they had suffered and sacrificed, would Elcon now reject Emmerich?

"Are you all well?" Craelin said near Kai's ear.

Kai considered the question. "Well enough. We sustained injuries besides the ones you knew, but most have healed. Some take longer than others." *And some never heal.* "How did you and Eathnor fare on your return to Torindan?"

A smile lit Craelin's face. "Well enough, also. We

reached Torindan in advance of Freaer's charge and just managed to take away a small group of messengers. We rode like the wind to summon the loyal Shraens of Faeraven but had to dodge welke riders to save our own lives."

"Ah." An image of dark riders pursuing through the mists of morning came to Kai. "We had a bit of trouble with them ourselves."

"If not for Eathnor's skill as a tracker we would not have survived to spread the alert."

Kai nodded to Eathnor. "Well done. And so you have joined the ranks of the guardians. I commend Craelin's choice in you."

Eathnor clasped Kai's hand. "Thank you. I hope to prove myself worthy of the company I keep."

Dorann dismounted in one leap, and the two brothers gazed upon one another with eyes that shone. At last, Eathnor dipped his head. "You've healed."

Dorann put a hand to his once-blackened eye as a slow smile spread across his face. "In truth, I'd forgotten it." He took in the garb his brother now wore as part of the lof stapp. "Green suits you."

Eathnor laughed. "That it does."

With Eathnor beside him, Dorann led his dark gray wingabeast, Sharten, through the archway into the outer bailey, where the stables lay.

"Welcome back."

At Craelin's greeting, Kai smiled for the first time since entering Torindan. But he also felt like weeping. "Thank you. I'm glad to see you."

The bright blue eyes nested more deeply in Craelin's face. "And I, you."

Kai cleared his throat. "We should hurry, although I dread facing Elcon again." With slumped shoulders, he led Fletch after the others into the outer bailey, where smoke hung heavy and the stench of charred meat fouled the air. Dogs snarled and yipped, fighting over a bit of offal thrown to them. A scarred wooden door hung open in a doorway, through which emitted the clash and clang of cooking.

With Craelin keeping pace beside him, Kai took the side path to the stables, which squatted across the sward from the kitchens. Waiting for a groomsman at the stable door, he breathed in the heavy scent of hay. Thudding hooves, soft whickerings, and calming voices drifted to him. A lump formed in his throat. He'd forgotten what it meant to come home.

Craelin touched his arm. "Give it time, Kai. None but a fool would think you gave less than your all for Elcon or Shae."

Kai wanted to shout that his all hadn't been enough. He'd failed Shae, and he had failed Elcon.

2

Reunion

"You're weary, Lof Shraen. Come and rest by the fire." The steward of Rivenn, in a blue-cushioned chair which contrasted with his russet surcoat, waited in Elcon's outer chamber.

Elcon frowned. He'd not summoned Benisch.

The steward arose, the chair creaking beneath his girth, and executed a bow.

Elcon inclined his head to acknowledge the belated gesture and then took a stance before the flames in the hearth. He would deal with Benisch later. Other matters occupied his mind at present. As dried pitch ignited, the burning logs snapped and sizzled. Heat radiated to him. He held out his hands as if he might wrest life itself from the fire. His focus shifted inward and, instead of the flames before him, he saw the rounded eyes of the Elder youth, looking as if they saw all Elcon was and would ever be.

Standing turned to pacing. Elcon started when he came across Benisch, still waiting where he'd made his bow. In truth, he'd forgotten the steward's presence. "Did you need something?" he rapped out.

"I?" Benisch gave a small smile and coughed. "Not I, but perhaps *you* might do with something to eat or drink?"

"I want nothing." He paced to the fire and clasped his hands behind him as he watched its flames claw the air. "But if I do Anders can tend me."

"Perhaps—" Benisch hesitated with delicacy. "Perhaps a listening ear?"

"What?" He looked away from the flames. "No. Benisch, I thank you, but really I don't see—"

"I received word of a strange Elder brought to Torindan by Kai."

Benisch's quick knowledge of the affairs within Torindan had served Elcon on more than one occasion, but now it irritated. He raised his brows. "Do you intend to gossip, then?"

Benisch sniffed. "I overheard another speak of it."

Elcon repressed a smile. "I've a mind to leave you wondering as penance for eavesdropping, but it won't hurt for you to know. Yes, Kai brings an Elder upon his return from…an errand." Benisch opened his mouth to speak again, but Elcon forestalled him with a raised hand. "I know little more than you do at present."

"This comes at an awkward time." As Benisch moved closer, he clicked and jingled.

Diverted, Elcon angled a look at Benisch's feet. The toes of his slippers curled upward, each ending in a tiny golden bell.

Benisch cleared his throat. "Your youth does not benefit you, Lof Shraen. You should be more circumspect. You have yet to secure Faeraven, and allowing an Elder within Torindan's gates will bring ill favor in some quarters."

"I'll not let the thoughts of others guide me." His words, meant to ring with boldness, sounded plaintive even in Elcon's own ears.

"Better their thoughts than their armies." Having delivered himself of this verdict, Benisch said no more, but stood with hands clasped docilely before him. The jewels in his many rings flashed in the light of the chamber's torches, already lit against the growing darkness. "Shall I have a footbath brought to ease you?"

Elcon would have laughed at Benisch's puppyish expression if his eagerness to please hadn't been such an irritant. "Thank you, no." He waved his hand in dismissal. "Really, Benisch, I need nothing but privacy now. Pray, consider your duties for the day at an end."

Benisch looked as though he would argue but instead nodded and swept from the room.

Alone save for his servant Anders, who would remain discreetly closeted unless summoned, Elcon sat in the chair Benisch had vacated and let his fingers curl against the smooth wood of the armrests. Leaning his head back, he released a long sigh.

An image flashed behind his closed lids.

He opened his eyes to stare at the vaulted and gilded ceiling. Why did the face of the Elder youth haunt him?

He pushed aside an uneasy emotion he refused to name and set his thoughts instead on Shae. Why had she not returned? Surely Kai would have kept her from harm. After all, Kai had known and loved Shae long before Elcon had even learned his sister lived. He pushed off the arms of the chair to rise. Odd that resting his body only meant he exhausted himself in thought, whereas movement wearied his body but eased his mind. He strode to the side door connecting to the servant chambers, summoned Anders, and ordered food and drink for those who would soon arrive in his meeting chamber.

Kai came first, and as he entered, Elcon noted the sadness that mantled him. Whatever had happened on the journey did not sit well. Kai met his glance, but his own slid away. He seemed distracted, little able to give attention to even simple matters.

Elcon indicated the benches before the fire. "Make yourself comfortable. The others have not yet arrived."

Kai obeyed, seating himself on one of the benches, but his posture remained stiff.

Elcon's conscience smote him at the harsh words he'd spoken earlier. He took a steadying breath, raked a hand through his hair, and then joined Kai on the bench. "Tell me about Shae."

Kai spread his hands. "She's gone. She went through Gilead Riann to allow the DawnKing to enter Elderland."

Elcon shifted forward on the bench. "You said as much earlier, but I don't understand. Where is this DawnKing?"

"You've already spoken with him."

Elcon's brows shot up, and his eyes widened. "*Not…*surely not—"

Kai nodded. "I speak of Emmerich, the Elder who rode with us. He is Shraen Brael, the DawnKing we seek."

Elcon found his feet. "It's not possible! Must the Kindren look to a youth—and one of the Elder nation, at that, for deliverance?"

"I know it's hard to acknowledge. I can barely credit it myself, yet I saw Emmerich waiting within the gateway of Gilead Riann with my own eyes."

"I'm not sure I believe this, but I'll agree to listen to all you say this night." Elcon seated himself again and crossed his arms. "But first, has harm come to Shae?"

"I don't believe she suffers, although we all did in reaching the Caverns of Caerric Daeft. Misfortune reduced our number until only two of us, Dorann and myself, remained to guard Shae. Welkes attacked us in Laesh Ebain, and we became separated.

"I found and helped her, at least for a time. Dorann followed also, at great sacrifice, and came upon me lost in the cavern without a lamp. Shae went on alone, for time grew short, and she could see by an inner light.

"Dorann and I found Shae standing on the natural bridge that spans Lohen Keil, the Well of Light below Gilead Riann. Freaer tried to lure her away, but Emmerich called from within the gateway. Shae wavered, but in the end, sang the death song as she crossed into Lohen Keil and changed places with Emmerich. He stepped out as she went in."

"She sang the Mael Lido? Why?"

Kai's long eyes gleamed. "To ensure her own safe passage to Shaenn Raven. When she passed through Gilead Riann, Shae gave her life with all her heart. The gateway closed after she entered. Emmerich tells me she wants for nothing in the land beyond, and I—I somehow know she's well. I grieve for her, but I'm certain that, if she had it to do again, Shae would make the same choice."

"I hope she has no cause for regret."

"Her song carried far and wide and brought healing to many."

A tap came at the door. Aerlic and Emmerich entered together, followed by Craelin, Eathnor, and Dorann.

Craelin made his bow, echoed at once by his companions. "Guaron remains behind with the wingabeasts but will join us after they settle in."

Elcon inclined his head. "Let's go through to my meeting chamber. Sit you down at my table. I've ordered food and drink." He spoke to Craelin but could not prevent his gaze from straying to Emmerich. Freshly washed, the Elder youth looked even younger than he had upon first acquaintance. He must be no more than fourteen summers.

They ranged around the massive slab of strongwood set on sturdy trestles that dominated the center of his meeting chamber. Elcon took his place in the elaborate carven chair at the table's head. Silence reigned for a time as they examined one another.

Anders appeared at the door and admitted servants bearing steaming platters piled high with meats and tubers, fruit pastries, and chilled tankards of cider. Elcon plucked an apple from a passing tray, biting into its crisp, cool flesh and letting its sweetness soothe his tongue. "Tell me everything that happened after I left you."

Kai carried the weight of the narrative, with others chiming in various details although Dorann spoke little. The story unfolded for Elcon in bits and pieces. The small band had navigated the canyons of Doreinn Ravein to spend a harrowing night at Paiad Burein. They'd resisted the terrible beauty of the Smallwood of Syllid Mueric only to meet peril in the ruins of Braeth.

Kai frowned as he described the rush to carry Guaron, near death from the bite of a waeven, to Graelinn Hold. "He lived, but Praectal Caedric gave no hope for a full recovery."

A tap came at the door, and Guaron slipped into

the room. He straightened from his bow and looked from one to the other, his brows lifted. Elcon sat forward. "I thought no cure existed for a waeven's bite, and yet you seem well."

"I am well."

Elcon leaned forward to catch the murmured reply.

"Speak up." Craelin commanded. "None can hear you."

Guaron hesitated, but then stood taller. His voice rang with conviction. "I am well because the DawnSinger's song healed me."

Elcon cradled his forehead between steepled fingers. "Tales come to me, tales of sightless eyes opened and of hearing restored." He dropped his hands and looked to Craelin, who nodded. Elcon turned to Emmerich, seated between Dorann and Aerlic. "What do you know of this?"

"Shae, like Kunrat before her, sang a song of sacrifice to fulfill prophecy."

"How do you, an Elder, know Kindren prophecy?"

Emmerich gave no response.

"Why do you keep silence?" Elcon heard the rising note in his own voice and cautioned himself, for he did not care to show this Elder his consternation.

"What can I speak that you will hear?"

The words struck Elcon like a blow. His head came up. "Do you presume to know my heart?"

The Elder looked at him with piercing eyes.

Elcon stirred himself. "Don't deceive yourself that I'll accept a youth, and an Elder, as Savior. Speak the truth. How came you to Gilead Riann in the place of Shraen Brael?"

Emmerich bowed his head.

Elcon jumped to his feet. "Your silence condemns you! Craelin, place him under guard in one of the suites above the gatehouse."

"Lof Shraen—"

"*Take him away!*"

Craelin hesitated, but at Elcon's look, moved to comply.

With a look of nobility, Emmerich rose, and Craelin stopped short. He motioned with his head to Eathnor, and the scrape of the tracker's chair came loud. Silence mantled them all as Emmerich was escorted from the chamber.

Elcon waited for them to go before seating himself again. He clasped his fingers together and heaved a breath. "Now, then. Continue." Blank faces stared back at him, but he prompted them again. "What happened when you left Graelinn Hold?"

அ~ஓ

Kai entered the allerstaed through its central archway, his footsteps ringing across gleaming strongwood floors. Stained glass windows set in high arches glowed like jewels in a setting of gold. He reached the golden railing at the foot of the altar and there knelt. It seemed a lifetime ago since he'd bent his knee here with Shae and Elcon. He touched his forehead to the cool metal of the railing as his vision blurred.

If another gateway into Elderland could open to release Shae, it would be here in the allerstaed. If love could call her forth, she would come to him. Although tears fell to bathe his hands, he could only summon the memory of the girl he'd found weeping here, so long ago, at the foot of the altar.

He spoke aloud. "Lof Yuel, help me bear this pain, for an arrow lodged within my chest to bleed away my strength could not wound more."

Kai raised a hand to dash the tears away, for they did not ease him. He could not afford to linger in sorrow, regardless. He had slipped away from his regular duties for a time only. He waited in prayer and silence, understanding all at once why Shae loved the place of prayer. A gentle touch, Lof Yuel's caress, felt but not seen, soothed him. He lifted his head and let the breeze that found him dry his tears.

Footfalls carried in the silence, following the invisible current into the chamber. Elcon stepped through the main archway and into the allerstaed. Kai rose and gave his bow.

Elcon inclined his head in greeting. "I didn't think to find you here, but I'm glad of it now. Will you stay beside me while I pray?"

"I will. Why do you go about unguarded?"

A rueful expression flitted over Elcon's face. "I'm afraid I slipped away from Weilton."

"Shae often freed herself thus from the restraints of others."

Elcon returned Kai's smile. "We are siblings."

"And both of you were delivered into my care." Kai frowned. "I can do no more now for Shae, but I should this day relieve Weilton from duty to you."

"I mean to let you rest first, Kai. You are weary and laden with sorrow."

Kai averted his eyes. "It comforts me to pray."

Elcon measured Kai with a look. "You do not ask why I seek the allerstaed."

"You will tell me if you wish."

"I've come to pray, too. It occurs to me...I ask myself.... Have I done the right thing in confining Emmerich?" Elcon reached out, and his fingers circled the prayer railing. "I reacted rashly, perhaps."

Kai waited for Elcon to speak again.

"Things have changed with the Elder nation. It's no longer easy to know friend from foe. "I must keep the Alliance of Faeraven safe."

Kai joined Elcon at the railing. "I would lay my life down to help you do so, Lof Shraen." He drew breath and considered his next words with care. "But I doubt success will come if we spurn prophecy."

Elcon bore the force of Kai's words. "Do you really think he is Shraen Brael?"

"I do."

Elcon released the prayer rail to pace before the altar, picking up speed and volume as he went. "But it makes no sense. Why send an Elder to the Kindren? And would Lof Yuel give a mere youth the responsibility to guide many?" He halted before Kai. "Well?"

Kai lifted an eyebrow. "Has not the High One given a mere youth the wisdom to rule Faeraven?"

Elcon's eyes widened, and he clutched the prayer railing again. "I wonder, Kai. Sometimes I wonder about that." He knelt and bent his head.

Kai watched Elcon for a time, and then joined him at the railing. His mind clamored, but Kai shuttered his thoughts and listened. Echoes of voices, long stilled, reverberated through time to reach him, a line of rhythm *here* and a snatch of melody *there*, as of the pulse of life beating. He caught a shadow of movement. Shae came to him, then, for he heard her

step, felt her phantom touch. He stood with Elcon and
left her there at the altar.

3

Courtship

Aewen plucked another handful of plaintain leaves from beside the stream and let them slide from her palm into her satchel. She would make a poultice to draw the poisons from young Caedmon's wound. A bird trilled from a broadberry bush as wind touched Aewen's face and fingered her hair. Its icy breath lingered in the shadows, despite the midday heat penetrating the forest.

She gathered another handful of leaves and paused when a fat, shiny fish slithered by in the stream, parting the water with its back in shallow places. She smiled. Perth would like a chance at the fish, she knew, but other duties engaged her oldest brother. Perth and Conn, the next oldest, journeyed this day to Lancert to trade a matched pair of high-stepping Anusians for a fine destrier Conn had his eye on. He would train hard through the winter in preparation for Darksea's spring tournament. Rumor already spread far and wide that the winner of the jousting competition might ask for the hand of Vanora, daughter of Devlon, King of Darksea.

Aewen picked her way across the stream on the backs of flat stones, but one rocked underfoot. To save herself a fall, she stepped into the swirling water. On dry ground once more, she sat on a fallen log and wrung out her skirts. When she pulled off her elk-leather shoe and tipped it over, water ran out to puddle on the muddy loam underfoot. She put her shoe back on, wincing as she walked, for it squelched.

She followed a path that traced the course of the stream before striking out for a sunlit patch. Forest shadows fell away behind her, and heat beat down on her head as the path meandered through fields cleared for grazing beasts. Here and there stumps of felled trees remained, attracting bramble vines and ivy to their rotting wood. She passed through fields where sedges and grasses with feathered seed heads tangled with dagger weeds, thistles, and wild roses. Familiar with the sting of thorns and burrs, she kept her skirts and hands away from the edges of the path. The wind picked up in the open, sweeping through to ripple the grasses in long waves.

She sighted the thatched cottage belonging to Willowa, set back from the path and half-hidden beneath a draetenn tree brought thence by Willowa's grandfather in the days when the Kindren still ventured into the Darkwood of Syllid Braechnen far away and to the east of Elderland. Draetenns did not grow in Westerland by choice, but this one seemed happy enough to drape itself over the dwelling huddled under its care.

With just time enough to check on Caedmon and apply a poultice, Aewen turned aside from the path. His mother would welcome both her company and help with the task of curtailing a lively toddler. Camryn, Willowa's huntsman husband, spent long days afield and could not often relieve her burden.

Willowa bent over a huge iron kettle in the yard,

which she stirred with a stick as clouds of steam boiled about her. She tugged at a dirty scarf from which tendrils of dark hair escaped and lifted a dirty face to call to little Caedmon, who chased a squabbling fowl. The bird ran before the child, screeching its terror. Caedmon's eyes shone with glee as his fat hands reached for the object of his desire, but he did not pursue with his usual energy.

Willowa set the stick aside and moved toward her son. *"Caed!"*

At the note of tired desperation in Willowa's voice, Aewen quickened her pace. Willowa snatched up her son, clucking at him. Aewen reached the pot and picked up the stick. Willowa nodded to her. "Careful there. Don't get spattered. I'm rendering fat."

Aewen stirred the pale, bubbling liquid. "How fares Caedmon?"

Willowa gave a weak smile and kissed the top of her son's head. "Well enough, as you see, although his burns trouble him at night. Poor child. I can't forget his screams when he fell at the edge of the fire. "

"I'm glad I was gathering herbs nearby."

"Thank you for cleansing his wounds. It was more than I could bear."

Aewen pushed away the memory of the young child writhing in agony. "He seems better today. I've a new poultice to make for him."

Willowa offered the child to Aewen. He held tight to his mother but when he looked into Aewen's face gave a happy chirp. Chubby arms encircled her neck and a soft cheek pressed hers. The boy's weight shifted, and she pressed a hand into the soft curls at his nape. Starting for the cottage, she left Willowa to tend her duties at the rendering pot in peace.

Aewen blinked in the dark interior of the cottage and paused to let her eyes adjust. She untangled Caedmon's fingers from the long, dark curls which escaped her plait, wincing as he tore out several strands. She set him on his feet, prepared to chase after him while she made the poultice, but Caedmon propped against the wooden bench at the small trestle table and watched her. She unwrapped the bandages and discovered his wounds looked worse. Small wonder he fretted at night. She cleaned his burns and applied the poultice and fresh bandages, persisting despite his horrific cries.

Willowa looked in. "Is all well?"

"I've just finished. I can go and stir while you comfort him."

She released Caedmon, and he ran to his mother's arms. Aewen walked into the yard and took up the stick again, drawing comfort from the simple task before her. She smiled at the sudden mental image of herself—Aewen, Princess of Westerland—standing in wet skirts with hair unkempt while stirring a kettle of fat in a cottage yard. Over time, in the course of ministering to the poor, she'd been called upon to do many such tasks.

Thoughts of home reminded Aewen of duty. Already the sun had descended halfway to the horizon, and she had a fair distance to walk before reaching home. She didn't fear the forest by day, but night brought predators down from the hills. The dagger sheathed at her waist would not serve against a shaycat or bruin. Besides, she'd be missed at table if she did not return in time. Her parents allowed her to comfort the poor, just so long as she did nothing to draw attention to her activities.

When she ducked into the cottage to say goodbye, she found Caedmon asleep in his mother's arms. Willowa laid him in a hand-hewn cradle and followed her outside.

"Thank you for your help."

Aewen gestured toward the cottage. "It's well he sleeps."

"He seems...less than himself since the accident."

"Let him rest as much as he will. I'll check back tomorrow, if I may." Aewen set her feet once more on the path. She backtracked through field and forest, and at the fork, took the turning for Cobbleford. The path slanted upward and narrowed, going through a stand of kabas that creaked and swayed in a growing wind. The scent of water hung heavy in the air. No doubt a storm would buffet the landscape in the night, if not sooner. A feeling of unease followed her, and she wished she hadn't lingered at Willowa's.

At last she reached the bridge over the Cobble River, but she slid on its slick planks and clutched the handrail to stop herself from falling. Below her the river churned and spewed foam. Lightning flared across the sky, thunder boomed, and rain drove into her face. Panting a little, she proceeded with more caution across the bridge and stepped with relief onto the long bar of rounded rocks from which Cobbleford derived its name.

The garrison had not yet secured the gatehouse against the night. She shouted to the watchguard, ran through the open gates, and followed the covered corridor that skirted the bailey to slam into the keep through a side door. She leaned against it, blinking as her eyes adjusted. She'd made it home before dark, although with little time to spare.

Aewen stepped from the puddle of water forming at her feet and crept to the side stairway, her shoes squelching across the dressed ironstone of the floor. As she made her way up the stair she met no one, which was just as well in her present state. The door to her outer chamber gave beneath her hand, swinging inward with such rapidity she almost fell.

"I see the storm caught you."

She recovered her balance and peered up at her mother.

Inydde, Queen of Westerland, clad in a garment of blue silk and with her black hair dressed and gleaming, held an expression of bemused exasperation.

Aewen sighed. "It did."

Inydde frowned at her. "Come then and change before you catch your death of cold. I have news for you, but I'll wait until your maid tends you to give it."

She swept past her mother and into the outer chamber where Murial awaited her, drying cloths in hand. Her maid, long familiar with Aewen's comings and goings, never met her unprepared.

Murial handed her the cloths and bent to the hearth where flames embraced a steaming iron kettle. Her knees creaked, and she groaned a little as she lifted the heavy kettle and filled a brass ewer. The sideways look she gave Aewen would normally have held a twinkle, but today her wrinkled face could not be more somber. Aewen followed into her inner chamber without further delay.

Her servant made her presentable and Aewen returned to her outer chamber, more dry than wet now and much improved. Inydde waited for her in the outer chamber, having moved to the white-and-gilt bench nearest the fire. Aewen joined her, moving close to the fire's warmth. Inydde patted the cushion embroidered in colorful silk flowers. Aewen sat, perching on the cushion's edge with her back straight, and waited for her mother to speak.

Inydde smiled. "You look quite another matter now. If I did not know you as the same drowned waif who entered your door, I'd not credit it."

Aewen lifted the corners of her lips in what she hoped passed for a smile.

Inydde took a breath. "You are beautiful, daughter, and of an age to marry."

Aewen fastened her gaze on the sapphire brooch pinned to her mother's bodice. How the gemstones gleamed and threw back the firelight.

"As you know, King Devlon of Darksea honors us with his presence. He and his son, Prince Raefe, come to us on a *special errand*."

The silence stretched so long Aewen wrenched her gaze from the brooch and looked instead at the sapphire of her mother's eyes.

The hint of a smile curved Inydde's lips. "King Devlon has asked for your hand in marriage on behalf of his son, Raefe."

Aewen could not have spoken even if she had summoned the wit. She stared at the hands twined together in her lap. Her knuckles showed white.

"Your father has accepted on your behalf. You will wed after the harvest feast, but before winter when transportation of guests would bring difficulties."

"I—but that is so soon."

Inydde stood. "True enough. We'll need to hurry our preparations, but we'll make them just the same. Come to table now and meet your bridegroom."

Air sucked out of the room. Aewen made a small

sound and put out a hand to catch hold of anything that would prevent her from sliding into the pit of darkness rising to claim her.

⤞⥀

"Aewen, awaken." The whisper came out of the darkness, sounding, in its nearness, somehow louder than the ragings of the storm outside the castle.

She pulled upright and put a hand to her head. "Wh—what?"

"It's me, Caerla." A gentle push guided her back into her pillow. "Lie still. You've had a shock, and no wonder. How do you feel?"

Aewen's brows drew together, but then realization dawned. She must have fainted. Memory returned in full then, and she sat up again. "Caerla! Such news Mother brought me."

"I heard."

Why did her sister speak in so flat a voice? "I can scarce take it in. It all happened so fast. *I must think.* At least I've escaped meeting him for tonight."

"I'm cold. Move over."

She obliged Caerla and felt the depression as the feather-filled tick took her sister's weight. Caerla's cold body pressed against her side, stealing her warmth so that they both shivered. She didn't really mind. They would warm again soon enough. Caerla would forsake her own bed this night to curl beside her, as she had done since childhood.

She closed her eyes to sleep again but curiosity drove her to speak. "Have you met him?"

"Prince Raefe? He's dark and brawny and handsome with eyes of deep blue—all a maiden could want."

"Then you are not glum on my account."

Silence stretched between them until Caerla spoke at last, although her tone sounded a little strange. "I wish I were to marry instead, that's all."

"We both wish that, but you can't marry before me, more's the pity. I'm the oldest daughter."

"You don't need to remind me."

She sighed. "Why snap at me? What have I done?"

Caerla rolled onto her side. "I'm sorry, Aewen."

"You'll have a husband of your own soon enough, Caerla." But Aewen spoke without conviction. With her skin eruptions, frizzing brown hair, and wide-set eyes so pale as to seem colorless, Caerla did not inspire ballads of love in her honor. In fact, she had no admirers.

A small hiccup gave way to Caerla's silent weeping. Aewen longed to comfort her although she knew nothing would ease Caerla's pain, so she offered the only comfort she could by pretending not to hear her tears of humiliation. In truth, her own tears waited to fall. She should not give way to emotion, though, for she needed her wits about her.

She could tell from Caerla's even breathing that her sister had fallen asleep. Aewen tried to follow her example, but slumber eluded her. The howling of the storm echoed her dark reflections. Being told she would marry was one thing. Actually doing so was another. She did not care whether Prince Raefe was the handsomest and worthiest of men. She doubted he, or any other man she might wed, would allow her to continue in service to the poor. Therefore, she could not ever marry. Wavery light leaked into the chamber before Aewen found refuge in sleep.

But not before she'd formed a plan.

⮞⧫⮜

Aewen pushed the wooden side door to and latched it with as much stealth as she could manage. She wanted no company. The garden's fresh-washed heather and roses beckoned. She could not wander its paths now but moved with purpose toward the square herb beds at the rear of the chapel. Here, from long experience, she knew Brother Robb could be found every morning. She only hoped he'd not abandoned his home in favor of a steaming mug in Cobbleford's kitchens. But, no. She came around the corner of the chapel and saw his brown-robed figure bent over a patch of parsley. Heaving a sigh, she closed the gap between them, her feet sinking into the fresh straw scattered across the paths.

Brother Robb straightened at her approach and a beatific smile wreathed his face above the fold of fat at his neck. "Good morn."

She stopped before him and nodded in greeting, breathing in the sweet pungency of damp straw and moist earth. Making an effort, she returned his smile, but her own faltered. She launched into words, unable to bear the speaking of pleasantries. "I have much to discuss with you." She hadn't meant to jerk out her words like that.

Brother Robb's smile fled, replaced by a look of concern. He set down his hoe and dusted off his hands. "What troubles you, child? Although, perhaps I know."

At the kindness in his tone tears stood in her eyes. She had grown up at Brother Robb's knee, tottering about the garden behind him as a child. He'd been tall and thin then, with a full head of nut-brown hair, not bald and comfortably rounded as now. In all that time, she had never seen a hint of any harshness in his manner except when the deer dined too freely upon his garden.

"Have you heard, then?" *Do all know?* Aewen could not fathom such a loss of privacy. She had spent too long doing nothing worthy of notice.

Brother Robb's arm came about her shoulders, warm against the chill that penetrated her cloak. "*Whhst* then, child. You'll make yourself ill. Such news carries, whether you will it or not. Now tell me why you seek me."

Aewen's hands found one another and twisted together. "I wish to take a vow of celibacy—to devote myself to the church."

Brother Robb's eyes widened, their blue clear as a summer sky. "Have you taken leave of your senses?"

"It's law. A maid may take a vow of celibacy in order to dedicate her life to the service of others." He shook his head before she even finished speaking. Clutching the arm he withdrew, she raised her voice. "I wish to give my life in service to the poor."

Brother Robb lifted his hands as if in surrender. "You speak without thought. Such vows belong to those destined not to marry. You are young and comely and full of life, a rose ready for the picking."

"Roses wilt and die the sooner when plucked."

"Give it a chance, child. I cannot encourage you to dishonor the word your father has already given."

Aewen eased her clasped hands and massaged the little circles in her palms her fingernails had dug. Tears rolled down her face. "I thought you would help me—

that you cared about my happiness."

His arm went around her shoulders once more. "I do, but we have different ideas of what will bring your happiness."

"You know how giving alms to the needy and watching over the children gladdens me."

"Just as it will bring you joy to watch over your own children. Trust those in authority to guide you, Aewen." He shrugged. "I cannot give what you ask. I will not sanction your taking such a vow."

She dashed her tears away and tore herself from his embrace. "You could if you would. You pretend to know my heart better than I do. You think by refusing me this I will marry as my father has rashly committed me. But I won't. It would have been easier with your help, that's all."

"Aewen—"

"There's nothing more to discuss." She backed away as fresh tears fell.

He called after her, but she fled to wander beneath the green forest canopy until nightfall. She emerged then from the shadows and crept around the dark hulk of the chapel and into Cobbleford Castle through the side door.

Torches burned in their brackets at intervals along corridor and stair. Light pooled beneath the torches but did not penetrate the darkness between. Aewen climbed the stairs, moving freely across the lighted stretches but slowing to feel her way where darkness found her. At the top floor her chambers waited. The sound of weeping bristled the hair on the back of her neck. Cobbleford had its share of specter stories, but upon entering her outer chamber, she learned this sound came from among the living.

4

Rejection

Elcon swept into his outer chamber, unsurprised to find Benisch admitting him. Without greeting his steward, he continued into his inner chamber, where he cast off his robes. Anders emerged from his own chamber and gathered Elcon's discarded garments from the chair where he'd flung them. At the tinkle of bells, the servant lifted his head and widened his eyes. Elcon paused while removing the circlet of Rivenn, but then set the circlet on a side table for Craelin to return to the strongroom. He didn't have to look to know Benisch had followed him into his inner chamber. He kept his voice quiet. "What do you want with me here?"

"I came to see if there is anything I can do for you." Benisch spoke after a small pause.

Elcon shook his head and faced Benisch, who hesitated near the door. "Anders sees to my needs. It's not your place."

Benisch recoiled as if wounded. "I thought only to see to your comfort, Lof Shraen."

"There's no need, as you can see. I'm well-tended. Now, if there's nothing else..." He suspended his sentence, hoping Benisch would take the hint.

"Wait!" Benisch pressed forward into the chamber.

Elcon raised his eyebrows.

"I wonder...I wonder if I might have a word with you, Lof Shraen, in private?"

Elcon sighed. He needed to take Benisch to task but weariness dogged him now. "Very well, come into the outer chamber and you may speak that which weights your mind." He slipped through the door behind Benisch, seated himself on a bench angled before the hearth, and then sent his steward what he hoped was a quelling look. "If you are long-winded, I do not promise to attend."

Benisch, when he had arranged himself on the bench opposite Elcon's, tilted his head to one side. "Have you decided what you will do with the Elder boy?"

"I don't know at this point."

Benisch sent him a sage look out of watery gray eyes. "Tongues wag in Torindan—throughout Faeraven, for that matter. I deal with the merchants who travel between the ravens. I hear things."

Elcon eyed him, repelled by his gossip but drawn to make the inquiry that Benisch must await. "What do you hear?"

"There are those who question your authority to sit upon the throne of Rivenn and to wield the scepter of Faeraven. They say you are too young to carry such authority. Freaer and the three shraens who support his claim will vie again for the alliance of Faeraven. There are those who say he takes his cause to the Elder nation. And now some of those who supported you at the siege of Torindan watch and wait." Benisch drew close, and his breath rasped near Elcon's ear. "Don't misstep regarding the Elder youth."

Elcon backed away and looked into Benisch's face,

which had settled into lines of asperity. "What would you have me do? From what you say, if I do nothing I may lose supporters. But, if I charge him with treachery, I risk turning the Elder nation against me."

"I say, banish him. Take him into the mountains and leave him there."

Elcon pushed a hand through his hair. "I'll consider your words, Benisch, although I don't well regard them."

"Consider your own position, and you will make the right choice."

"That's enough." Elcon abandoned any attempt at politeness. "Leave me."

Benisch's face settled into cordiality. "Good night, Lof Shraen." He bowed. The outer chamber door thumped behind him with force.

"Latch the door behind him, Anders."

❧❦

Arillia won this time, but only just. Elcon found her waiting at the edge of the kaba trees that stretched from Rivenn through Westerland and Darksea to the shining waters of Maer Ibris. They laughed together as Elcon pulled his charger up beside her. "Vixen! You've been practicing. I'll warrant I could leave you behind every time until now."

The late summer sun, coming bold at this hour, glinted off the gold of Arillia's hair and backlit her pale skin. Elcon's laughter died. "You look stunning."

Her smile gave way to a look of desire. Their eyes locked, and he bent to place a kiss upon her cheek. He meant only to brush her skin with his lips, but she turned her head and their lips met and clung. Elcon drew back, narrowed his eyes against the sun, and took a calming breath. She looked so luminous he wondered if, to enchant him, one of the Fiann had changed places with the Arillia he knew.

She fixed her pale gray eyes upon him. "Do you remember, Elcon, how in our early days we promised to marry one another?"

He tilted his head and looked at her, trying to connect a memory to her statement, but his mind went blank. "Yes?"

Her smile faltered. "Oh, that you would forget your promise to me." Her voice changed, took on warmth. "I cherished it, you see."

"Pray remind me."

"I should let you suffer longer, but I'll not. We only agreed to wed one another because our parents wished it and to protect ourselves from other suitors."

"I remember something, now that you mention the matter."

Her gray eyes took him in. "I think it, now, not so bad an idea."

"Have you a suitor you despise?"

She chortled. "I didn't mean it that way."

"Then you have no other suitor? I shall take comfort in that knowledge, although I can scarce credit it."

"I want no other suitor, Elcon. You are quite enough."

He raised an eyebrow to let her know he did not miss her irony and he knew that she gave no direct answer. He turned his black charger upon the trail. Torindan, fortress of Rivenn and high hold of Faeraven, rose pink and graceful in the near distance. They passed through a long meadow painted in shades of gold and green. Birds sang and flitted from bush to bush or winged across the dome of sky. Beyond the meadow, southern mountains thrust up their peaks. Weild Aenor edged the meadow to the north, its sparkling waters foaming as they combed through rocks poking above the surface.

Arillia drew alongside him, demure in her gray riding garb, or, she would have been demure, did not her hair escape the edges of the feathered cap she wore. He preferred her hair unfettered, not braided and coiled as now. He knew a sudden desire to tear the cap from her hair and free it from its constraints, but he did not. Arillia had worked hard to reach adulthood, and he would not take it from her.

His brows drew together. Why had she mentioned their childish promise to marry? Did she view the prospect of marriage to him as a protection against undesirable suitors? Or did she desire him? The thought of a union with Arillia brought a queer feeling to his stomach.

Her gentle voice called him back. "Stop scowling so. What dark thoughts burden you?"

"I'm wondering who your other suitor might be."

"Perhaps I have none but only wish to make you jealous."

"Then you may congratulate yourself."

Her laugh danced in the air. "It seems I won twice this day."

~∞∽

Blue crobok wings fluttered in the stand of weilos that shimmered down the hill and bent at river's edge to wash their long tresses. The river sucked and sloshed against its banks and, further from shore, eddied into whirlpools. Kai skimmed a flat pebble across its bright surface. The stone arced once, twice, thrice before sinking.

He sighed and straightened. Although he did not blame Elcon for wanting time alone with Raena Arillia, he thought it a poor choice for the Lof Shraen to go out without a guard. Elcon would no doubt call for him upon his return, but for now Kai was free to climb the earthen path that skirted the hill, a trail no doubt made by deer. The sun beat on him as he emerged from beneath the trees, but he didn't mind it. Soon enough they would trade summer's warmth for the cold, overcast days of winter.

A crashing in the brush warned him of the stag before it appeared. As the magnificent beast leaped past him Kai had little time to sidestep. *Thwack!* The stag arrested midair and crashed to the ground below the path. Kai looked, not toward the slain deer, but uphill, one hand going to the hilt of his blade, the other to the dagger tucked into his belt. His posture relaxed. "Well, then. Good day to you."

Dorann lowered his bow and gave a nod. "I'm sorry I startled you."

"You came a bit close with that arrow."

Dorann slung his bow across his back and half-slid down the hill to draw abreast of Kai. He pulled a hunting knife that gleamed and dove into the brush below the path. "You were safe enough." Kai followed, coming upon Dorann in time to see him slash the dead beast's throat. "I suppose I'm used to lesser marksmen—excluding, of course, Aerlic."

Dorann bent to examine the motionless animal, then stood and gave Kai a grin.

"It's well I came across you. The Lof Shraen requires at his meeting table this eve all who accompanied Shae."

Dorann gave him a long look but nodded without speaking. He turned to hoist his kill upon his shoulders. The great head hung backward, its antlers branching down, and swung as Dorann started up the hill, dragging the dead beast behind him.

"Here, let me help you."

Dorann shook his head. "I'm balanced this way."

"How is it you still hunt and track while your brother serves as a guardian of Rivenn? Should I speak to Craelin on your behalf?"

"He already asked." Dorann puffed out the words. "I said no."

"You said no? Why?"

Dorann paused at the top of the hill. "Each man has his place in this world. Here's mine."

~∞~

"How did you come upon the Elder youth you brought into Torindan?"

Why did Elcon ask the same question twice? Kai, seated beside Craelin, frowned. Had Elcon not heard their answers when he first asked, or did he look for another truth?

Across the Lof Shraen's meeting table Aerlic, Eathnor, and Dorann quaffed steaming cider after a fine meal. Beside Kai, Guaron kept his own counsel. Farther down the table Benisch still attacked a roasted *crobok* leg.

Kai tried again. "Emmerich came into Elderland at Gilead Riann in place of Shae."

Elcon's green eyes lit. "You saw this?"

"I saw this."

Dorann cleared his throat. "As did I."

Elcon said nothing for a time then gave a curt nod. "I believe you."

Benisch waved the half-eaten crobok leg. "Begging your pardon, but whether or not you saw the Elder come from the gateway matters not. That's not the question t'ask at all. You want to know just *who* came through the gateway." He looked first to Elcon, and then swept a glance to all those seated. "*Who* is this Elder?"

Kai considered Benisch's question. How could he say with certainty he knew the answer? And yet he felt he did. Try as he might, he found no words to speak his heart.

Elcon lifted a tankard to his lips, his expression meditative.

Benisch eyed them. "Am I to understand none can answer my question? And yet you brought this Elder, *whoever he might be*, into Torindan and into the presence of your Lof Shraen." He shook his head in apparent amazement at such perfidy.

Elcon put his tankard down. "Thank you, Benisch. You've clarified matters."

Benisch sat back with a grunt and gave himself once more to his food. Kai averted his eyes. Although Benisch had excellent manners, he did not like watching him eat. He looked instead at Elcon and wished he could explain that accepting Emmerich as DawnKing required a knowing that started first in the heart.

5

Backlash

"Aewen." Inydde stood to her feet and held herself in stillness. "What became of you this day?"

Aewen looked from her mother's upright figure to the slumped and sobbing bundle of clothing that pulled upright. She gasped when she recognized Murial as the source of the weeping. She seemed older, the lines etched deeper into her face than when Aewen left her—had it been only this morning? Murial wrung her hands and smiled through tears. "You've returned safe, Lof Yuel be thanked."

"Be still, Murial." Inydde rapped out. "My daughter's welfare is no longer your concern. Gather your belongings and take to the road. You'll have no reference from me."

"*Mother.*"

"Silence. I'll have no protests from you, Aewen. Murial should not have allowed you to wander off as she did this morning. She's entirely too lenient with you."

Aewen's jaw dropped. Her voice, when she found it, sounded strangled. "How can you say such a thing when you, yourself, look the other way and allow me freedoms? You're embarrassed because I was not here to receive Prince Raefe. That's what this is all about, is it not?" She stomped her foot, past caution. "I'll not have Murial punished in my place."

Inydde advanced, red-faced. Catching Aewen by the hair, she drew back her arm, and her slap rang out as Aewen's cheek took fire. The blow spun Aewen backward against the open door, which crashed into the wall as she fell. She pulled to her knees and raised her arms to protect herself, but Inydde only jerked her upright by the shoulders. She gained her feet, and they faced one another, panting.

"You will not instruct your mother." Inydde paused to catch her breath. "Do you understand?"

She lowered her head. "I understand."

Inydde released her and huddled by the fire as if chilled. "Leave us," she flung at Murial, who had not yet moved.

Aewen looked to her maid with silent tears sliding down her face. She could not imagine her life without the woman who had watched over her since before she could remember. Murial gave her a tender look, straightened, and walked through the doorway to her own chamber.

Aewen spoke to the back her mother turned to her. "The fault is mine. I should not have run away today. I was upset."

Inydde stood in profile, the flames in the hearth behind her. "Brother Robb said as much."

Aewen managed to contain her surprise. She had not thought Brother Robb would go to her parents. "Did he tell you all?"

"He said you wished to take a vow of celibacy."

She put her arms around herself. To refuse her request was one thing. To tell her parents what she'd asked was another. "Well then. You know he refused me."

Inydde faced her. "You must keep your father's word, which he gave with your happiness in mind."

Aewen gave a short, bitter laugh. "And so my life is decided for me. My father, whom you remind me has my happiness in mind, did not even bother to ask me what I wanted."

"I warn you, Aewen, do not provoke me further. You will marry Raefe of Darksea."

"And if I refuse?"

Inydde's face went red again and her hands balled into fists at her sides. She took the strides that brought her close, and Aewen flinched.

"That option does not belong to you." Her mother struck only with words this time, but she delivered a harsher blow.

Murial returned from her chamber bearing a large carpet bag and a cloth bundle that looked like it contained bedding. She wore a cape, a hood of black wool, and sturdy shoes. At least she would not be cold, although Aewen could not bear the thought of her upon the road by night.

"Mother, please don't send Murial away, or at least let her go by morning."

Inydde's eyes narrowed to slits of sapphire as she looked at the old servant, who huddled in her cloak before her. "Very well, then. You can stay." She cocked an eyebrow and shot a look at Aewen. "But mind your mistress does not stray again, and that she acts with good faith toward Prince Raefe, or you'll find the road your bed."

Aewen caught her breath as Murial's gaze flew to hers.

Inydde swept toward the open door, pausing as

her hand came out to touch Aewen's face. "Bathe your face and tidy yourself, daughter. There's yet time to meet Prince Raefe at table. We'll await you."

Inydde departed, and it seemed she took the air from the chamber with her. Aewen pushed the door closed, listening for the click of the latch before she turned back to embrace Murial, who wept in her arms. She soothed her servant, although she wanted to weep herself.

∾⊱

The maiden who looked back with enormous eyes of palest blue from Aewen's mirror glass seemed to have no resemblance to herself. The skin beneath those eyes bore a faint smudge of purple—the result of sleeplessness. Her black hair, so like her mother's only served to draw attention to skin that seemed pale, drained of life, except for the red stain on her cheek. Aewen sighed and put her hand over the tender place. She could do nothing to hide the mark. With a sudden surge of anger, she drew her hand away. Let Prince Raefe and King Devlon guess the truth. It didn't matter. She would find a way to free herself yet. Murial finished dressing her hair, and Aewen turned away from the mirror. She must not involve her maid in her troubles again.

Aewen, with Murial holding a lanthorn to light her way, descended the side stairs and took the corridor that ran the length of Cobbleford Castle. An archway at its center led into the great hall. The sound of chatter reached her long before she entered the enormous vaulted room with its gilt and crystal. She blinked in the sudden light of many torches, fires, and candles. A footman came forward to offer his arm. She walked beside him toward the raised platform at the north end of the hall where her family and guests waited. She kept her pace slow, wondering how she would be able to eat anything. Her head ached and her stomach churned with nausea.

She saw him then, youthful and handsome, with eyes that sparkled. No wonder Caerla recommended him so. And yet, despite Prince Raefe's handsomeness, the lift of his head hinted of arrogance.

Her father, King Euryon of Westerland, watched her, too. Although Aewen avoided his eye, she could not detect any sign that her father knew of her rebellion. She curtsied to her parents. Inydde stood in greeting and went to her at once. She might look the picture of motherly grace to others, but Inydde dug the tips of her nails into Aewen's arm.

Raefe rose from table and came forward with his father, Devlon of Darksea, to give his bow to her. With a parting squeeze, her mother released her grip, and Aewen made her own dutiful curtsey. Her face grew warm under an inspection from deep blue eyes. "You have much of beauty about you."

She bowed her head. "Milord, I thank you."

"I hope you are now well? Your mother gave your apologies earlier—a headache, I understand."

"Thank you, I am better now."

"I'm glad to hear it. May I escort you to table?" Raefe took her arm without waiting for permission. "You will sit beside me."

Aewen looked away from her mother's hard sapphire eyes and let Raefe draw her to the table. She felt small beside him, for he stood a head above her and had breadth of shoulder besides. She smiled across to Caerla, seated on his other side. Her sister had taken pains with her appearance, but the result could not have been more unfortunate. Braiding and twining her hair about her head did tame its unruliness but also drew attention to Caerla's short neck. Her cream gown of finest silk played against the tawny color of her hair, but washed out her complexion.

Beside Caerla red-headed Perthmon, the oldest of her brothers, slanted a gleaming glance from his dark eyes at her before turning back to his conversation with King Devlon. Of them all, Perth understood her best. He would know, even if no one told him, how she felt about marrying Raefe.

Next to King Devlon sat her mother, a well-groomed miracle of composure whom Aewen could not credit as the same woman who had struck her with such passion.

Her father rested one arm about Mother as he engaged King Devlon in fervent conversation. On Father's other side, another brother, Connor, spooned pudding into his mouth with an appreciative gleam, obviously more interested in food than conversation, but then Conn was nothing if not practical. From his sturdy build to his pale blue eyes and curling brown hair, Conn took after their father.

"…and lively, would you not say?"

When Raefe's intense blue eyes pierced hers, Aewen gave a vague nod, hoping that whatever he'd said needed no contribution on her part.

"Perhaps I shall ask permission to take you there on the morrow, then. Would that please you?"

Aewen could only nod again and smile, although the enthusiasm on Raefe's face dimmed at her cautious response.

"Oh how wonderful. I love Lancert." Caerla burst out, her eyes shining.

Raefe turned to her. "You're most welcome to come along."

Lancert? Aewen's confusion cleared. Raefe planned to take her to Lancert. She could think of other places she'd rather visit. The hustle and bustle of the city did not strike a chord within her as it did Caerla, but any escape from Cobbleford after today's horrible episode came as welcome.

She gave Raefe her first genuine smile since meeting him. "My thanks."

Raefe's smile returned, full force, reaching his eyes. Of all the people she might have found herself betrothed to, he at least seemed kind. What if she did marry him? Would that be so unpalatable? She tried to put the thought from her, but it persisted.

Servants brought food and they ate a plentiful feast of boar's head, venison and wild onions, a salad of greenings, stewed plums, slurry nuts, and assorted puddings. Caerla carried the conversation, which centered on the delights to be found in Lancert. Aewen had naught to do but attend, smile, and nod at appropriate times. While the two laughed together over some joke that escaped Aewen, she could not help but wish Caerla had been the older sister who must be given in marriage first, so suited did her temperament seem to Raefe's. Her betrothed lowered his voice to speak for her alone, perhaps fearful she'd become jealous of his attention to her sister. "I love exploring places like Lancert, but in the end I'm always glad to return to Darksea."

She smiled and lifted her cup but paused before drinking. "Tell me about your home."

"It's a place of wild shores and tall trees that love the morning mists. The people of Darksea are a tough breed. We work hard and we play hard, too." Raefe gave her an intimate smile. "But I plan to do more than tell you of it, Princess. I will make it your own."

Aewen's smile faltered, and her hand shook as she lowered her cup.

"What's this?"

He saw too much. "Forgive me, Prince Raefe. I'm grateful for your intentions. I simply find them overwhelming."

"Have you not been told of our fathers' agreement?"

She recovered something of her lost composure. "I know of it, yes. But two days hence I had thought to pass my days in service to the poor." She met his gaze. "My future changed in the blink of an eye."

"I hope you will find that change agreeable."

She managed a smile. "We are of the same mind."

He answered with a robust smile. "Come then. Let us enjoy ourselves now. You may find tomorrow pleasant despite your fears." He raised his cup. "To our future."

She drank his toast, gazing at him above the rim of what seemed a cup of poison.

❧

"Move over."

Aewen recognized the voice whispering in the darkness. She shifted to allow her sister into her bed. Caerla's company came as a welcome distraction, for her thoughts kept her from sleep. Light flared behind the bed hangings, followed by another crash of thunder. Caerla, already shivering, shook also and ducked her head beneath the counterpane.

She smiled and put her arms around Caerla. "*Whhst.* You're safe. I don't blame you, though. Tonight's storm rages."

They lay still until both the storm's fury and Caerla's fears abated. "Do you think you will miss me coming to your bed at night after you marry?"

Aewen tightened her arms about her sister. "Of course, I'll miss you."

"I wish you did not marry Raefe."

"Not more so than I."

"You do not wish to marry Raefe—even having met him?"

Sudden tears threatened to choke Aewen. "I do not wish to marry him, *especially* after having met him."

Caerla stiffened in her arms. "How can you say such a terrible thing? Raefe is wonderful, and he has set himself to woo you, to see to your every need. Think of whom else he might have been—someone harsh or horrible or hideous. How can you be so ungrateful?"

"Peace, Caerla. It has nothing to do with Raefe's worthiness. I appreciate his kindness, but even if I wished to marry, I would hope for a husband I suited better."

"Why do you say you're unsuited?"

"Can you not see it for yourself? You're with us most of the time. Each day Raefe grasps life by the throat as if to wring all he can from it. Such zeal alarms me. And he desires nothing better than festivities and the company of others, whereas I seek the quietude of nature."

"You name the things I admire most about him. How can you despise him?"

Aewen bit her tongue to keep from blurting out her wish that Caerla, who thrived on Raefe's energy, might be the one to marry him. It wasn't fair to mention such an impossible idea, especially since Caerla might wish, as she did, that Aewen were not the older sister who must marry before the younger. How different these days might be had that been the case. "I don't despise Raefe, but he exhausts me. I've tried to keep up with him these past weeks, but I feel myself growing thin around the edges, as if I will fade away at any moment."

"I've noticed you seem quieter than usual."

"That's because I'm so unhappy. Sometimes in the early mornings before anyone looks for me, I slip outside the castle gates to walk along the banks of the Cobbleford and watch the mists play above the waters. Only in these moments can I revel in the small freedoms remaining to me. Marrying Raefe will deny me even those."

"But you will marry him, regardless?"

Aewen dashed the back of her hand across her eyes. Her voice came as a whisper. "I can't."

As Caerla sat up the tick shifted. "You must. How dare you think only of yourself. *What about me?* I can't marry until you do. Would you have me wilt on the vine? Don't you see I have little time left? I—I'm no beauty like you. It will take a bit of time and a little doing for me to find a husband. And yet you dally and dig in your heels as if your own desires are the only that matter." Caerla threw back the bed covers and yanked the hangings aside to stand, limned in the light leaking into the room around the wooden shutters at the window. She looked, in her fit of heightened emotion, almost beautiful.

"I'm sorry." Aewen bowed her head. When she looked up again, Caerla had gone. She turned onto her stomach and wept until her tears ran dry.

అలా

"Come in, Daughter."

Aewen stepped into her father's outer chamber. He rose from a bench cushioned in elk-leather. Stuffed fowl perched on the mantel behind him—pheasants, croboks, several wingen, and even a rare kairoc. Tapestries woven in faded wool eased the graystone walls behind the mute creatures.

Her father gestured to the footman at the door. After a pause, the latch clicked and they were alone. "Sit, Aewen. I wish to speak with you."

She sat on the bench opposite his and smoothed the blue wool of her kirtle. When she had removed every crease and wrinkle, she risked a glance at her father.

He looked at her with intensity, but then sighed and seated himself also. "Your mother wanted to speak to you, but I decided to do so myself. I'm told you plan to refuse Prince Raefe."

Caerla! No one else knew her secret thoughts. Aewen stared into the fire as the knife of her sister's betrayal twisted inside her. "I can't lie. I don't rejoice in the match."

Her father hesitated. "I can't take back my promise, Aewen. Do you plan to dishonor my word?"

"Why did you give it without inquiring into my

wishes?"

"A king does not bow his knee to his offspring, but only to God."

"And have you done that?"

His eyes widened. "Does a child instruct her father? Whether I have or not is my own concern. It is up to you to obey."

She met his blue gaze and felt her resistance crumble. She could not fight them all. "No, Father. I'll not do that. May God help me when I marry Raefe."

6

Banishment

Dawn pinked the sky with promise, and the very air seemed to hold its breath in anticipation. At the edge of the fountain, Kai trailed a hand in water of cool silk. A small trough formed and filled behind his fingers as ripples radiated outward. A shadow passed below, and a fin split the surface. A fish rolled to expose a sleek brown side before disappearing into the depths. Kai leaned back and let his gaze wander over the bronze figure of Talan astride an arching wingabeast topping the fountain at the pool's center.

He turned his head and caught sight of Elcon, who lingered beneath the twisted strongwoods. The Lof Shraen had slept little in the night. Kai knew this because he had occupied the small cot in Elcon's dressing room. In truth, he'd had little slumber himself due to the incessant pacing in the adjoining bed chamber. Something had upset Elcon. That much he knew. Only the day before, a messenger had arrived on a lathered horse, sent by Shraen Eberhardt of Whellein in the north. Elcon had closeted himself with the messenger and afterward spoke to no one.

When he at last stood before Kai, he looked him over with grave attention, and then tilted his head. "Will you sit there all the morn?"

Kai squinted at him and flashed a smile. "That depends, Lof Shraen, on your wishes."

"Come then."

When they reached his chambers, Elcon motioned Kai toward his meeting room. "Wait in here. I'll have Anders send for Craelin."

Kai took the seat he normally occupied, leaving a space for Craelin between himself and Elcon. The room was not yet lit for whatever meeting Elcon planned, and in the small fireplace the ashes looked gray and dead. Elcon joined him and they sat together as Anders lit the torches. Elcon dismissed the servant when he bent to revive the fire. "The day warms."

Kai regretted the loss of the fire. Although sunlight heated the outside world, the chill of night had not yet left this chamber. But he rubbed his hands together and said nothing.

"Kai, it occurs to me I never said thank you for all you did for Shae."

The words hit Kai in the stomach. What had he done for Shae, after all? "I left her there."

"She stayed."

Kai acknowledged the truth of Elcon's words, but his heart could not yet accept their peace.

Craelin entered with Anders behind him and glanced sideways at Kai before facing Elcon, who waved for him to sit. "Anders, leave us and shut the door." Craelin had barely seated himself when Elcon spoke again. "I've news from Shraen Garreth of Tallyrand. His spies report that Freaer denies my right to rulership of Rivenn and Faeraven and approaches King Corbin of Norwood in an attempt to curry support within the Elder nation. He claims himself as the true Lof Shraen of Faeraven." He flattened his hands on the table before him. "I don't know what to do."

"Does he really think the Elder nation will take up a fight not their own?" Craelin spoke from beside Kai.

"They may choose to ignore Freaer." Elcon voiced what could only be a hope. He frowned. "Or they may blame me for recent disturbances and wish to remove me from power."

"We must act in swiftness to counter Freaer."

Elcon eyed Craelin. "How do you suggest we do that? I'll not pick a fight where none may exist."

"Why not go on your own tour of the Elder kingdoms and dispel ill will?"

Elcon put his hands over his face, but with a sigh lowered them. "Your idea has merit, Craelin."

"Ask Shraen Brael for help." Kai spoke the words almost before he knew their presence in his mind.

"Are we back to that, then?" Elcon's tone bespoke impatience.

Kai drew air into his lungs. "He's come to help you, if you will only give him the chance."

Elcon's head came up. "You speak out of turn, Kai. I'll not grovel before an unproved Elder youth. I've already decided his fate."

❧◦❦

Garbed in blue and gold, Elcon sat in state before the three great arches framing two carven and canopied strongwood thrones. From his position behind and beside the throne Kai gazed over a crowd swelling the chamber beneath an enormous golden chandelier suspended from the vaulted ceiling. Light fell in beams through tall clerestory windows above pillars that marched down the chamber on either side. Beyond them, strongwood leaves lifted in a breath of wind.

A herald took his position before the throne platform. "Bring the prisoner."

Craelin and Dithmar came forward, Emmerich between them, but somehow it looked more as if Emmerich brought the two guardians, rather than the reverse.

Emmerich, but a slender youth with tousled dark hair, nonetheless stood with quiet dignity and a bearing that bespoke nobility. He did not speak but fixed deep brown eyes upon Elcon.

Elcon curled his fingers on the arm of the throne. "Tell me the truth of your identity, and you may find lenience."

"I am Shraen Brael, the DawnKing of prophecy."

"So, you hold to your story?"

"You asked for truth."

"What is this insolence, Lof Shraen?" The voice, which came from the forefront of the crowd, belonged to Benisch.

Elcon raised a hand to silence the roar in response from the crowd. His voice sounded thin in the sudden silence. "Very well, then. Let your presumption decide your fate. I hereby banish you. You will be taken to the border of Westerland and there released. If you ever return to Faeraven, you will be put to death on sight. Do you understand?"

Emmerich lifted his head with an expression not unlike pity on his face but gave no reply.

Elcon's voice shook. "Take him, then! I loathe the sight of him."

Craelin and Dithmar escorted Emmerich from the

presence chamber.

From beside Kai, Benisch sighed as if in contentment.

Kai's face felt chilled, and touching his cheek, he found there tears.

శితಾ

Kai woke in the night to hear Elcon pacing. He rolled over and tried to sleep once more, but nothing could drive the sound from his mind. He rolled to his feet and abandoned the warmth of the cot where he slept when he needed to watch over Elcon in the night. The door that separated the inner chamber from the dressing room gave way beneath his palms. Moonlight pooled on the floor from the tall, arched windows, for the hangings were drawn and the shutters open. Elcon entered from the outer chamber and began his circuit of the room with bowed head and clenched fists.

"Lof Shraen."

Elcon turned at his call. Kai stepped into the inner chamber and came to stand before Elcon. He could not see Elcon's face with the moonlight behind him. "Are you well?"

Elcon shrugged. "Well enough. My body does not trouble me, only my thoughts."

Kai waited. Elcon gave a short, bitter laugh. "When I accepted the scepter of Faeraven I didn't know I would pay a price in sleeplessness. I did not know the costs of rulership but saw only its privileges."

Kai fell into step with Elcon, who resumed pacing. They completed a circuit of the inner chamber and passed through the connecting door into the outer chamber. Elcon stopped before the fireplace. "You think me wrong."

The statement lay between them, harsh and final. Kai searched for words but found none.

Elcon stared at him for several heartbeats in the light of the glowing embers. When he turned away, Kai did not follow.

7

Departure

"Come back to me."

Arillia's gentle call summoned Elcon's thoughts from the gray wasteland they wandered. The garden path they walked appealed to him more, for the vibrant garments of fall dressed the trees. A piquant breeze stirred the leaves and searched his collar as he bent his head to focus on her familiar face. "I'm sorry, Arillia. I have much on my mind."

With a gloved hand she touched his face. "What a weight you bear, Elcon. I hope you will not let it overcome you."

He captured her hand and carried it to his lips in a courtly gesture that brought a sparkle to her eyes. Tucking her arm into his own, he took her farther into the scented shade. She matched her steps to his and, when he paused, turned into his embrace. This time he kissed her in earnest, much as a thirsting man quenches the need for water. He drew away to look at her and caught his breath at her dewy skin, reddened lips, and pale oval lids. She opened her eyes, gasping a little, and he backed away, for honor's sake.

She gave a slight smile. "That was not a goodbye."

"It will have to serve as one, since you intend to leave me this day."

She sent him a coquettish look. "You must find occasion to visit Chaeradon, Elcon."

He sobered. "It will be some time before I can do that, Arillia." He tucked her arm in his and strolled back along the path. "I depart tomorrow on a peace-making tour of the Elder lands."

"Is that what so occupies your mind?" Jealousy tinged her tone.

"I'll come to Chaeradon when I return, Arillia. I promise."

A contented look settled over her face. "I'll look forward to your return."

They walked on in silence, but when he started toward the fountain where Kai waited, Arillia touched his arm and stopped him beneath a strongwood tree. "Wait. I'm not ready to go back. I need to know something, Elcon, and I want the truth."

He lifted an eyebrow. "Go on."

She looked full into his eyes with shadow and light playing over her face. "Do you mean to court me?"

At her words, laughter shook him.

Horror crossed her face. She stumbled backwards, turned and ran.

Elcon recovered his wits and caught up to her. He took her by the shoulders, but she averted her face. "Forgive me, Arillia. I don't laugh at the idea of courting you, just that you would ask such a question after…" He sent a look Kai's direction and lowered his voice. "Do you think I would embrace or kiss you if I did not mean to honor you?"

Her face lit with sudden joy, and he flicked her tears away with his thumbs. "Stop weeping, dear one. I have a journey to make, but when I return, if you will have me, I'll court you."

She smiled and reached to place a kiss on his cheek. "Keep safe on your journey, Elcon. Remember, I await your return."

He laughed at the satisfaction in her tone and pulled her into his embrace. "With that in mind, I'll take even better care of myself."

8

Desire

"Aewen." Murial's quiet summons cut through the morning.

Aewen gave a wry half-smile and stopped moving but did not turn back.

"Time to return, flitling. The household will awaken soon."

That Murial named her after the tiny birds that flitted from bush to bush in freedom seemed more irony than she could bear. Her life had become a cage. Each day she spent as Raefe of Darksea's betrothed showed her more clearly how unsuited they were for marriage. Did he see it, too? If he did, he gave no sign.

She could not fault his attentiveness, except that he scoffed at her need for quiet and called her "bookish" because she could read. He also informed her that wandering in nature was no proper occupation for a woman. "Leave that to the commoners." She understood by his tone that he would not welcome a wife who tended "peasants."

Aewen looked across the Cobbleford to the other shore just as a fawn emerged from the trees. She put out a hand to silence Murial, and the little creature's ears flicked. She held her breath. The fawn reached down to drink. Tears stood in her eyes. When its head lifted and the delicate creature vanished into the underbrush, she barely saw it go. How could she bear it? Except for those tournaments and social gatherings he favored, Raefe meant to confine her indoors, away from nature's beauty.

Murial touched her arm with a gentle hand, and a smile split her weathered face. Her maid seemed more fragile these days. She kept silence more and startled easily. The change in her made Aewen's heart sink. She wished she could do something to ease Murial's peace of mind, but could not even save her own, not with the wedding banns soon to be nailed outside the chapel door for all to see. To soothe her maid, Aewen attempted a weak smile that, when they started back, failed entirely.

Upon her return to the castle, garment fittings, discussions of jewelry, and hair stylings soon overtook Aewen. Mother at first included her in the excited discussions of fabrics and flowers and friends but, when she failed to respond, no longer consulted her. Aewen could summon only a lackluster interest in such things, whereas Caerla brought into the conversation all the enthusiasm a mother could want.

Raefe called for Aewen partway through the morning, and her mother, laughing, drove him off until after the midday meal. Mother seemed gay these days, almost as if she herself became a bride once more. Aewen, by contrast, sank deeper into gloom with each passing day.

That afternoon Raefe took Aewen and Caerla riding in his carriage and urged his driver to whip the horses until they bolted down the rutted track. Aewen shrank into a corner of the carriage, which rocked and jostled her so severely she nearly tumbled from the seat. Her white fingers gripped the elk-leather armrest as she fought the urge to vomit. She could not even enjoy the benefit of scenery since the red velvet curtains were drawn against the dust, although it entered anyway. She felt its effects in her stiffened hair and aching eyes. Caerla and Raefe seemed unaffected by these discomforts. When the carriage canted at what seemed an unsafe angle, they laughed out loud. Where Caerla found such an appetite for danger, Aewen did not know.

She was thankful when they arrived home. It took Murial a long time to wash the road dust from her hair and change her into clean garments for the evening meal. Aewen stared at her bed, longing to crawl into its comfort and forget the ordeal she'd just experienced. Soon she would find no refuge in her bed. Mother had explained physical duty to a husband as a distasteful burden she must learn to bear.

Aewen stood still and allowed Murial to fasten her new garments and untangle her hair. Protocol required she present herself in the great hall for the evening's feast. She might contrive to slip away early, however.

She sat beside Raefe throughout the meal, smiling and commenting whenever politeness required, but for the most part ignoring him. His blue eyes sought hers repeatedly, as if he sensed the distance she placed between them, but she could not, after that frenzied ride today, manage anything more.

"You are quiet tonight." Raefe refused to be ignored.

At the annoyance on his face, her irritation melted into remorse. The fault was hers. A man should find more of a welcome from his intended bride. Raefe was handsome, but he didn't attract her. What would it be like to yearn for her bridegroom? The thought made her sigh, but she instantly regretted it. From the way Raefe's eyes narrowed, the sound gave away more than she intended. "I am weary." She shifted forward in her chair, and he grasped her wrist with a restraining hand, as if he guessed she meant to flee.

"They're about to start. If the music pleases you, we'll invite this troupe of minstrels to play for us at Trillilium." The name of her future home, seat of Darksea, spoken by her betrothed, should have brought delight to her. She sighed again. How far she was from the bride he would want her to be.

Caerla leaned toward Raefe, her tawny eyes alight, and Aewen saw again her sister's hidden beauty. "Another sort of entertainment will follow." Excitement infused her voice. How Caerla could look forward to an evening's entertainment after the battering in the carriage, Aewen had no idea. She hadn't lied to Raefe. She could barely keep her eyes open. Still, for his sake she lingered. Minstrels strummed lutes and psalteries while timbrels and finger cymbals lent percussion. There was even a timpani, carried into the minstrel's galley on the back of a brawny youth with deep brown hair. That particular minstrel struck her as a little strange, although she couldn't decide why.

King Devlon, seated on Aewen's other side, glanced across her to his son. "That one bears Kindren blood. They'd better watch the silver."

"And the women." Raefe's laughter sounded course. "He'll be a half-cast, probably a son of Ellendia."

Aewen knew the story as well as any Elder maiden. The huntress Ellendia of Sloewood had fallen under the enchantment of a son of Rivenn who found her after she was thrown from her horse in the canyonlands. The Kindren were no more ready to accept her as an Elder than her own people would condone her marriage to a son of Rivenn. Aewen didn't know all the details, but Selfred, one of the Kindren kingdoms, had formed when it divided from Glindenn as a result of the strife that followed. Ellendia and her husband had vanished together into the wilds of Dyloc Syldra to live hand-to-mouth, under constant threat from the garns who dwelt there.

Aewen stared at the minstrel with unabashed fascination. While he had the Kindren's long eyes, his darker coloring was that of an Elder. Could he be a son of Ellendia?

He swung the timpani into place and boomed an accompaniment to "A Pirate's Rolicking Tale." Another minstrel stepped forward to sing, his bright voice threading the jaunty music.

Oh, I'll away 'cross the rolling sea
To an isle overlooked by all
But the lively men of Dead Man's Key
Who never forget to call
Wandering ships into the lea
Of their hospitality

As verse after bantering verse enlivened the hall, Aewen's exhaustion fell away, and she tapped her foot in time. Raefe, after ensuring she remained at his side, all but forgot her as he laughed with Caerla.

Now was her chance to escape. If she hurried, she could distribute leftover food to the poor when they gathered at the castle gatehouse. How she longed for her accustomed task and to hear news of little Caedmon. Had his wound healed? She hadn't been able to keep her promise to check on him again. She made to rise from the table, but Raefe caught her wrist. "Stay with me." His tone brooked no refusal.

A frisson of fear touched her. What did she really know of Raefe of Darksea?

She sat back down with her cheeks burning and rubbed the wrist he'd squeezed too tightly. Wood scraped as servants cleared the trestle tables from the floor below their dais, and a troop of acrobats ran in. They wore jerkins and leggings but kept their feet bare the better, she supposed, to perform their feats. The acrobats climbed on one another to form impossible towers. When they tumbled in a beautiful free fall, Aewen gasped with the others, but the acrobats landed on their feet.

Her weariness returned. When Raefe forgot her again in favor of Caerla, she managed to slip from his side at last. This time she did not murmur polite words in his ear but whispered instead to a servant she instructed to deliver her apologies to Raefe and her mother after she left. She sidled out of the hall by a servant's door and followed the narrow passageway to the kitchen. Raefe might be angry to find her gone, but he should have let her go earlier. He didn't own her, after all, at least not yet.

She descended worn wooden stairs illumined by wall-hung torches as voices drifted to her from below. She could put names to most of them. Maered, a dark-haired serving girl about half her own age, looked up from the rush baskets which held scraps of food and the trenchers of bread from which they'd eaten their meal. Maered smiled when she saw Aewen and held out one of the baskets from long habit.

Maered's mother, Brianda, turned from scrubbing

pots in a sink supplied with water piped into the kitchen from the Cobble River. "*Tsk*, girl! Don't be disturbin' the princess wi' such."

"Nonsense," Aewen declared in robust tones as she laid hold of the basket. "I've come this night to tend the poor."

Brianda gave her a hesitant look. "Are you certain, milady?"

Her heart sank. Why did Brianda address her with formality? And for that matter, why did the others gathered about the battered trestle table stare at her so?

She swept from the room, going up another flight of stairs made of equally worn wood. A small arched door gave onto the bailey and the side passage leading to the gatehouse.

"Who goes there?" The watchguard's voice halted her.

"Let me pass, Lyriss. It's only Aewen."

From behind the portcullis above the watchtower, Lyriss gaped at her in surprise, and then broke into a toothy grin. "I thought to see you giving alms no more."

"I will serve while I may." She choked on her brave words but took a steadying breath. "Raise the portcullis so I and the others who will soon follow may distribute leftovers from the king's table."

Chains clanked as the portcullis raised with a groan. Outside the castle, the poor waited. She walked among them, not fearing these faces she knew. Her friends hailed her with gladness and without jostling stretched out thin hands to take the portions she gave. She smiled to herself. She'd taught them that, to consider one another even in their need.

She recognized the face of Jost, a weaver whose

cottage stood just north of Willowa's farm, and gave him the last trencher. "Do you have news of Caedmon? Does he heal?"

"Aye, he heals." Jost delivered himself of this speech and bowed his head with a jerk, acting as strange as had those inside the kitchen. She swallowed against a lump in her throat. When had she become someone else?

Movement caught her eye. At the edge of the torchlight pranced a black horse with wings—a creature of surpassing beauty bearing a Kindren youth with fair hair tinged red in the torchlight from the guardhouse. She took a step toward him but halted, speechless.

"Well met, fair one." His voice, soft and cool, stirred her.

She stared back at him with wide eyes.

His brows drew together. "Do you speak?"

She dipped her head and found her voice. "You are of the Kindren."

He smiled. "I am indeed of the Kindren, as are my companions. Pray tell the watchguard that Lof Shraen Elcon seeks audience with King Euryon. But if the hour be too late, we can return tomorrow."

His light gaze went over her as he spoke, touching her hair, her eyes, her mouth, speaking things his mouth did not say. She stumbled backward and ran from him as laughter broke from the Kindren riders who accompanied him.

"Princess Aewen, are you unharmed?" The voice of Darbin, one of the gatehouse guards, rang out as she approached. The sounds of mirth behind her ceased, and she realized the Kindren riders must have overheard. They'd taken her for a servant before, despite the rich garments she wore. It was one thing, it seemed, for a Kindren to laugh at a servant, but quite another to mock a princess of Westerland. She turned her head and shamed them all with a glance. But her gaze snagged with the light-eyed Kindren's.

൜൜

Never had Elcon seen hair so glossy and black that it shone like an eberrac's wing. She seemed an exquisite gem, or a rare flower, one he might never find again. She watched him from eyes of palest blue with all the grace of a doe. He could not look away. She spoke to the guard, then without a backward glance entered the gatehouse. Bereft of her presence, the moon's glow surely dimmed.

Kai drew up beside him. Elcon heard the sound of his voice but looked at him in helpless confusion, for he did not know what he said. At sight of the dark-haired Elder flower, Princess Aewen as the guard named her, Elcon's life had changed forever. Never had he desired anything as much as he yearned for another glimpse of her. He resolved to find a way to meet Aewen again, to drink in her soft voice, and feast on her beauty. She was an Elder and he a Kindren. It could never be more, but he would have that much.

"Lof Shraen?" Kai interrupted his thoughts.

"I'm sorry, Kai. I'm befuddled. I've just lost my soul."

Kai whistled beneath his breath. "The Princess Aewen?"

Elcon answered him with silence.

The guard signaled their admittance to Cobbleford Castle, and they rode into the gatehouse, the graystone walls closing about them. Elcon dismounted and flung the reins to the groom who met him. He followed the servant who led them by lanthorn light into the rectangular outer bailey skirted by covered cobblestone paths.

Cobbleford's great hall was small compared to Torindan's but elegant nonetheless. New rushes strewed the floor, windows stretched tall, and the ceiling vaulted into shadow. Elcon bowed before Euryon, seated on the dais. Euryon stood and returned his bow, although Elcon thought he bent a measuring look upon him. "Welcome, Shraen Elcon of Rivenn, Lof Shraen of Faeraven."

"I am glad to receive Westerland's hospitality at such short notice. I thank you."

Euryon inclined his head with perfect manners, although his lady, Queen Inydde, looked upset. Elcon greeted her and kissed her hand, but she snatched it back sooner than might be considered seemly. His gaze roamed about the room as he sought for his beautiful Elder flower.

"Will you not take food?" Inydde asked.

Elcon would have liked to accept her hospitality, but he knew better than to strain Inydde's welcome. He shook his head. "We ate upon the way. But we will take something warming to drink, if you please."

Inydde nodded to a servant who waited nearby. Another servant whispered in her ear, and Inydde cast a look down the long table to exchange glances with a black-haired, brawny youth he recognized as Raefe of Darksea. She stood. "Please, take your ease. There's room at our table. I've a small matter to attend but will soon return."

Elcon watched her go, disliking the way she

carried herself as if going into battle. Cautioning himself to tread lightly with Inydde, he gave swift sympathy to whomever she sought.

He drank mulled cider while bards played lively strains and a line of men formed in what seemed a traditional dance with much balancing and quick footwork. He sat beside King Euryon, a place having been made for him, but real speech was not possible in the cacophony of music and voices. The subject he wished to broach called for privacy, at any rate. He would wait until he had the king's undivided attention, hopefully on the morrow.

And then he forgot why he'd come to Westerland, for Princess Aewen accompanied Inydde upon her return. Her gaze cast downward, she approached with seeming reluctance but curtsied smoothly. It occurred to him to wonder if she had been the object of Inydde's earlier wrath. She seemed uncomfortable, of a certain, but perhaps his presence bore the blame for that. He set himself to ease her if he could.

"I'm grateful for the chance to meet you, Princess Aewen."

She looked at him in question, and he realized that in the general din she could not hear what he said. He stood and gave a polite bow to her father, and then came around the table to repeat himself close to her ear. She blushed and drew away. He looked up to find all eyes upon him. Rather than embarrass her further, he returned to his place at the table.

He saw that she seated herself beside Prince Raefe, and that Raefe took possession of her hand. A flash of discomfort went through him. Something was wrong between them. Aewen seemed only outwardly present. How he understood this, he did not pause to wonder.

It seemed he could read Aewen with the ease of breath. He tried to hide his interest but could not keep his gaze from straying to her. Indeed, he knew her every movement. When she chanced to look his way, he caught her gaze and held it, at least until Inydde, beside him, troubled herself during a lull in the music to inquire about his journey from Rivenn.

Elcon pulled his attention from Aewen and turned to her mother. "We fared well enough, Your Majesty, although travel by wingabeast wearies both mind and body."

She looked blank but then clasped her hands together. "Of course! You refer to the winged horses of Torindan, do you not? Have you brought them with you then? I wish to see them and perhaps ride one on the morrow."

He smiled despite his misgivings. Riding a wingabeast required balance and training. Perhaps she would forget the notion by morning. An image rose before him, unbidden, of Aewen riding before him on Raeld, his wingabeast named for the darkest marches of the night. His arm held her in safety as her unbound hair caressed his face, and he bowed his head to kiss the back of her neck.

His face warmed, and he wondered if he blushed, especially when Inydde gave him a strange look. He needed to guard his thoughts. It would be best if he dealt with matters in Westerland and moved on, but he could not, somehow, bring himself to contemplate a quick departure, at least not until he knew why Aewen seemed a silent ghost whose smile did not quite reach her eyes.

Caerla pulled Aewen aside on the landing at the top of the stair. "Why the sad face?"

"Hush! Speak softly." Aewen peered into the darkness beyond the light from the lanthorn Murial held.

Caerla gave her a gentle push. "Silly. No one follows us or cares what we say. Have you been reading books again? Mother says flights of poetry sicken the mind."

Aewen kept silence on *that* subject. She alone of her household valued books except, in a small way, her father, who loved his histories but did not put any store in other works.

Murial opened the door to Aewen's chambers, and Caerla followed them inside. "Tell me what's wrong."

Aewen gave Caerla a quelling look, but at the concern written on her sister's face, relented. "All right, but you'll not like what I say."

"Only if you refuse to marry."

She curled her hands into fists. She longed to do just that, but it seemed she must endure marriage after all. Because she'd offended Raefe by leaving the feast, Mother had this night almost turned Murial out as threatened. Aewen had only just prevented disaster, and she doubted her mother would relent again.

She longed to tell Caerla the truth, to explain that Raefe had crushed her wrist to prevent her from leaving, and that she feared him now in a way she had not before. She wanted to speak of the green-eyed Kindren king who had cast a spell over her, but she told, instead, a simpler tale. "My head hurts."

Caerla's tawny eyes gleamed in the lanthorn light. "Do you speak truth?"

Heat rose into Aewen's face.

"Come, and when you are ready for bed, I'll rub lavender oil into your temples." Murial's call from her inner chamber saved her from responding. Caerla drew breath to say more but relented with a swift embrace. "Rest then." She picked up the lanthorn and shook her head at Murial. "See to my sister. I can find my way next door, where Donia waits to tend me."

But Murial took the lanthorn from Caerla's hand and led her from the room as if she had not spoken. Aewen did not blame Murial for ensuring she neglected no duties. Mother did not treat her maid with kindness. She frowned, and a stray drop of moisture tracked down her face from the corner of her eye. Later, when she was alone, she would let tears dampen her pillow.

Murial readied her for bed, and she took comfort in her maid's quiet ministrations. But no amount of lavender oil could remove the Kindren king from her thoughts. It seemed he followed her even into her dreams.

9

Betrothal

Elcon took a seat at the polished kaba wood table that dominated the king's meeting chamber. Kai's presence beside him leant him strength.

Euryon rose from his chair and looked out one of the chamber's tall windows.

Elcon waited for him to speak.

"Tell me, Lof Shraen, what brings you to Cobbleford?"

"I've come to clear my name among the Elder. I had nothing to do with the raids by wingabeast riders."

Euryon turned back to Elcon with a frown. "I don't believe you."

Kai went still.

Euryon took a step toward him. "I don't believe you came all this way on these matters. Why did you not come earlier? Why wait until the raids stopped?" He sat at the table and laid his hands flat on the polished strongwood slab. "Now tell me the truth."

Elcon smiled. "You are astute, King Euryon. I did come for another purpose, but also for the one I gave. I did not lie. The wingabeast raids have long troubled me, and I came, in part, to clear my name. I had nothing to do with them. I never discovered just how they came about, but they stopped after Freaer left Torindan. I believe we can assume he instigated them."

At mention of Freaer, Euryon's head came up.

"The other reason I came to Westerland was to ask you to pledge your loyalty to me as Lof Shraen. I rule as a legitimate son of Rivenn. Freaer, an illegitimate son, holds no real claim to the throne of Rivenn and even less to the title of Lof Shraen."

"I see." Euryon's eyes grew distant.

"Freaer has visited you." Elcon voiced his suspicion out loud.

"He has. He is quite...convincing."

"He possesses a power for deception. His greatest desire is to control all of Elderland."

Euryon's gaze snapped to him.

Elcon leaned forward in his chair. "We must unite to overcome him."

"You ask much of me, as did Freaer. Why should I concern myself with the affairs of the Kindren?"

"Kindren affairs may soon become your own, whether you will or no."

"I can tell you I will not side with Freaer against you."

"I'll content myself with that."

Euryon smiled. "Come, I'll show you around Cobbleford."

Elcon overcame his disappointment enough to nod agreement, and with Kai and several of the king's guards following, he strode with King Euryon through the presence chamber doors and into an outer chamber where kaba wood gleamed. This chamber gave onto a vaulted side corridor that ran the length of the castle. Arches marked each section of the long hallway, and at regular intervals clerestory windows cast the light of day across the scarlet carpet underfoot. Euryon paused before an arched doorway and glanced behind them. "This corridor helps cool the castle in the heat of summer, but in winter, it collects drafts."

Elcon laughed, and some of his tension eased. "I can well imagine."

"And yet it serves a practical purpose. It is possible to vacate Cobbleford quickly. In times past this was important."

Elcon's nerves twanged back full force. "Of course, you refer to the revolt of Lancert." A revolt, he did not add, that had been fueled by the Kindren. When they abandoned Pilaer after it fell to garns, they moved westward into lands formerly used by the Elder for hunting. Amberoft, king of Westerland and Euryon's grandfather, welcomed them but Haldrom, pretender to the throne, called for the Kindren to be removed from Westerland, thus stirring the resentment that gave rise to the revolt.

"Among other incidents, yes." Euryon nodded to one of the guards, who opened the door. Outside a cobblestone path cut through a mown sward toward the chapel Elcon remembered from one of the infrequent visits he'd made to Westerland in his early days. Those visits had diminished over time until they became nonexistent, an omission of his mother's. He didn't blame her for not continuing relations if they were as strained as this. He was here to right matters, if possible.

As they walked the path Elcon reveled in the tang of kabas, which carried on a freshening breeze. At the entrance one of the guards pushed open the door, and Euryon turned to Elcon. "I think we'll find the chapel quiet."

Elcon followed, but halted where a scroll nailed beside the door flapped in the wind. Curious, he flattened it, holding it still long enough to read it. Afterwards, he lifted his head in surprise.

Euryon smiled. "In your hands you hold my daughter, Aewen's, banns. She and Prince Raefe will soon unite two kingdoms."

࿔ঌ

Inydde would have her wingabeast ride, it seemed, even if it meant giving up propriety. Her daughters and the visitors from Darksea waited as she rode before Elcon, her back stiff and unyielding. He kept a hand about her waist with as light a touch as possible. He wanted no misinterpretation of a safety precaution. Feathered wings lifted about them and beat down as Raeld's muscles bunched and heaved. The wings lifted again and air rushed over them. As they spiraled upward, Inydde let out a scream and grasped Raeld's mane with both hands, bending so low Elcon feared for her safety. His hand tightened around her waist and he leaned forward to instruct her.

"Let go of me!"

Raeld quivered, and Elcon spoke calming words to both the wingabeast and the woman.

Inydde threw her arms around Raeld's neck. "I want off! Take me down!" she shrilled near the wingabeast's ear.

A shudder went through Raeld, but he held course. Elcon felt immediate sympathy for his wingabeast. He did not want to be in the air with Inydde either. He released his breath between his teeth. He could not bring Raeld down until they leveled out above Cobbleford Castle. To do so before then might mean a disastrous landing.

Inydde hid her eyes against Raeld's neck and refused to move even when their flight leveled. The castle shone in the afternoon sun, its baileys small green squares amidst walls of brown and gray stone, the garden behind the chapel marked off in a neat grid. He whistled the command to descend so that Raeld might hear it above Inydde's piteous wails.

The landing in Cobbleford's outer bailey was rough, perhaps hindered by the death grip Inydde maintained on Raeld's neck. Even now she would not let go, despite the fact all four of the wingabeast's hooves rested on the ground. Elcon dismounted and reached to help her, but she had gone too far into hysterics to recover easily. Raeld pranced a little, and he issued a sharp command that quieted the beast. He hesitated, not sure what else to do short of wresting Inydde by force from Raeld's back.

At a gentle touch on his arm, he looked sideways. At sight of Aewen's beautiful face his pulse picked up speed. She spoke near his ear. "Let me."

He gave way, going to Raeld's head to hold him steady. Aewen moved to the wingabeast's side and lifted her arms to her mother, all the while speaking in a low, soothing voice. Inydde released Raeld's neck and clung to her daughter instead. Elcon stepped forward to assist Inydde, who dismounted without grace. Aewen gave him a weak smile from across her mother's bowed head. A jowl-cheeked maidservant came forward. Inydde sagged against her and allowed the woman to lead her along the cobblestone path to the keep. In her distress Inydde left her daughters alone among men. "Thank you, princess." Elcon's voice was not quite steady.

"She's my mother. I could not leave her thus." Aewen's face shone with compassion. Utterly smitten, he watched as she rejoined her sister on the sward beside Raefe and Devlon of Darksea.

Shaking from emotion and in the aftermath of a situation that could have turned out much worse, Elcon put a hand to Raeld's neck to steady both himself and his wingabeast. But Raeld was not ready to be soothed. He gave a series of snorts, and his prancing hooves made dull thuds in the grass as the wingabeast let his opinion of recent events be known.

Craelin and Kai approached, leading Mystael and Fletch. Inydde had requested the Kindren offer wingabeast rides to her guests but had insisted on going first. Sending an inquiring look to Raefe and Devlon, Elcon stood away from Raeld.

"I mislike this idea." Craelin said in response to Elcon's greeting.

He gave a swift nod. "Let us do what we can for peace."

Craelin squinted toward Inydde and her maid, now entering the keep. "I doubt today's adventure will have a pleasing outcome."

Elcon firmed his jaw. "You and Kai take the two from Darksea, and I'll let the daughters admire Raefe. He's done more than his share this day."

"As have you." Kai's smile didn't quite reach his eyes.

Elcon turned to the waiting group. "We are at your service if you still want to ride, but think well. As you have seen, the prospect of riding a wingabeast can be somewhat different from the reality."

"I have no need to *think*, Kindren. I will ride one of

the beasts alone!" After making his bold statement, Raefe turned his head toward Caerla, and a glittering look passed between them. All at once Elcon understood. The Elder prince showed off for the younger daughter, not the older. He shook his head. "I am sorry, Your Highness, but none can ride a wingabeast alone without training. Even the guardians of Rivenn do not do so."

"I care nothing for your trifling *rules*." Raefe stood taller. "I will ride alone. Now give me the white one. He looks quick."

Kai's long eyes narrowed. "No one rides Fletch without me."

Elcon raised a hand to warn Kai to silence. He spoke, with an effort, in even tones. "I am sorry, but I must insist for your safety, Prince Raefe. The wingabeasts are trained to know certain signals that, if absent, may confuse them. Besides that, it's easier than it seems to become unseated by a sudden change of direction in midair. Riding a wingabeast requires balance gained by much practice. If you want to ride Fletch, Kai will be happy to accompany you."

Raefe stood his ground, looking so furious that Elcon balanced on the balls of his feet, ready to intercept a blow. He felt Kai and Craelin move to stand just behind and beside him. Raefe, whose eyes shifted to take in this change, huffed as he glared into Elcon's eyes. "Never mind then. I'll not be coddled like a babe." With that, he stomped off toward the gatehouse in a childish fit.

Aewen bowed her head at Raefe's display. Elcon ached to comfort her, but that privilege did not belong to him. A slow blush crept up King Devlon's neck. He dipped his head in a quick nod and set off for the keep.

Only the two daughters remained, but Caerla, bemused, made her apologies. "I'll check my mother." She left them, but seemed to lose her way. She did not set off for the keep, but followed instead the path Raefe had taken.

At a touch on his arm, Elcon met Aewen's gaze. "I'm sorry. You've done no wrong." She spoke barely above a whisper, and tears brightened her eyes.

He put a hand over hers. Her words, soft as the hand he held beneath his own, brought him comfort. "Come." He walked with her then, taking her toward Cobbleford's gardens, leaving Raeld in Craelin's care. Kai followed him at a discreet distance, a fact he welcomed. With Kai near, he might better remember his manners in Aewen's presence.

They were of the same mind it seemed, for they passed the chapel's cultivated beds to lose themselves in the natural gardens beyond. Here, weilo trees dangled long leaves in the silvered waters of a stream lined with cobblestones. Wild roses unfurled and native plum trees bent under the weight of their harvest. Bees buzzed, and the aroma of sun-warmed fruit scented the air.

Elcon plucked two ripe plums and offered one to Aewen. She took the treat from his hand, the corners of her mouth lifting in a quick smile. He bit into his own plum and smiled with her as its sweetness filled his mouth. He held a branch as she sought the banks of a quiet pool, inky in the shadow of a thicket of broadberries overhung by weilos. She stood upon a flat rock at water's edge and looked back for him. His heart stirred at the sight of her there, awaiting him. He knew without being told she had brought him to a quiet place she cherished, a place of peace. He joined her on the stone slab and crouched to rake his hand through the cool water. As he watched, a silver fish flashed beneath the surface. He stood, droplets falling from his fingers to splash on the stone at their feet. He turned to her. "Thank you." The words resonated between them.

She tilted her head to look at him and dimpled. He longed to reach for her, to take her into his arms, to run his hand through her dark hair and free it from its plait. Instead he smiled and memorized her face, so that he might not forget her, ever.

She gazed at the pool. "I love this place."

"I can see why."

She sent him a sideways glance. "*Can* you?"

"Sometimes I steal away to the inner garden at Torindan, and there listen to Lof Yuel's voice."

Her brows drew together. "Lof Yuel?"

"The 'High One,' or God as you Elder call Him."

She sighed and her face grew sad. "I feel Him here also. But soon I will not be able to come again. I will dwell far away in a land of cold mists."

He caught her hand, brought her around to face him, and cupped her face. "Aewen."

"*No!* No, please." She broke away. "I should not have mentioned my sorrow to you. I forget myself because you are so kind."

"Know this"—he paused to bring his voice under control—"I would do anything to ease your path. I would do anything if only I had the right."

She flinched and a bruised look came into her eyes. She turned away from the pool, away from him, and stepped from the flat stone to the path.

"Wait."

She paused but did not turn back to him.

"Are you in trouble of some kind? Do you need

help?"

She looked at him then, and he saw that tears stood in her eyes. "None can help me, least of all you."

She ducked back under the weilo branch and left him there. Elcon hesitated, on the verge of following her, but then restrained himself. He did not have the right to follow.

When he emerged from the hidden pool he found Kai waiting on the path. He didn't try to hide his feelings. Kai read him too well for that. He sighed. "Trouble calls my name, it seems."

Kai's silver eyes gleamed. "But you decide whether to answer."

∂∞৶

"Flitling, what troubles you?" Murial looked up from her needlework. "You're pale as death and can scarce catch your breath. I've lit a fire. Come warm yourself."

Aewen sank onto the bench by the fire in her outer chamber and watched the flames licking around the logs they consumed. Hypnotized, drawn into them, she forgot their danger in the beauty of the light they made. She took with gratitude the cup of cider Murial brought her. Her maid brushed her hair, all the while crooning beneath her breath. With deft fingers, Murial replaited her hair and tied across her forehead a doeskin strip with a sapphire stone at its center. She kissed the top of Aewen's head and, as a last gift, rubbed lavender oil into her temples.

Aewen caught Murial's hand when she would withdraw it and dropped a kiss upon its weathered surface. "You are good to me, and I thank you."

Murial smiled and her dark eyes warmed. "I only do what my heart speaks." She sobered. "Today your mother suffered a misfortune."

Aewen gave a deep nod. "Indeed, she did. How does Mother fare?"

"She received a sleeping drought and now rests in her chambers."

Aewen stood. "That's well. She took a fright."

Murial asked no more questions but probably knew the details already. News traveled quickly within the walls of Cobbleford Castle.

A memory returned to Aewen, of Caerla following Raefe. "And my sister? Has she come back?"

Murial looked blank. "Was she not with you?"

Too late, Aewen realized her error. Murial had thought she and Caerla chaperoned one another in the absence of their mother. She shook her head and wondered if Murial would hear the falsehood in her voice. "I—I walked in the garden alone to—to soothe my nerves after all that happened with Mother. I didn't see where Caerla went. Perhaps she sought the chapel." She added the last part despite the fact Murial would know Caerla never sought the chapel of her own volition.

Murial gave her a long look, and Aewen knew she blushed. Elcon's image rose in her mind's eye, as he had looked when he touched her face at the pool. She had thought she would drown, then, in his eyes. Murial gave a little cough, as if to clear her throat, and looked away. She asked nothing more.

For once Aewen had the chance to capture a stretch of time, for Raefe did not call for her, Inydde slept, and Caerla, for all she knew, remained absent. She sat in the light of one of the tall windows in her outer chamber and occupied herself in needlework while in memory she wandered along garden paths with Elcon. She heard again the timbre of his voice, which stayed with her, as did the feel of his hand in hers and the tender look on his face. As her needle flashed in and out of the linen she embroidered, she fell to humming. At some point Caerla must have returned, for the door to her room slammed. Aewen paused, but then continued with her needlework. She would go to her sister in time, but she needed a breathing space before taking up the threads of life. And so Aewen embroidered bright silks into delicate patterns until the light lessened, leaving Caerla to tend her own wounds.

She set her needlework aside and stretched, yawning. The simple task had restored her, as if silken strands could repair the rent places in her life. She would not admit, even to herself, that thoughts of Elcon brought her joy. She could not seek happiness from such a source, despite the longing that plagued her like a sickness. The fact that Elcon was high king of his people only made her infatuation with him worse. Even if she were free, he was already claimed by duty. Besides, a marriage between a Kindren and an Elder would tear the very fabric of life in Elderland. Such a union had occurred only once in history, to Ellendia, and that had been a disaster. Some Elder children did have light hair and long eyes, but the polite did not inquire into their backgrounds. The rude threw stones. The mothers of these children most often fell upon hard times, and the children themselves lived lives of poverty and shame. She would not wish such a fate on any offspring she might bear. And so, when Raefe came to her door to escort her to the evening's feast, she linked her arm in his and smiled a welcome. She would put the Kindren king from her mind, if she could not remove him from her heart.

Caerla did not show herself in the great hall that evening, having sent word of a headache. Neither did Inydde or King Devlon of Darksea appear.

Her father seemed distracted, and Aewen caught him sending Elcon a pensive look more than once. She noticed her father's interest because she could not deny her own. Try as she might to concentrate on Raefe, her attention drew of its own will to Elcon. And as much as she sought him out, she felt his gaze on her. Each time their glances met something happened inside her, a curious jolting sensation that caused her to stumble in speech and her hands to falter as she gripped her cup. She spilled her honeyed ale and Raefe stood, cursing in a way she'd never heard before, as a stream of pale liquid ran from the table and into his lap. He gave her a violent look, but then a mask came down over his anger. She shuddered, nonetheless, for now she had seen and had no doubt that, when they married, nothing would shelter her from his wrath.

10

Interlude

"Don't move or I'll stab you."

Aewen knew from experience that the dressmaker Glynnda's pins could draw blood. While balancing on a precarious footstool, she glanced down at the wedding gown snugged about her. "It's too tight. I can barely breathe."

"Stop struggling and you'll find it comfortable."

With a sigh of her own, Aewen sought relief in the view from the window. Beyond the castle wall the Cobbleford River broadened and bent southward as clouds gathered with the promise of rain and the surface of the water grew murky.

Aewen scowled. Even in nature she found no solace. The violent weather seemed to echo Raefe's thinly-veiled rage the night before. What would marriage to him bring?

"A bride should not frown so. Come now, Aewen. Anyone would think you were tormented rather than favored with all manner of wedding finery."

As a pin pricked her skin, Aewen bit back a cry.

Glynnda *tskd* and raised her hands. "I did warn you."

She blinked away tears that had little to do with the pain that pierced her side.

"Careful!" Mother, neat and prim in cream brocade, appeared self-possessed and beautiful, incapable of her hysterical outburst of the day before. "Perhaps you sulk because Prince Raefe has taken himself without you to Lancert. Well, never mind. He'll return soon enough and miss you the more for having gone without you."

She had not known of Raefe's departure and didn't long for his return. In truth, she rejoiced in his absence and hoped he would linger in Lancert. How could her mother possibly think otherwise? It was better not to ask. "Are you recovered from yesterday's upset, Mother?"

She sniffed. "Had that *Kindren* warned me of what it would be like to ride such a beast, I would never have risked my life on its back. Pray, speak no more of it, Aewen, for I do not wish to remember the incident. It is well the Kindren leave our gates soon. Perhaps even today."

"Ouch!"

Glynnda sat back on her heels. "Aewen, please. You'll bleed on this fine linen and ruin your wedding dress."

"The Kindren leave today?"

"You sound as if you care. I can't think why. Your father plans to ask them to leave after all they've put me through."

"Did he say as much?"

"No, but I'm sure he will do so. Besides what I endured at their hands, I am told the Kindren visitors humiliated our guests from Darksea."

"Look what you've done now!" Glynnda's protest sounded sharper than usual.

Aewen stared at the small spot of blood that

stained the side of her wedding dress. "It's an omen."

࿇

A flurry of white feathers greeted Elcon. He released the weilo branch as the egret he'd startled winged across a steel-gray sky. Balancing on the flat rock at the edge of Aewen's pool, he peered into its green depths while listening to the wind stirring the grasses. He shook his head at his own folly in expecting her to find him here, as if his need might call her to him.

He'd dragged himself from bed early and ducked out alone, without Kai's knowledge. Although he never censored him, Elcon thought Kai did not entirely approve of his actions. He should leave today rather than linger here pining like a love-struck youth. Euryon already hinted he would like the Kindren to leave. Inydde must have blamed Elcon for her own foolishness. Whether or not Euryon believed her, the king would want to please his wife. It was past time to move on to Norwood. Euryon had already given him the only promise he would make. No reason remained to stay at Cobbleford—no reason save one.

He could not forget the tears in Aewen's eyes the last time he'd seen her. Through a long, sleepless night, he'd made an uneasy peace with the fact that, once he left, he might never look upon her again. Perhaps it was better that way. But he couldn't leave without knowing she was safe. Something was not right with this betrothal of hers, and after seeing Raefe's treatment of her yesterday, he could not settle to the thought of leaving her in the power of such a man. He let out the breath he hadn't known he'd held. To find release, he needed to hear Aewen say she wanted Raefe and no other.

He turned to go back, for peace eluded him.

The weilo branch swayed and Aewen, wrapped in a black woolen cape, appeared. He blinked, not quite believing she stood before him. With her pale eyes and wan face, she looked insubstantial, like some wraith sprung from his imaginings. He touched her arm to make sure of her. His laugh caught in his throat. "I could almost believe you come to me in a dream."

She did not smile. "I do wish this a dream, one that I might return to at will. Then I would ever after find my way to you."

His hand tightened on her arm. "Take care. Do you not know the effect of such words?"

She looked at him out of pale eyes and said nothing.

He groaned and drew her into his arms, pressing his lips to her hair, her forehead, and finally her mouth. She went to him willingly, lifting her arms to enfold him, kissing him back with innocent fervor. For a time he knew nothing but the taste and feel of her.

They pulled apart, gasping for air, and gazed into one another's eyes. He traced a tear, just forming at the corner of her eye. "I believe I have fallen in love with you, Aewen. I can't deny it. You've occupied my mind and my heart from my first sight of you."

She covered his hand with her own, the tips of her fingernails blunt against her skin. "Then we are a pair of fools, for I love you, too."

He kissed her to seal their pledge of love, however ill-fated it might prove.

"When do you leave?"

He heard the catch in her voice and laced her

fingers in his own. He would let her go, but not yet. "That depends on you."

Her brow creased. "I cannot hold you, Elcon." She faced the pool. "I am promised to another and must give penance for all I have said and done this day. And you are not altogether safe here."

"Aewen." He turned her toward him. "It's true. All you say separates us, and more besides. But I can't leave without knowing you give yourself to Raefe willingly."

She shut her eyes and took a breath that shuddered. When she opened them again, her eyes shone with unshed tears. "I do."

He had not thought she would lie to him. He released her hands. "No."

"Yes!" Her cry came so loud she looked about in alarm. "I will marry Raefe. I care nothing for him, but I will one day be Queen of Darksea. Do you think I would give that up for you?"

He stared at her. Had he been blinded by love? What did he really know of this Elder Princess?

She tossed her head. "You must leave Cobbleford at once. I—I no longer wish you near me."

❧❦

Kai stopped polishing his boots and gave Elcon a long look. The Lof Shraen's pinched expression made it clear he needed to keep his own counsel. Although Kai did not know for certain what had happened, he could guess Princess Aewen lay at the center of Elcon's distraction.

Not so long ago, Kai had faced a similar dilemma over love and honor. He had chosen honor, as had

Shae, but the integrity of their choice did not remove its pain. He wondered, not for the first time, if he would make the same choice again, knowing what it would cost him. Did Shae miss him as he did her? How long before he could hold her again? *A lifetime?*

A tap at Elcon's chamber door pulled Kai from his musings, and he admitted Craelin, who flashed a carefree smile. "Good morn. Do we depart for Norwood this day?"

Elcon scowled. "Not this day."

Craelin's smile faltered. "Perhaps on the morrow then?"

"I'll decide the matter, Craelin." Elcon turned away with a huffing sigh.

Craelin's eyebrows rose and his eyes widened. "Well then... I'll just check on the wingabeasts." With that, he withdrew.

Silence reigned in Craelin's absence. Kai finished with his boots and, setting aside his cleaning cloth, quirked a look at Elcon, who paced the room.

Elcon came to a standstill before him. "What would you do, Kai, if you loved a maid whose path was already set for her—someone who could not return your love without bringing dishonor to herself, to you, to her family, and even to her people and yours?"

"Ah." Kai ignored the twist of sorrow Elcon's words brought him. "You must find your own way in this, but forsaking honor does not nourish love. It brings destruction. Pure love refuses dishonor. I believe that with all my heart." He swallowed and looked away.

"You speak with passion."

"Even I know something of passion."

☙❧

"How come you to be so silent?" Aewen asked, although in truth she had spoken as rarely as her sister. She'd sought refuge in the simple rhythms of needlework, although she seemed to have made a mess of her pattern. Her memory strayed to place her in Elcon's arms, and she stared unseeingly at the embroidery she held. She felt again his touch, his look, his kiss… The needle jabbed her finger. Pinching the wound, she watched as a drop of blood beaded against her skin.

"Now you've made me lose count!" Caerla raised puffy eyes from her own embroidery. Had she been crying? They sat in the queen's parlor, a pleasant chamber in rich hues of red, purple and blue accented in white and gilt. No expense had been spared in outfitting the chamber, for Mother whiled away much time here and must be kept comfortable.

Aewen set aside her embroidery and put her hands in her lap. "Are you well?"

"I don't know what you mean. Of course I'm well. Why would I not be well?" Caerla threw down her needlework and burst into tears.

Her sister's tawny, frizzing head bobbed as she rocked in an excess of grief.

"You seem quite upset over losing count."

Caerla gave something that closely resembled a snort. She glared at Aewen. "Go ahead. Make fun of me. I am, after all, only an unlovely second sister who will never marry. "She jumped up and might have fled the room had not Aewen risen also and put out a hand to stop her. "Wait."

Caerla paused but did not turn.

Aewen let her hand fall from her sister's sleeve. "I'm sorry. I've grown selfish of late. Tell me what troubles you."

"Will the cause of my tears comfort me?"

As comprehension dawned, Aewen sucked in a breath. "You love Raefe."

Caerla wrung her embroidery in her hands. "I didn't mean it to happen. I only thought to entertain him, to make sure you didn't drive him away with your coldness."

Aewen had to do something to make matters right. Through the window she glimpsed a kitchen maid in the sunlit inner bailey. Shayla carried a basket toward the gatehouse. Alms for the poor. A sudden thought caught at her. "Does Raefe return your love?"

"He does not." Caerla wept again, with gut-wrenching sobs. Aewen cradled her sister in her arms, her shoulder dampening with tears long before they eased. She wished she might comfort Caerla, but could offer no more hope than she found, which was none.

She put Caerla to bed and gave her a headache draught, glad when her sister slept. Tomorrow was soon enough to rediscover her sorrows.

With a sigh, she ran the back of her hand across her forehead. Life seemed dull and her every movement leaden. The thought of presenting herself to Raefe this night galled her.

Murial sat on a bench in her outer chamber. Her needle flashed as she drew it through a length of woven flax.

Aewen knelt and put her head in Murial's lap.

Murial's hand stroked Aewen's hair. She crooned a question. "Flitling, what worries bring you to me?"

Tears pricked Aewen's eyes, and her thickening throat choked off speech.

"Here now." Murial lifted her head with gentle hands.

Aewen's tears fell without restraint now, and she gave up trying to stop them.

Murial continued to stroke her hair while she wept. "What troubles you? Although I ken well enough, I think."

Controlling herself with an effort, Aewen sat on the bench. Taking Murial's rough brown hands, she kissed them and ventured a small smile. "What would I do without you?"

"Perhaps you would not marry amiss."

Aewen opened her mouth to object, but Murial lifted a hand to stop her.

"When Queen Inydde first turned me out I should have gone. No protests now. Just listen. You must refuse to marry Prince Raefe, just as your heart tells you to do, and think no more of what will become of me. If you do not, you will spend the rest of your life in a prison of his making. I've seen enough of his ways to know what he'll do as a husband."

"But I can't refuse to marry him now. The invitations have gone out and the preparations—"

"Bah!" Murial raised her hand in a claw and swept the air as if she battled invisible insects. "Don't look to such things. And don't concern yourself about me." Her lips curved in a smile. "I can impose on my sister in Norwood, when all's said and done, though being ornery she will of certain complain, and I'd miss you more than I can say."

A small seed of hope stirred to life within her. It was madness to dream she and Elcon could ever marry, but at least she might not have to wed Raefe. She would never marry, just as she had wished from the beginning. The thought somehow did not bring her the peace it once had.

She dreaded a confrontation with her mother, but better that than a living hell with Raefe. She smiled at Murial. "Thank you."

In the great hall Raefe met her with a gleam in his eye. Whatever he'd been up to in Lancert had put him in a fine mettle. When he took her hand and led her to table, she went without complaint. She would reject Raefe but after Elcon left.

As Elcon's green gaze meshed with hers, a small jolt went through her. Raefe caught her hand and twisted it under the table, and she gasped. It felt like her wrist would break. "Why do you stare at the Kindren king so?"

"I'm sorry. He strikes me as so different. I suppose I'm curious." The glibness of her own lies shocked her.

"Don't cross me, Aewen." He glared at her, but then released her.

Gritting her teeth, she rubbed her wrist beneath the table. She had endured enough of Raefe's company for one night. When Perth leaned over to say something to Raefe, Aewen slipped from her seat. He reached for her wrist again, but she backed away in time. Elcon rose halfway from his chair but sat down again. As she fled, she glimpsed the look of venom Raefe turned on Elcon.

11

Intrigue

Someone hissed.

Kai pivoted, balanced and alert. Craelin, on Elcon's other side, also peered down the vaulted corridor.

Aewen's servant emerged from the shadow of the stair into a pool of torch light. "Didn't mean to give you a start. It's only me, Murial."

"What business brings you?" Elcon asked. "Is Aewen well?"

Murial hesitated and then stepped toward Elcon. "Milady needs you."

"Why say you this?" Elcon rapped out the words.

"I don't know what to do. She places herself in peril." Murial clutched Elcon's sleeve. "I beg of you, come at once." Her intent seemed harmless, but Kai shifted closer to Elcon. As if realizing she touched the Lof Shraen of Faeraven before his guardians, Murial let go and backed away, fright in her eyes.

But now Elcon grasped Murial's arm. "Tell me, where is your mistress?"

"She has gone to the wild garden near the forest's edge."

"Why would she do such a thing? The forest by night is not safe."

Murial cast a glance both ways down the empty corridor and lowered her voice so that Kai barely caught her words. "To meet with you."

Kai read on Craelin's face the same uneasiness he felt.

"If you will excuse me, I seem to have an errand." Elcon faced Kai but turned his head to include Craelin as he spoke.

Craelin's chin came up. "Surely, you do not go alone."

"Pray do not concern yourself." Elcon's tone brooked no argument.

"But we must. You risk yourself, Lof Shraen, without thought." With an effort, Kai kept his voice level. "Remember, we are a long way from Rivenn."

Elcon gave a mirthless laugh. "If we are honest, I can no longer count on safety anywhere, even in Rivenn. But perhaps safety should not be my first concern."

No, that should be Faeraven. Kai did not voice his thought, for Elcon was in no mood for the truth.

❧

Frogs sang in the darkness, as a milky path of light descended from the full moon and crossed the pool at her feet. The flat rock shone blue at her feet. She stepped to the side, where shadow hid her. Night wind tugged her cloak and teased stray tendrils of hair from beneath her hood. Creaking in the weilos at her back made her jump, and she raised the dagger Murial had pressed into her hands.

She stood poised, scanning the dark branches, but finally spotted an owl watching her. Before she could fully recover from the fright, furtive rustlings from the broadberry thicket on the pool's other bank sent her heart racing again. She strained to see in the dark. A jaggercat might crouch there.

After a tense interlude, she released her breath on a long sigh and scolded herself for yielding to fancies. It had been a long time since a jaggercat had actually been reported around Cobbleford Castle, and that starving creature had only come down from the mountains in a time of deep snow and little game. Still, she could not prevent herself from peering into shadows.

The back of her neck bristled, and she spun about. Elcon ducked beneath the weilo branch nearest the path. He stood before her on the flat blue stone, on his face a guarded look that shredded her heart, for she'd placed it there.

"You came." After their last meeting, she hadn't been sure he would.

He faced the pool so that she saw him only in profile. "How could I not offer you my protection? If harm came to you I couldn't bear it." He turned back to her with anger on his face. "But you should not have called me."

"I had to. There was no other way…" She stopped short, the need to make him understand robbing her of words.

"To torment me? Does it bring you such amusement to toy with me that you would risk yourself in the wild at night?"

"No—"

"And what of your betrothed? Would he not object to this meeting?"

"You don't understand."

"You've made it clear enough." He slid his hand beneath her elbow as if to lead her away.

She shook free. "Stop this. You must listen. I would spare you."

"Speak your mind, princess, but then I'll escort you back to the castle and you'll summon me no more."

She drew a shaky breath. "I would spare you. I saw the way Raefe looked at you tonight. I don't know what he intends, but I think he's guessed our attachment."

His eyes widened, and then narrowed. "Why should I believe you?"

"Because I love you." She hadn't meant to blurt it out like that.

He went still and stared at her. Was that a flicker of joy in his face, or had she completely killed his love for her? And why should she care when she meant never to marry? But, God help her, she did. "Aewen." His voice shook as he drew her to him. Their lips met in a kiss that lingered. When a nightbird whistled, they broke apart. Black wings passed across the lighter gray of the night sky, and Aewen laughed. "It was only a graylet."

Elcon returned her to his arms. "You're trembling."

Her fingers curled into his woolen surcoat while she resisted the urge to shake him in frustration. "Why didn't you listen when I asked you to leave?"

He pushed her from him. "Is your concern for me or yourself? Do you want me to leave to make sure Raefe still makes you his queen?"

She stared at him, aghast, the words she'd spoken to him earlier convicting her. She'd succeeded too well in driving him away. He no longer trusted her. Should she let him believe her so horrible she would choose all Raefe offered over her love for Elcon? The thought tormented her, but better that than for him to meet with Raefe's cruelty. The prince of Darksea was not a man who lost with grace.

"He will make me his queen, I assure you. I want nothing better."

Tears blinded her as she ran from him. She stumbled, and a sob escaped to betray her. Elcon caught her, and she found herself once more in his arms.

"All the treasures of Darksea cannot replace love."

He bent his head, and she yielded to his desperate kiss.

Light fell over them as wood splintered, and they broke apart.

"They're here!" Raefe's voice intruded to break them apart.

Aewen blinked in the light from a lanthorn held aloft by a servant. The weilo branch that had hidden the pool from the path lay broken at Raefe's feet.

Elcon pulled Aewen back into his arms as if to shield her, but nothing could protect her from the stunned look on her father's face. From behind him, Mother gasped.

"When Raefe said his servant followed Elcon here and found you, I did not believe him. I had to see for myself." Mother moved forward in fury, but when she looked into Elcon's face, subsided. She glared at her daughter, her eyes sunken pools in the lanthorn light. "Have you lost all reason? You've tarnished yourself. You do not deserve to marry a nobleman like Prince Raefe."

"She'll not." Raefe gritted out the words as his glare raked over Aewen.

Aewen swayed on her feet, but Elcon's grip tightened on her arm.

"My queen must be without taint. I'll not have her, and I'll make certain no one else will either."

"Surely you don't mean to ruin Aewen!" Mother gasped.

"The *Kindren* you harbor has done that, not I."

"Will you not reconsider your course, milord?" Mother wheedled. "It's understandable that you would not want Aewen now, but to spread rumor is cruel."

"Rumor? Is that what you call truth in Westerland? And let us not speak of cruelty. I had already come to regard Aewen as a wife."

That Raefe should pretend heartbreak was too much for Aewen. She pulled away from Elcon. "The only thing I've wounded is your pride. You never loved me but merely thought to possess me as you do a fine destry or a jewel for your crown."

"Aewen!" Mother's shocked protest barely penetrated her wrath.

"I'm well rid of you."

Mother turned to her maid. "Lock her in her chambers until she remembers her manners."

Mother's maid grasped Aewen by the arm. "Come Aewen."

Raefe looked her up and down insultingly. "Your plain sister is worth two of you."

Rage flared white-hot within her. How dare he speak so of Caerla? But Aewen went still. She wouldn't give Raefe the satisfaction he sought by baiting her. "Very well, Mother. I'll go. All I ask is that you'll not touch Elcon."

"Oh, I think none will touch Elcon." Kai answered as he and Craelin emerged from the shadows beneath the weilos to flank their Lof Shraen.

Elcon touched Aewen's cheek, his eyes deep pools. "I'm so sorry, Aewen. Never forget that I love you."

Mother's maid already pulled her away, but she resisted long enough to answer. "You were right, Elcon. I did lie." His face blurred as tears hid him. "I love only you."

࿐

Elcon's hands fisted at his side as he faced Raefe and Euryon in the flickering lanthorn light at the edge of the pool. Kai and Craelin waited, tense and watchful, beside him.

Raefe stood tall. "Euryon, you should imprison these Kindren and overrun their kingdom! Look how they repay your open hand of friendship."

A shadow of pain darkened Euryon's face. "Well? What have you to say for yourself?"

Elcon flinched. Raefe was right. He deserved to pay for his misdeeds. "I'm sorry."

Euryon's eyes widened. "You repay my hospitality by frightening my wife and dishonoring my daughter, yet now you expect forgiveness?"

"I can make no defense save my love for Aewen."

Euryon barked with laughter. "You speak of love, and yet you shame my daughter before her people. You act as the untried youth you are, giving little thought to your deeds. Aewen would have been better served had she never met you."

"I would lay down my life for her." Euryon was right. He loved Aewen enough to die for her, but he'd given Raefe the opportunity to forever destroy her reputation. Not only that, but Raefe's story would also spread ill will among the Elder against the Kindren. He'd failed both Aewen and duty.

He bowed his head before Euryon. "I ask you to forgive me and let me take Aewen to wife."

12

Repentance

Raefe snorted in derision as Euryon stepped forward, the lanthorn light falling over his face. Elcon read no kindness there. "I'll not allow her to marry a Kindren. Take yourself from here come morning." Euryon turned on his heel, and a footman stepped forward to light his way back down the path.

Raefe strode toward Elcon as Kai and Craelin tensed at his side. Raefe gave a mirthless laugh. "Relax. I'll not touch your king. Anyway, you've done me a favor, *Kindren*. You showed me Aewen's unfaithfulness before I cursed myself with her as a bride."

Kai and Craelin moved as one to shield Elcon with their bodies. Did they also mean to block him from attacking Raefe? Elcon's hand went to his dagger, and he fought the urge to push Kai and Craelin out of the way and launch himself at Raefe. He longed to shove Raefe's words down his throat, but retained enough sense to remember that nothing good ever came of letting his emotions rule him.

Raefe gave a low growl. "Hide behind your servants like a coward if you must, but make no mistake, *Kindren*. If you ever enter Darksea, I'll kill you on sight." The last lanthorn withdrew its light as footsteps thudded away.

Craelin and Kai faced Elcon, the moonlight falling over their shoulders so that their faces hid in shadow. He would scold them for following him—right after he thanked them.

ৡৢৡৢ

Aewen wept into her pillow until exhaustion claimed her. But she found no peace in sleep, for strange dreams tormented her. She stood on one edge of a chasm with Elcon on the other. He climbed upon a fallen tree bridging the gap and balanced as he crossed over the chasm. She ran to help him, to steady the tree, for it rocked. Before she reached it, the tree rolled and Elcon fell.

She started awake and gasped with relief, but then turned her face into her pillow to weep again.

Mother did not lash her, as she expected, but instead locked her alone in the darkness of her chambers. Aewen caught herself listening for the shuffle of Murial's footsteps, but they would come no more. Murial, Mother informed her, had been put out of Cobbleford at last.

Her mother's white-lipped silence frightened Aewen much worse than her anger. She'd lain on the floor where she had fallen when pushed into the room. The bar of lanthorn light beneath the door thinned and faded. Crawling to the bed, she climbed onto its tick fully clothed and let her tears flow. She wept over Elcon, now lost to her forever. She wept for Murial, who might even now cower in the dark forest. She wept for her own ruined life and for the shame she'd brought to her family. She even wept for Caerla, who loved the horrible Prince of Darksea and who could now never hope to marry. How could a second daughter wed when none would have the first to wife? She did not even begin to hope Raefe would not ruin her reputation. His wounded ego would demand satisfaction. He hated her now.

A gray day dawned, sending dull light across her bed to wake her, for none had closed the hangings or shutters the night before. She stirred and lifted her head from her pillow with a groan. Now she had found sleep, she longed only to forget herself in its rest. But, although weary, she couldn't surrender to its embrace again. Sitting, she blinked to comfort her aching eyes.

A grating at the latch alerted her. Someone entered her outer chamber. She did not call out, but waited. Through the open connecting doorway, Caerla swept into the inner chamber, her erect posture a reminder of Mother's. With her unbound hair frizzing about her and her eyes wild, she looked almost like a madwoman. From the foot of the bed, she glared down upon Aewen. "Are you content now? You have destroyed all my chances!"

Aewen stared back at Caerla, not sure how to respond.

"Have you nothing to say for yourself?" Caerla's volume raised a notch.

"What can I say? You are right. Your fate is linked to mine. Why should we bind ourselves to a form without substance? Why should it matter which sister marries first? And yet, once in times past and for reasons now lost to us, it did." New tears gathered in her eyes. "I would not harm you for anything, my sister, but it seems I have."

Caerla's tawny eyes glinted. "Do not call me *sister*.

You had everything *I* could want and you despised it. You drove from my life the only man I will ever love." Silent tears slid down her face. "Raefe and his father left at dawn. They couldn't get away from here soon enough."

"You make no sense, Caerla. How can you reproach me for not wanting the man *you* love?" She just stopped herself from giving her opinion of Raefe's worthiness of Caerla's love.

"If you had married him, I might have spent time with Raefe as a sister, at least. Now I'll never see him again." Wrenching sobs wracked her.

Aewen wished she could comfort her sister. "What a wretched life that would be."

"Don't talk to me about my wretched life!" Caerla flew at her, hands curved into claws.

She caught her sister's hands and struggled against the sudden strength that possessed Caerla, enduring pain as her sleeves fell back and fingernails rode paths down her arms. And then the fight went out of Caerla, and she dissolved into tears. Aewen held her slender body in an awkward embrace, but her sister pulled away. "I've made up my mind. I will take my vow of celibacy."

"Mother will not allow it."

Caerla arched an eyebrow. "You think she will not?"

Aewen fell silent as she rubbed the stinging scratch marks on her arms. She was not sure of anything anymore.

འ➻⬳

Cobbleford Castle stood against a pewter sky that

gathered clouds to hide the sun. It seemed fitting to Elcon that such a day as this should dawn overcast and cold. At the clack of hooves on stone, he turned. The grass of the outer bailey glowed green against the cobblestone path where Craelin and Kai, already mounted, waited beside Raeld.

Craelin squinted at him. "Ready?"

He leaped to Raeld's back, taken by the urgent desire to be quit of this place of shattered dreams.

"Halt!" Four of the garrison watchguards approached, two armed with swords that clanked at their sides and two with bows slung across their backs.

Elcon's hand went to the hilt of his sword.

Kai and Craelin rode to position themselves between the guards and Elcon.

"What business have you with Lof Shraen Elcon?" Craelin called a challenge.

"King Euryon requires the Lof Shraen's presence in his meeting chamber." As the group reached them, one of the swordsmen answered.

"Name the king's business." Craelin demanded.

Silence. One of the guards shifted, the leather of his armor creaking. "We cannot."

Elcon dismounted. "Never mind. For good or ill, I'll go to Euryon."

Craelin and Kai dismounted as well but the swordsman who had spoken stood in their way. "King Euryon asks only for Elcon."

Craelin jutted out his chin and drew breath.

"I'll present myself alone." Elcon said before Craelin could speak.

When Elcon entered with the watchguards Euryon looked up from the head of a long table of reddish kaba wood.

Elcon inclined his head in greeting.

Euryon did not return the gesture of respect, although he waved to dismiss the guards. He sent Elcon a piercing look. "Sit near me."

Elcon obeyed.

"Raefe and Devlon departed for Darksea early today."

He waited.

"I tried—" Euryon cleared his throat. "I tried to persuade Raefe to keep silence about what he—about last night. He's bitter, though, and he promised me he would not." He hesitated. "I've spoken with Inydde. We've reached a decision." His voice strengthened. "You don't deserve her, but you may take Aewen to wife if she will have you. Her reputation is in ruins. She can no longer hope for a husband among the Elder. She will only suffer if she remains in Westerland, and we must think of Caerla. As you may know, among our people a younger sister cannot wed before the older. We can only hope that, with Aewen gone from Westerland, Caerla might someday rise above her sister's shame."

"I'll wed Aewen with gladness."

"You will take her with you to Rivenn, to your people, and marry her there. That is best, under the circumstances."

Elcon frowned. It was too late for his peace-making visit to succeed now. He'd given little thought to what he'd lost in winning Aewen and even less to the reaction of his own people to his marrying an Elder princess. He pushed away the doubt that nagged him. "As you say. She will return with me to Torindan, where I will make her Queen of Rivenn and High Queen of Faeraven."

Euryon pierced Elcon with a glare. "Mind that you do." He pushed to his feet and, uncurling one fisted hand, gripped Elcon's a little too tightly. "Aewen waits to receive you in the queen's parlor."

Aewen stood with her back to the door but turned as he entered. Limned in light from the tall window, dressed in blue silk, and with one long plait falling across her shoulder, she looked beautiful. "I thought never to see you again."

He took a step toward her, and she met him. She felt fragile in his arms. They stood locked together as he savored her nearness. At last he drew back to look at her. "To think I almost lost you."

At the glint of tears in her eyes, he pulled her to him again and spoke against her hair. "Your father has given us permission to marry."

"I know. Mother told me." She twined her arms about his neck and lifted her face as if for a kiss.

"Then...you will?"

She drew away this time, and he saw that she smiled. "I will, Elcon, with pleasure."

He caught the contagion of her smile but schooled his features. "Will you come with me to Torindan? Will you reign with me?"

Her face sobered, and she looked away. "My people will reject me now, Elcon. But will yours accept me?"

He tilted her face. "They will love you as I do." As he lowered his head to kiss her, he pushed away his lingering doubts.

Part Two: The Elder Queen

13

Restoration

Hiding her surprise, Aewen backed into her outer chamber to allow her father entrance. The scratch on her door had sounded timid, as if not made by a king.

Father flicked a glance about the chamber. "Does a princess of Westerland now answer doors? Where is your maid?"

Tears thickened her throat. "Murial has left my service." She would say nothing in complaint on her last morning at Cobbleford.

"Then I will instruct your mother to send a replacement."

"Thank you, Father."

"Any child of mine will make a good impression wherever she goes." Although he spoke in a gruff voice, his eyes looked suspiciously bright.

Aewen squelched a rueful smile. Her father hadn't added "even amongst the Kindren," but from his sour expression, he might as well have. "Yes, Father."

"Well, then…" He cleared his throat. "Have a pleasant journey with joy at its end." He walked toward the door for all the world as if she departed for a social engagement and would return later that day.

"Father?" Her voice shook. As he spun around, she flung herself into his arms.

He patted her back like he had in childhood after she'd scraped her knee. "There, there."

After the storm of weeping passed, Aewen straightened and dashed her tears away. "Promise me we will see one another again."

"Now you've dampened my surcoat."

"Promise me."

He sighed. "You ask something not in my power to give, Aewen. Age creeps upon me, and you go to a new life in a land where you may not even remember you have a father."

Her smile was tender. "Don't think you are so easily forgotten."

He cupped her chin. "Nor are you, my daughter."

"If I did not love Elcon, I would wish I didn't have to go."

"Children must wing away from the nest."

"I've failed our family."

His face reddened so much she wished she had not spoken. "None more than yourself. Godspeed."

He walked quickly from the room, leaving the door open behind him.

"Goodbye Father."

⁓⁖

Curiously disconnected from her body, as if she

had thinned to become a spirit, Aewen floated toward Elcon. He waited for her inside the gatehouse near his guardians astride their wingabeasts Raeld, saddled and laden, stirred beside him. Although the dimness of early morning would obscure Aewen's identity from a chance observer, she still wore a dark cloak with the hood up. The maid supplied to her wore similar garb and followed behind bearing only a few satchels. So little.

Elcon offered a hand to her, looking so handsome she almost forgot her sorrow. Almost.

"My love, why do you hesitate?"

She blinked away tears. "Mother and Caerla remain absent, even now. I might have sought them myself, but my new maid warned that I should not. I didn't have the heart to inquire further."

Elcon's jaw firmed. "If only I could bear your pain. Perhaps we can return to Cobbleford after matters settle."

She attempted a smile, for his sake. "Yes."

"Come, I'm eager to carry you away."

He lifted her onto his wingabeast, and she gathered the folds of her cloak so they wouldn't billow in the wind of their flight. Mother had arranged for them to depart in the early morning when few would be about and had sent the plain woolen cloaks. She must still cling to the delusional hope that she could keep Aewen's shame a secret.

Kai dismounted to take the satchels from her maid and passed them to Craelin. As he attempted to lift her onto his wingabeast, however, she backed, wringing her hands and weeping.

"What's this?" Aewen called. "Why do you carry on so?"

Rushing to Aewen, the maid clung to her leg and lifted a tear-streaked face. "I don't care if milady beats me. I won't go to the Kindren lands."

She was little more than a child and probably still lived with her mother. Why should the innocent bear the burden of the guilty? Surely there were maids at Torindan. "Hush now, I won't make you go."

The maid caught her hand and kissed it. "Thank you. May God protect you, princess." She stumbled away, and then ran through the archway into the outer bailey. With a shake of his head, Kai mounted his wingabeast. Elcon vaulted into position before Aewen, and they passed beneath the raised portcullis.

As they emerged from the gatehouse, a cloaked beggar woman lurched into their path, and Raeld reared.

As Elcon reined in Raeld, Craelin rode to intercept the beggar. "Step aside!"

"Wait." Aewen found a coin to toss to the woman, but as recognition sparked, cried out. The peasant woman threw back her hood and lifted a beaming face. Aewen's throat unlocked. "Murial!"

Elcon had barely halted the wingabeast before Aewen slid to the ground. She took Murial into her arms, but then drew away to give her a light shake. "Why do you linger here? Have you nowhere to go? It frightens me to think of you in the woods alone."

"Well now, I did have a fright that first night, but I reached Willowa's farm safe enough. I scared her to death pounding on the door. Her husband, Camryn was on a hunt that night, you see. Willowa welcomed me, especially as I could lend a hand with little Caed."

"You're staying with Willowa? How wonderful. And Caed—has he recovered from his accident?"

"His burn left a scar but it will shrink as he grows. He's full of energy. I could not stay with Willowa long. She would never turn me out, but I went nonetheless. They can barely feed themselves as 'tis."

Aewen dried her tears. She did not ask why a huntsman had little food. She knew that most of what Camryn caught went to her parents' table. "And so I find you begging outside Cobbleford. You suffer for my sins."

Murial waved her hand as if to erase all sufferings. "Nay. I saw it coming and already knew what I'd do. I even hid a wee lanthorn, a blanket and a little food outside the gates. I can look for my sister in Norwood, but I couldn't leave without knowing what became of you. I didn't dare show my face near Cobbleford again, so I disguised myself as a beggar at the gate and kept my ears open. It seems that things have turned out well, though *some* might not think so."

"Elcon and I will marry. But you—what will you do now? I won't rest until I know you are safe."

Elcon cut into the conversation. "Bring Murial with you to Torindan, if you like. You'll want a maid."

She beamed at him, her heart full.

Murial smiled. "You've married a fine man, whether Kindren or no. I'll go with you, if you want me."

She blinked away tears of gratitude. "Want you? Just try to refuse."

With Murial safely seated behind Kai, Aewen pressed her cheek against Elcon's back and felt his muscles flex as he guided Raeld into flight. She smiled to herself, well pleased to give herself up to the kiss of sun upon her face, the wind that freshened her heated skin, and the dizzying sensation of flight on this first day of her new life.

Rivenn, in tales she'd heard as a child, had seemed an enchanted place filled with sparkling waterfalls and towering mountains. What would it be like to live among the peaks, as they did at Torindan? Despite its forested hillsides, Westerland boasted no real mountains. The blued peaks that shone in the sun rendered her speechless, even at a distance.

Did she dream? How else could she explain the joy that sprang to life within her as Elcon's intended wife? It had seemed impossible. She would cherish her happiness all the more because it came at great cost. Did not the sweetest roses guard their scent with thorns?

She might never return to Westerland or receive her parents as visitors to Torindan. They had only sanctioned her marriage so that others would know she'd not lost her virtue to Elcon without gaining its benefits. They'd chosen a higher course for her despite the disgrace she'd brought to them.

∂∾∿

Torindan caught the sun until its walls and turrets glowed with pinkish light. The green, rose, and gilt flag of Rivenn flapped with lazy abandon from the south and north towers. The flag of Faeraven, ten white diamonds against a background of red and black, adorned the towers to east and west. Each diamond represented one of the ten existing ravens that together made up the alliance of Faeraven. Or at least they once had done so. He might need to have the flag amended to show only seven diamonds. He hoped it would not lose more. He would wait to revise the flag, however, for he still hoped to restore Glindenn, Selfred, and Morgorad, the three ravens under the shraens Veraedel, Taelerat, and Lenhardt, traitors all.

He eased his jaw, which had tightened as memories intruded—memories of his coronation day and the attempt by Freaer to assassinate him. The presence chamber ran with blood that day. He'd escaped with his life, as had Freaer and the three traitorous shraens.

Aewen nestled against him, her touch recalling him, and he smiled to himself. As he carried home his future bride, he should not reflect on things that worried him. He contemplated instead their wedding night when he would comfort her shyness and show her both gentleness and passion. But they would wed before Lof Yuel first. He would make certain of that.

The waters of Weild Aenor swelled their banks below. Autumn rains must have visited in his absence. The river's familiar sweet and tangy scent filled his senses. He breathed deep, giving himself to the pleasure of homecoming. When Aewen's arms tightened around him, he caught one of her hands and warmed it in his own.

They approached on the side by the river, going past the water gate with its hewn steps and defensible platforms. Raeld dipped and leveled alongside Torindan's middle ward, the balding grass strip outside the inner curtain wall and above the wall retaining the motte upon which Torindan rested. Two guardians kept watch at a bastian. Manning the bastians was a new precaution. Freaer would return, without doubt. Even now the guardians marshaled their defenses in preparation for another siege.

Raeld rounded the side of the castle and spiraled

to land before the drawbridge that led to the barbican with its tall, wide towers and twin turrets. Water lapped against the moat's sides and sent wavy light upward. Fletch and Mystael stirred the air with the batting of wings as they came to rest on either side of Elcon. "Lof Shraen!" A voice rang from battlements above the gatehouse.

Metal screeched as the portcullis raised and the drawbridge lowered. Craelin moved into the lead and Kai dropped behind Elcon as they rode into the shadowy interior of the barbican and, emerging, crossed the second drawbridge. They dismounted inside an archway giving onto the outer bailey from the inner gatehouse. Elcon stretched to ease his stiffness, and then took Aewen's slight weight into his arms. He steadied them both before assisting her to stand on her own.

Aewen looked about her. "This is much larger than the guardhouse at Cobbleford, but then Torindan is altogether larger."

"You'll grow used to Torindan." He gave her a reassuring smile.

Murial drew near to her mistress in silent support.

"I'll find the grooms." Craelin offered.

Elcon smiled. "You and Kai shall dine in my chambers as a reward for your diligence."

Aewen smiled at him, and he felt a twinge of conscience for what he left unsaid. In truth, he balked from presenting his future bride before the Kindren in the great hall. He did not know the reaction Aewen at his side would bring. Craelin emerged from the stables with several grooms, and Elcon turned to Aewen. "Come."

He walked beside her but did not take her hand as

they followed the fieldstone path crossing the outer bailey. Murial trailed after her mistress while Kai and Craelin fell into step behind. At sight of the inner garden and its fountain, both Aewen and Murial exclaimed with delight, but Elcon did not let them linger, urging them away from the garden with a promise to return. He wanted only rest within the quiet safety of his chambers.

When they reached the keep Aewen exclaimed with delight, but he hurried her toward his chambers without giving her time to admire its fine architecture.

As they reached his outer chamber, Aewen touched his arm. "Elcon, what troubles you?"

He evaded her eyes. "I'm only weary. Can I not show you the wonders of Torindan on the morrow?"

She put her hands on either side of his head and gazed into his eyes. "Do you deceive me, my betrothed?"

Heat rose into his face. "I—I'm sorry, Aewen. I'm uncertain of—well, I…"

A knowing expression came over her face. "Do you fear my reception here?"

The door to Ander's room opened, and Elcon's servant stepped into the outer chamber. He stared first at Aewen, then Murial. He appeared to have forgotten his bow. Perhaps Anders had never seen Elder women before.

Elcon took a breath. "Well, Anders, what greeting have you for my intended bride?"

Anders' eyes widened. His mouth opened as if to speak but then closed. He tried again, only to squeak something unintelligible. At least, when he closed his mouth at last he remembered his bow.

"You will treat her with all the respect due your

future *Lof Raelein*, for I intend to make her High Queen."

Anders seemed to master himself. He pulled his gaze from Aewen and Murial. "Yes, Lof Shraen, of course I will." He bowed to Aewen. "Welcome to Torindan."

The small victory warmed Elcon and gave him courage.

"Anders, this is Murial, Aewen's maid. She and her mistress will require the guest room closest to my chambers."

"Very well, Lof Shraen."

Elcon gave Aewen a reassuring smile. "There, that's settled. I will have the Lof Raelein's chambers prepared for you and your maid soon. But until then, it is best that you stay close to me. Don't be alarmed, but I plan to post a guard outside your door."

"If you think you must."

"I do, but only for a time. I would have you safe."

"Anders, we will wash away the dust of travel and then take food and drink in my meeting room."

Anders bowed and went to the outer chamber door just as the steward Benisch gained admittance. Dressed in blue silk trimmed with gold, Benisch made a fine figure. He gave a deep bow. "Lof Shraen."

Elcon inclined his head in acknowledgement. "Benisch, I'm afraid you catch us at an inopportune time. You may return on the morrow."

Benisch glanced at Murial and then ran a watery blue gaze over Aewen. He frowned and clamped his lips together, but then executed another bow before Elcon. The jingling of bells accompanied him from the chamber.

Aewen dimpled and her eyes danced with

laughter. "Who, pray, was that?"

Elcon laughed. "That, my flower, was someone overly concerned with my affairs."

At thought of his meeting with Benisch tomorrow, he sobered. From the look on the steward's face, he did not welcome Elcon's decision to marry an Elder princess.

Early the next morning Benisch requested an audience. Elcon strode into his meeting chamber, shut the door with a thud, and rounded on his steward. The day was much too early for a disagreeable discussion, but Elcon would not sidestep. Benisch peered at him out of watery eyes and gave his head with its wreath of sandy hair a shake. "I doubt you'll survive the reaction to your new concubine, Lof Shraen."

Elcon's jaw tightened. "I must warn you, Steward Benisch, never to use that term for my betrothed again."

Benisch's jaw dropped, but he recovered himself in swiftness. "Many will use harsher terms to refer to a Lof Raelein of Elder blood."

The urge to cast Benisch from the room and from his service seized Elcon. He had not faced the wrath of the Prince of Darksea and the fury of the king and queen of Westerland in order to be chastised by a servant, no matter how highly-placed. His hands curled into fists at his side, but he held onto his temper by a thread. Benisch meant well. "We will marry as soon as possible."

"You make a fool's choice."

Elcon moved toward the door. "I've satisfied your curiosity. Should you happen to make this known, also state that I'll exact punishment against any who oppose my choice of bride. Please show yourself out."

With that, Elcon left the chamber and the annoyance of Benisch's presence. The encounter had stiffened his spine. He would allow none to tell him he could not have Aewen as his wife. He loved her and would not abandon her. He would follow their marriage ceremony by crowning her Lof Raelein of Faeraven. That should still most of the whispers. Thereafter, if any tongue wagged against Aewen, the speaker would be named a traitor to the throne.

$$\approx \infty$$

Anointed and bejeweled, Aewen gazed at Elcon through a wedding veil. For now, it didn't matter that the crowd should be greater. Certain shraens and their raeleins had refused to sanction Elcon's wedding to an Elder, despite her nobility, and rumors circulated that several shraens meant to withdraw from the Alliance of Faeraven. Aewen let herself look away from such concerns and into the sea green eyes of the husband who loved her. Light poured into the allerstaed from its high windows and flooded over her as she received Elcon's pledge and gave hers in turn. They knelt, and the black-garbed priest thrice rang the bells of unity above their joined hands and bowed heads. The priest blessed them and offered supplications on their behalf. They arose together, and Elcon removed the veil from her face to warm her lips in a lingering kiss. He grinned and faced the crowd. With a deep breath, Aewen did the same.

"Good Kindren all, receive Elcon, Shraen of Rivenn, and his wedded wife, Aewen of Westerland." The priest's voice gave way to cheers.

She smiled her relief. Not all despised her union

with Elcon, it seemed. Elcon took her hand with a smile. She wanted to cling to his hand but turned and knelt before the priest alone. Above her head the priest held a bejeweled circlet similar to the larger Circlet of Rivenn Elcon wore. "Aewen of Westerland, daughter of Euryon, son of Garadrel, son of Amberoft, son of Mercedon, son of Rhys, begotten of the Ancient Kings of Elderland, receive the Coronet of Rivenn."

As the priest helped her to her feet, the weight of the crown pressed against the head she held high.

"A new raelein rises over Rivenn." A tumult from the crowd, still joyous but quieter, overrode the priest's declaration.

Elcon's hand at her elbow steadied her. A second priest emerged from a small archway behind the chancel. He bore a gleaming scepter of beaten gold, its jewel-embedded staff crowned by a rampant gryphon with a star sapphire orb suspended in its claws—the Scepter of Faeraven. Elcon took the scepter, kissed it, and held it toward her. Enmeshed in his sea green gaze, she joined her hands with his upon the staff. "Aewen, Raelein of Rivenn, receive with me the Scepter of Faeraven."

They turned together and held the scepter aloft. The crowd murmured in tones of wonder at its beauty.

The priest made his final proclamation. "Good Kindren all, receive Aewen, Lof Raelein of Faeraven."

The crowd hesitated, but then broke into restrained cheering. Aewen understood. She would have to prove herself.

They surrendered the scepter to the priests and submitted to a final prayer.

Elcon escorted her from the allerstaed by means of a vaulted corridor to the foyer of the great hall, where they greeted all who entered the wedding feast. The clang of dishware punctuated bright melodies. As the chattering crowd issued from the presence chamber to press around them, the fragrance of food reminded her she'd been too excited to eat earlier.

Many long eyes sent Aewen inquisitive glances. She must seem as exotic to the Kindren as they did to her. She ignored her jangling nerves and greeted those she met with warmth and kindness, no matter how much they stared. She must not once allow her composure to falter or she would shame Elcon. Had she done him a disservice in wedding him? Would they both have been better off if she'd taken a vow of chastity? Brother Robb would probably have granted her request if she'd asked again, under the circumstances. She might rather have given Elcon a broken heart than a broken kingdom.

She pushed such thoughts to the back of her mind. Beside her, a golden-haired maiden held Elcon's hand and gazed at him in a way that struck Aewen to the heart. The tilt of Elcon's head conveyed its own story.

Elcon turned to her with an unreadable expression. "Aewen, I present to you Raena Arillia of Chaeradon, a dear friend since my early days."

Aewen took the delicate hand extended to her and smiled into gray eyes that shone with unshed tears. "I am happy to meet you." Aewen spoke a lie. She felt no happiness at meeting the beautiful Kindren princess whose pleased expression belied the sorrow in her eyes.

Arillia's parents, Shraen Ferran and Raelein Annora, greeted Aewen with cool politeness. She responded with equal courtesy. Later, she would ask Elcon the details of his association with Raena Arillia of Chaeradon. Or did she prefer not to know?

Her throat felt parched, and her stomach cramped with hunger by the time Elcon took her hand and guided her into the great hall. The crowd parted and applauded with restraint as they made their way to the dais to join the nobles waiting there. The other guests jostled one another at trestle tables below the dais. The guardians, ever present throughout the ceremony, filed to their own trestle tables nearest the dais.

Elcon seated Aewen at the center of a long strongwood table and then took his place beside her. The music, which had idled at their entrance, rushed on. The roar of conversation and laughter swelled and grew. Aewen's face heated and her ears rang. She took a draught of mulled cider, grateful for the tang which broke against her tongue and soothed her parched throat.

Elcon sat beside her with Benisch on her other side. Since she knew his opinion of her marriage to Elcon, she misliked such close proximity to the steward. Even so, as Elcon's distant relative, Benisch must be given precedence. After a brief but courteous greeting, to her relief Benisch said nothing more. Immediately across the table, sat Raena Arillia and her parents. They seemed similarly disinclined to talk. For her part, Aewen could think of nothing to say.

Conversation became altogether less important. Servants brought food in many courses, in a vast array such as she had never seen, despite Westerland's abundance. The table groaned under all manner of roasted meats, soups, breads baked of thrice-sifted flour, tarts, salads, and puddings. Indeed, so many offerings abounded she could not taste them all. Elcon stood and raised his goblet. "I toast the beauty and the virtue of the woman who has captured my heart, Aewen of Westerland."

After an awkward silence, others at the long table lifted their goblets. Aewen's gaze entangled with Arillia's, but she looked away, not waiting to see if the young raena joined the toast.

14

Heartache

Arillia raised her goblet in toast to Aewen, a wounded look in her eyes, and Elcon's conscience smote him. His marrying Aewen could only have alienated Arillia. He might even have broken her heart, and yet she and her parents still attended his wedding.

He drank his own salute to his bride and took his place beside her. When Aewen turned an adoring smile on him, the knife of guilt twisted a little deeper in his gut. He'd tarnished her reputation and given her little recourse but to marry him. He'd hurt Arillia as well, in the worst possible way. She'd grown up thinking he would wed her, but he'd broken his promise to court her. He couldn't fathom how she could sit in quiet dignity and make polite conversation with the bride he'd married in place of her.

Heat crept up his neck. In truth, he longed to cut the celebration short, but decorum made its demands. And so he engaged in small talk with the shraen and raelein of Chaeradon while their daughter maintained the carefully neutral expression he remembered from whenever Arillia had hurt herself in their early days. He wanted to comfort her now as he had then. He'd always been able to calm her upsets, until now. The thought brought him a curious twist of pain. Frivolous notions of romance had muddled what should have been a lifelong friendship, and it was too late to turn back now.

He found relief in conversing with Kai's father, Shraen Eberhardt of Whellein instead, which required he turn his back to Aewen and Arillia. Trying not to dwell on the falseness with which he'd served them both, he engaged Eberhardt in conversation until Aewen claimed his attention with a gentle touch of her hand. The trestle tables had already been removed to make room for dancing. Elcon offered his arm to Aewen at once.

"I don't know the Kindren dances."

Her blush brought a smile to him. "Come, I'll teach you."

"Please, no."

"Please, yes."

"I can deny you nothing when you smile at me that way." She rose with him, and he put a hand to her back.

"That's worth remembering."

Elcon led his laughing bride into the dancers but paused to explain the steps. Aewen stumbled and put her hands to her cheeks as if conscious of her blush. They laughed together and began again. He lost himself in the simple pleasure of dancing with his bride.

The partners shifted and the dance brought him face-to-face with Arillia. Her eyes widened, and he put out a hand to stop her, for it seemed she might break from him and run. He should prevent that for his sake and for hers. But Arillia did not run. How odd to dance with her in the same way as before when nothing was the same at all. The dance brought them close and he spoke near her ear. "I'm sorry."

"I hope you are not."

Did she deliberately misunderstand him? The dance moved them apart, and as Elcon turned to a new partner, he decided to let the matter drop. He'd made his apology, however inadequate. He could do no more to ease Arillia, especially since spending time in her presence left him with a strange feeling in his stomach. He loved Aewen, but it seemed Arillia could still touch him with regret.

He spent a restless night and, to quiet himself, slipped into the solitude of the inner garden. The mist parted to reveal Arillia walking with her maid near the fountain at the garden's heart. She'd already seen him, so it would be rude to withdraw despite his longing to flee. When they met he said the first thing that came to mind. "Forgive me. I'll leave you in peace."

Arillia's gray eyes, which he'd once found so calming, pierced him. "No Elcon, there's no need." She took a deep breath. "Perhaps you will join me."

He misliked the idea but paced beside her anyway as her maid trailed at a discreet distance. They passed beneath the strongwood tree where he'd once promised to court her. The memory of it took him and, from the look on Arillia's face, she remembered too.

"Each morning grows colder." Her words ended on a rising note he'd heard before whenever she'd wanted to weep.

He turned her toward him, but not for his kiss this time. "I meant what I said last night, Arillia. I'm sorry."

"The frosts of winter will soon paint the mornings." She would not meet his eyes.

"I broke faith with you, and I don't deserve your forgiveness, but I *am* sorry. When I met Aewen, I—I couldn't seem to help myself."

She put her hands to his chest. "Please, Elcon—"
Her husky whisper filled his ears.

"Will you not forgive me?"

Her eyes closed, and the eyelids fluttered. *"Speak
no more."*

He longed to continue his plea, to wrest from her
the forgiveness that would expunge his guilt, but this
time he would yield to her need rather than his own.
When she opened her eyes tears trembled on her
lashes. He saw, too, all he had taken from her, and
from himself. He had not known the future he'd once
held in his arms. He'd despised it as too attainable.
Now it was gone forever. He deserved to live with
guilt and regret, just as Arillia would live with the pain
he'd caused her. As Arillia's tears fell, Elcon caught her
hand and kissed her fingertips. He let go of her then,
backing until the mist shut her away from him, as it
must.

⧫

Aewen smiled and reached for her new husband
but found only bedding. Frowning at the silent
chamber, she pushed back the covers and dangled her
feet over the edge of the bed as she stretched.

An image of the golden raena with silver eyes
arose unbidden.

Aewen sighed. Raena Arillia embodied everything
she could never be. Where Arillia's locks resembled a
ray of sun on an overcast day, her own dark hair called
to mind the thickening shadows of night. Arillia would
always be a Kindren, whereas no matter how hard she
tried, Aewen would ever remain an outsider. Arillia

moved with ease within the social parameters at Torindan, but Aewen didn't even know when she blundered. She must embarrass Elcon, although he did not tell her so. Instead, he withdrew and left her to flounder alone. Hadn't he spent much of their wedding feast engaged in conversation with Shraen Eberhardt?

She called Murial to tend her and thus stilled the voice of introspection.

"You sleep late this morn." Murial pressed her lips together, but her eyes gleamed.

Aewen felt the rising warmth of a blush. "I do. My husband slept ill and disturbed my own slumber."

Murial looked puzzled. "What but the delights of the marriage bed keeps a bridegroom awake on his wedding night?"

Now her face truly heated. "Enough of such talk."

Murial brushed her hair in silent obedience, but Aewen could not keep her own rule. "Whatever keeps Elcon from sleep has to do with Raena Arillia. I'm sure of it. Have you heard of her, Murial?" She should not seek gossip from her servant in this way.

The brush paused mid-stroke. "Aye, I know of her."

"Tell me."

"You'll not like it."

"I like not knowing even less."

Murial continued brushing. "Well, then. Elcon was meant to marry Raena Arillia from childhood. He might have done so had he not met you."

She released her breath. "She loves him?"

"They say he broke her heart."

Aewen touched her hands to her cheeks. "I took him from her."

"You did, but he went willingly. He loves you. Let

it be."

How could she ignore the grief she'd given another, even without intent? Here, then, was another reproach at her door.

Elcon returned and swept her into his arms just as Murial tightened her girdle belt. She pulled away, fussing about the lacing, but Murial shushed her. "Laces be only laces, flitling."

With that reminder, she relinquished thoughts of Arillia and pulled Elcon down for her kiss. He responded with breathtaking fervor. Blushing when he released her, she glanced at Murial in embarrassment.

The corners of Murial's mouth lifted. The connecting door to the outer chamber closed behind her with a small click.

Elcon smiled at Aewen. "Do you blush in front of your servant, wife?"

Aewen tilted a smile up at him. "I suppose I do."

His laughter held an odd note that troubled her. "Are you well this morn?"

He sobered, and she almost wished she had not asked the question. "Why do you ask?"

She shrugged and looked away from him. "Sleep held little charm for you last night."

"That's true enough." He touched her shoulder. "With such a beauty in my bed, I lay awake thinking of my good fortune. I'm sorry if I disturbed you."

He lied. Such tossing and turning did not come from counting joys. She turned back to him. "Tell me about Raena Arillia."

Elcon looked as if struck. As he peered out one of the windows, she seated herself on the bench before the fire. Just when she'd decided he'd forgotten her, he turned. "You have a right to know."

She laced her fingers and waited as he crossed the room to her. "Arillia and I were raised with the understanding we would one day wed."

Murial had said as much, although she didn't inform him that she already knew. She examined her clasped hands.

Elcon heaved a breath. "No, it's worse than that, if I'm honest. I've not requited myself well, with either you or Arillia."

She jerked her gaze to his, and he gave her a sad smile.

"You see, I promised Arillia I would court her when I returned from my journeys. I came back with you instead."

She stared at him, waiting for what he would say next.

He paced before the fire. "You are not the only one who forsook another and bore shame so we might wed. I broke faith with Arillia and disregarded the understanding between her parents and mine in order to marry you." He came to stand before her. "I should not have asked it of you, nor should I have disgraced Arillia." Kneeling, he touched her face. "Despite my sins, I love you."

She caught his hand and brought it to her lips to receive her kiss. "I hope you find my love enough to sustain you, Elcon, and that you will not wish for what might have been."

His eyes widened. "We have made our choices, Aewen. Let us leave such speculation aside, for it cannot profit."

Outside the window in the inner garden a breeze stirred the leaves. Elcon was right. They had both chosen the path before them, a road paved in dishonor.

15

Conception

"What now?" Elcon did not bother to hide his irritation in finding Benisch at the door. When contrasted with the peace wrought by his avoidance of Elcon since the wedding, the steward's intrusion seemed all the more unbearable.

Benisch's face spasmed, and he pushed past Elcon into his outer chamber. "I must remind you, Lof Shraen, that you do not speak to a mere servant, but rather address one joined to you by your father's blood."

"I'm surprised you would reproach me with our relationship."

"We are cousins."

"Distant cousins."

"You tend to forget the truth of even that. If, like you, I had been blessed with the shil shael, you'd remember." Benisch had long rued the fact that he'd not inherited the hereditary soul touch of the sons of Rivenn. "You're reluctant to claim me, son of Talan that you are, and yet your shame is not that different from my ancestor, Iewald's."

"If we were not kinsmen that remark would see you to the dungeon." Elcon kept his voice light, but fury burned within him. Iewald, Kunrat's illegitimate son, had betrayed his legitimate brother, Talan, at the beguilement of Merriwyn of Old, thus weakening the virtue of the House of Rivenn and enabling Freaer to escape imprisonment. How dare a son of Iewald accuse Talan's son? And yet unease stirred within Elcon. Had he also betrayed his kingdom for love?

Fright stamped Benisch's features. He must realize he'd gone too far. He rasped a breath. "Lof Shraen, I have word of Freaer."

Elcon leaned forward. "Tell me."

"He now occupies Pilaer, which he fortifies daily, and readies for another attack of Torindan."

"How come you by this news?"

Benisch gave a cagey smile. "I have ears, Lof Shraen, in certain places."

Elcon waved that aside. "I'm not interested in gossip, Benisch. I need facts."

Benisch sniffed. "I overheard part of a conversation between Craelin and a messenger from Whellein Hold. Craelin will soon bring you this information."

Elcon eyed Benisch. "How came you to overhear a private conversation?"

Benisch waved his hand in a parody of Elcon's earlier gesture. "They need to take more care."

Elcon blinked. Whether or not Benisch should have eavesdropped, his logic was unassailable. Craelin should have been more careful. Still, Elcon had no wish to indulge in gossip with Benisch. He sat back in his chair. "Go find Craelin and tell him I wait for him."

Benisch opened his mouth as if to say more but then hesitated and inclined his head. "As you wish."

In Benisch's absence, Elcon paced through the room. When a tap came at the door, he turned.

Anders looked in. "Do you require food, Lof Shraen?"

Elcon waved him away in annoyance but then called him back. "Send Kai to me." While Kai had no formal duty to offer advice, more and more in difficult situations Elcon looked to his quiet presence and well-reasoned responses. His mother had done the same. Remembering his mother made Elcon smile but also hitch a breath at the thought she was no longer alive.

When Kai entered the room, he made no inquiry but waited in silence as Elcon concluded his pacing. Craelin arrived and Elcon moved to the table with a brief nod to acknowledge his bow. "Come then, we've much to discuss."

The men took their accustomed places at his side, and Elcon aimed a glance at Craelin. "Tell me how I come by news of Freaer's movements first from my steward Benisch."

Craelin's eyes widened, and he leaned forward in his chair. "I, too, would like to know that. We met under measures of utmost security."

Elcon lifted an eyebrow. "I am told he overheard the conversation."

Craelin drummed his fingers. "Impossible— unless..." He slapped his hand on the table and sat forward. "Word of mouth has it that a passage leads from one of the guardrooms to the stables. We've searched for it long and hard without success. Benish must know its entrance."

"Don't use that particular guardroom for matters of security again. And renew your search for the passageway. We will need to question Benisch further. I'm afraid his penchant for gossip may have led him astray."

"I'll see to it at once."

"Now, tell me all that this messenger said."

"Freaer rebuilds Pilaer Hold and lays claim to the fenland of Weithein Faen. Rumor holds that he arms for another attack on Torindan, and that he argues an earlier right as Rivenn's heir."

Elcon nodded. Freaer came from the same illegitimate branch of Rivenn's descendants as did Benisch.

Craelin pressed his lips together, as if to hold back words.

"Go on."

"Another two ravens have changed their loyalty to Freaer."

Elcon pushed to his feet and took the steps needed to reach the hearth where flames devoured and resin snapped as wood went up in smoke. He turned back to Craelin. "Name them."

"Merboth and Tallyrand."

"What reason do they give?"

"They say they will not follow a Lof Raelein of Elder blood." Craelin pressed his lips together once more.

"Speak all. What else do they say?"

Craelin glanced sideways to Kai and then back to Elcon. "They take offense on Arillia's behalf, although Chaeradon itself remains loyal."

"I see. Whether I will or not, it seems I must face my own people in battle. Did the messenger have any idea when Freaer might strike?"

"Shraen Eberhardt believes Freaer will strike before winter. We can't know for certain, but we may have a little more time than that. Pilaer's location within Weithein Faen suits it well for defense, but doesn't lend itself to offensive strikes."

Elcon tilted his head. If Freaer approached through the canyonlands to avoid crossing the Great Eastern Desert it would cost him time. But if he drove his armies across the desert without regard for loss of life, he'd arrive sooner. He pushed a hand through his hair, which had fallen across his brow. In truth, none of them could know what Frear would do, or when. "If Freaer were to strike before winter sets in, would we be ready to counter him?"

Craelin's gaze held steady. "Let us hope he waits until spring."

❧

Murial bathed Aewen's face and smoothed her hair. "There now, rest."

Aewen bit back the sobs that shook her frame and bent to vomit again. She had never felt so wretched in her life. The cloth, wrung of warm water, passed over her face. She caught Murial's wrist and pulled her near. "Don't tell Elcon."

"*Tsk!*" Murial stood back. "You'll not hide your condition long."

Another wave of nausea hit. She squeezed her eyes shut and spoke through gritted teeth. "I'll not tell him. Right now he has enough to worry him."

"What can be more important?"

The nausea ebbed. A measure of strength flowed back and Aewen pulled herself upright. "Promise me."

Murial snorted. "I'll follow your wishes although I think them daft."

Aewen eased herself onto a bench before the fire in what had been Lof Raelein Maeven's inner chamber.

She sent Murial a stern look but would not argue now. Nor would she mention the idea that made her toss upon her bed in the night—at least not yet.

She wiped her tears. "Summon Benisch."

Murial looked at her as if she'd lost her sanity, but inclined her head and went to do her bidding.

Aewen hated wresting Murial from yet another home, but there seemed no other choice. If Aewen disappeared, Faeraven could recover from the damage she'd wrought it. If he thought her dead, Elcon might marry Arillia and thus unify Faeraven. Aewen did not question the advisability of a marriage based on such a falsehood. In a sense, once she left Elcon, she would indeed live no more but only pass through life in shadow.

She had no idea where to go—there seemed no choices left to her—but perhaps Willowa would in kindness take her in. Or she could flee to the Abbey of Westernost and there spend her life in penitence. This last option appealed less, for they might take her child from her. She placed a protective hand on her stomach. She must do nothing that would separate her from her child. After all, the babe that thrived in her womb would be all that remained of the love she had shared with Elcon.

She gave a weak smile, thinking of that love, so ill-advised and yet so strong. She and Elcon had done nothing "right" save love one another. She would carry that thought with her. They'd been wrong in thinking love would transcend honor. She knew now that love and honor could not exist apart.

❧❦

Benisch seated himself in the embrasure of one of the windows in Aewen's outer chamber with a small smile.

Aewen lifted her chin. "At least I've found an ally in your hatred of me."

"Hatred is too strong a word. Shall we say that I find your presence inconvenient for the Lof Shraen?"

"Spare me your false concern for Elcon! Do you think I can't see that you have little thought for anyone save yourself?"

His eyes widened and then narrowed. Malice edged his smile. "Be careful the barbs you throw into a strong wind."

The truth of the ancient saying robbed her of breath. Why cast accusations onto Benisch when she had acted in naught but selfishness since meeting Elcon?

"I suppose I deserve that, but I want to make things right."

A smooth look came over Benisch's face. "I'll help you leave Torindan in secret. I'll provide you and your servant with a mount and a supply of food and water. I'll even put you on a back way that leads through the passes to Norwood."

She inclined her head. She would need to journey that way to Westerland, for roads had not yet penetrated the wild lands she and Elcon had flown over when she'd come to Torindan. Besides, she would be a woman alone. She might come upon other travelers willing to help her in the mountain passes, but only the roughest sort of huntsman and tracker could be found in the western wilderness.

"In return, you must leave at once, promise never to return and keep my involvement secret if you are discovered."

She took a steadying breath. "I agree to all but your first condition. I will leave when I am ready." She pressed a hand against her stomach. "But that will not be overlong. Now pray excuse me. I wish to be alone."

Benisch rose and unbolted the door. No sooner had it banged shut behind him than Murial opened it. She gave Aewen a strange look.

"What matters take you behind a locked door with Benisch?"

She sighed and squared her shoulders. "You will know soon enough."

❧

"Aewen, wake up." Elcon called from her dreams. When she opened her eyes, he leaned over her. "Come then wife, do you yet sleep?" He frowned. "It's past midday. Are you ill?"

Aewen came with difficulty out of slumber and sat upright. She shook her head, although her stomach did feel squeamish. "I'm just tired."

He gave her a weak smile. "Do you grow bored while I'm occupied? Perchance you are homesick. Do you miss your sister's company?"

She wished he did not speak of her people. She did think of Caerla sometimes, and of her parents and brothers at Cobbleford. They were all lost to her, as Elcon would soon be also.

He reached out and flicked away tears that had welled in her eyes and now spilled onto her cheeks. "What's this? Sorrow?"

She broke down in earnest, weeping until his arms came around her, and his kisses stopped her tears. Yes, she would leave Elcon to a better life without her, but not today.

Despite the joy of being in his arms, she could not ignore her nausea. Breaking free, she hurried to empty her stomach.

"You are ill." He opened their bedchamber door and called for Murial. "Summon Praectal Daelic."

Aewen was too weak to protest. She lay back against the pillows to wait with a sense of helplessness for the praectal's arrival. Her secret would soon be revealed. Her husband held her hand and smoothed her brow. Creases lined his forehead. He worried for her. She should tell him the truth now while it was hers to give.

And yet...what if the praectal missed her condition? Her belly had only just started swelling.

Elcon pressed his lips to her forehead and gazed into her eyes.

"Elcon—"

The door burst open and a large Kindren entered the chamber with Murial behind him. He had a kind face and carried a satchel by a strap across the front of his brown overtunic. After her examination, Daelic loomed over her bedside. "Are you aware you are with child?" Murial, waiting in the doorway, met her glance and backed away. Elcon, who hovered in the background, rushed to embrace her before she could respond. She breathed a thankful sigh, for what could she have said in answer? She'd meant to leave him, but in weakness could never bring herself to actually go. Her heart could not withstand such a loss. Each day spent as Elcon's wife, despite the distance he sometimes adopted, brought her comfort. Now that his joy overflowed at impending fatherhood, she could not bring herself to shatter it. Hope, which until now she'd counted as an enemy, embraced her. In bearing her husband a fine son, she would enjoy her husband's favor.

16

Duplicity

The cap for Aewen's soon-coming child blurred. Brushing away tears, she applied herself once more to embroidering the small garment. She would not allow herself to dwell on her fears for her child, its father, and herself. Now she knew what had so preoccupied Elcon. Civil war loomed. Snow had closed in to protect them over the winter, making it difficult to reach them. But the spring thaw would soon bring blossoms and new life. Would it also bring death?

Elcon did not say as much, but she'd overheard enough to be more certain than ever that their marriage had divided Faeraven. She snipped a thread, selected a strand of blue silk, and held up her needle to catch the light. She liked the quiet of her outer chamber with prisms and crystals hanging at the windows to create rainbows that swayed across the walls. Upon the mantel unibeasts and gryphons raised carved hooves beneath stuffed pheasants, graylets, and other fowl. A tapestry above the fireplace depicted the first Kindren who had entered Elderland at Gilead Riann, the Gate of Life. She paused to stretch and yawn, cupping a hand over her swollen abdomen.

Her child must sleep, for she'd not felt kicking since morning. She would not carry the babe much longer, for her lying in neared. Already, whenever she sighed, both Elcon and Murial turned anxious eyes upon her.

She put her needlework aside, for weariness took her. She should rest. Perhaps she'd awaken to a dream world, to a golden land where enemies filled with hatred and ambition did not lust for her husband's blood, or her own.

Murial assisted her to her bedchamber, where she settled for sleep. A tap at the outer door caught her attention as she shifted to place cushions about her. She would let Murial send away whoever knocked.

Benisch's voice roused her. He had no business intruding on the peace of her private chambers. What could he want? She'd kept secret his offer to assist her in leaving Torindan for her own sake, but if pressed, she'd confess all to Elcon.

Benisch must know she'd given up on leaving. It had been one thing to keep from Elcon his fatherhood but quite another for her to wrest it from him. Besides, she couldn't bear to go away or to separate her child from its father. She'd been wrong to think she could. The dark world she'd entered during the first throws of pregnancy now seemed distant. Right or wrong, she belonged with Elcon. They'd chosen their path and must walk it together.

Benisch's voice dwindled to nothing. Murial must have sent him away. Sleep laid a greater claim on Aewen. She woke to heavy silence and listened for Murial's quiet movements in the outer chamber as pale light filtered into the chamber. It must be late. She sat up. Why hadn't Murial awakened her? She should ready herself for the evening's repast. She gave a wry smile. Perhaps Murial had tried and failed. She slept soundly of late. She threw back her bed clothes and sought the stepstool with her feet. She glanced into the outer chamber. It reposed in semi-darkness, the fire smouldering to nothing. Why hadn't her maid lit the lanthorns?

"Murial?"

No response.

She hurried to her bedchamber and hastened to dress in a simple tunic. Something was wrong. She had to summon help. Before she had completed the task the outer chamber door clicked, the hair at the back of her neck bristled, and she went still. When no further sound came, she crept toward the connecting door, which she'd shut while dressing. She would throw the bolt, and then inquire.

Before she reached it, the door swung open. Benisch peered in at her. His face had changed, shed its concealing mask and now twisted to reveal the darkness within his heart. She shrank from the sight. "Wh—what do you want?"

Benisch gave a smile both evil and congenial. "I've come to help you, Aewen." He sounded as if he reasoned with a rebellious child.

Horror crept over her. She swallowed rising panic. "I—I thank you, but I don't require your help, Benisch. In fact, I expect Elcon any time now. He will be most unhappy to find you here."

Benisch looked troubled, but then his face cleared. He stepped closer. "I know you lie, *Elder*. With Freaer's armies camped but a few days' march away, Elcon engages in preparations for battle. And don't think your servant draws near. She's tucked in a place none will ever find her. I've come to help you leave Torindan. Remember that you want to prevent this war."

"I can't go. My labor nears, but even if I left, nothing would change now. It's too late."

Benisch gave a pleasant smile. "You are wrong. When you are no longer here everything will change. Elcon thinks he rules Faeraven, but he's wrong. I control Torindan and tell him what to say and do." He paused and took on the blank look she'd seen before. "Except I couldn't control his involvement with you. We used it to our advantage though, Freaer and I, to turn more Kindren against Elcon. And it served to alienate the Elder better than the wingabeast raids we carried out. But your presenting Elcon with an heir will never do. You and your unborn child must go."

She stared at Benisch, aghast, as her heart raced. She put a protective hand over her belly just as her child gave a mighty kick. Benisch could only mean to kill her and the child within her womb. What if she had gone with him before? Her remains might already be torn by forest creatures and scattered across the countryside.

She tried to scream but no sound came. She turned to flee. Benisch caught her wrist and twisted her arm behind her. His free hand encircled her neck. He spoke near her ear, so close it brought her pain. "If you struggle I will break your neck here and now. Understood?"

She gave a constricted nod, and he pulled her into a backward stumble. She didn't see what he did, but heard a grating. A blast of dank air hit her. He swung her to face an opening in the wall. A blow to her back sent her into gaping darkness. She struck damp stone and lay on her side, gasping for breath. The hidden door scraped, shutting her into darkness.

❧❦

Elcon pushed a hand through his hair as he paced before the hearth in his outer chamber. They had searched everywhere. He could not credit that Aewen would leave him, as Benisch seemed to think. No. Something foul had happened. Light edged the window hangings. Dawn neared. With sudden passion he struck the paneling. *"Think!"*

Craelin, at the strongwood table next to Kai, groaned. "We've looked everywhere."

Elcon willed himself to patience. "We must have missed something."

Craelin lowered his hands. "Should we—" He sent an anxious gaze toward Elcon. "Should we dredge the moat?"

"There's no time. Freaer's armies approach. Besides, she won't have fallen in. A person would have to climb over the battlements to land in the moat." *Or be pushed.* At the thought fear inched down his spine. Craelin shoved to his feet. "We'll search again, but we must turn our thoughts to war or perish."

A thudding came at the door, and Kai wrenched it open. Eathnor burst into the room, his chest heaving. "Lof Shraen, I heard—Benisch—the wingabeasts—"

Craelin slung an arm across Eathnor's shoulders. "Stop and breathe, so you may sooner give your news."

"The Lof Raelein—Benisch—"

A growing dread settled over Elcon. "Why do you speak of Benisch? Tell me at once, Eathnor. Kai, shut the door!"

Eathnor bent with hands on knees, gulping air. At

last he stood.

"Tell me." Elcon kept his voice calm.

Eathnor's pale eyes glittered in the lamplight. "As I watched the stables from the loft, I heard voices but only saw in outline one Kindren among the wingabeasts. I crept closer and found the steward Benisch grooming one of the blacks. He seemed not quite…right." He shook his head at the memory. "He spoke in a high-pitched voice and then answered himself in his usual tones, as if engaged in conversation. The hair stood on my arms, for he addressed his own womanish voice as Aewen and warned her not to complain of the cold and dark in the passage. That's when I realized—I realized—"

Elcon's calm deserted him. "Go on!"

"Benisch may have taken the Lof Raelein and hidden her in one of the passages beneath Torindan."

As the full import of Eathnor's words drove into him Elcon closed his eyes. The idea of Aewen trapped underground, wounded and terrified, perhaps giving birth alone ignited a terrible fire inside him. He fisted his hands and forced himself to concentrate. Taking time to indulge his fury would not save Aewen.

"Where's Benisch?" Craelin asked.

A smug expression crossed Eathnor's face. "He's under restraint in the east guardroom."

Craelin gave a curt nod. "That's well, then. The guardians can begin a search of the passageways beneath Torindan's motte while Eathnor and I have a talk with Benisch."

Elcon would have liked to have a conversation with Benisch, but he turned instead to Kai. "Hurry. Time presses."

৵৽

Aewen rolled onto her side with a whimper. Why had she made a hard stone floor her bed? Shivers wracked her body, and she curled into a ball—*so cold*. She must tell Murial to bring more blankets. She jerked her eyes open. "Murial?" Her voice, thin and frail, spun away into darkness.

A wave of horror rushed over her. Tears gathered. She wept not only for herself, but also for the child who would perish without knowing the warmth of a mother's arms. She wept for Elcon, who might never know what had happened. She spared tears, also, for Murial, who could even now have perished. *She's safely tucked away in a place none will ever find her.* The memory of Benisch's voice made her shudder.

She pushed to her feet and again searched the rock wall for some sort of device that might open the hidden door. Her hands found nothing but stone. She'd lost the way out. Darkness pressed past her eyes and into her mind. Her chest rose and fell as she panted. Steadying herself against the wall, she forced in deep draughts of moist air. If she did not take care, the child might come in this wretched place.

Perhaps the passage only opened from the Lof Raelein's chambers, anyway. That made sense for an escape tunnel built for time of war. A tiny light flickered in her mind. The passageway might lead to freedom, if she could traverse it in the dark. She might yet save herself. That thought brought her comfort and stiffened her spine. She was, after all, a daughter of the kings of Wester. She would not surrender to death without a fight.

Standing away from the wall, she slid a foot

forward. With her arms stretched before her, she took the next step and tested her footing. She advanced by slow measures until her foot found nothing, and then swayed backward. She'd thought to find a stairway leading down through Torindan's motte to an opening below. She lowered to her knees and patted the stone floor where it dropped away. Her hand found a flat surface below the edge. Could it be a stair tread?

She hesitated. What if she encountered flesh-eating rodents? Or wraiths? If she took a wrong turn, she could wander paths of darkness until the light of life snuffed from her. Or she might come to another door with a hidden mechanism she failed to find.

She could not allow fearful thoughts to rule her. Lowering herself with care, she blew out a tense breath. Her bare feet found another tread below. The stairs seemed endless but came at last to a landing where every small sound echoed. She rolled onto her back and folded her arms against the cold. Sleepiness dogged her, and a feeling of warmth she knew as false. She stirred, for to give in to sleep might mean she'd never wake again. She positioned herself to follow the stairway downward again, although her knees and toes ached. With painstaking care she lowered herself to the next step, and then the next. As time wore on, she lost count.

She took a weary step forward, but her feet found only air. She knelt upon the tread. A jagged edge of broken stone met her searching fingers. Rocks scattered and plunged to crash a long way down. She shivered. Perhaps with a lanthorn she might navigate, but she had no light. She pulled herself back up the stair to the landing, breathing in small bursts. An exhausted tremor went through her, and she lay still, too weary even for tears.

Metal grated and a light fell from above. Fear drove her to hands and knees. Did Benisch return to make sure of her death? She raised a hand to shield her eyes from the light which, although feeble, stabbed into them.

"Here! I've found her!"

Footfalls echoed. Arms cradled her. She thought she heard Elcon's voice. *"Aewen!"* She blinked and Elcon's form swam into view. She tried to say his name, but her voice was gone. Instead, she feasted her eyes upon his face, a face she'd never thought to see again.

They carried her to bed, wrapped her in blankets, and placed warming bricks around her. Servants bathed her cheeks and forehead with cloths wrung in warm water and gave her steaming cider to drink. Praectal Daelic peered at her with grave interest. She managed to speak Murial's name, but Daelic seemed not to understand her. She concentrated, trying to understand his words, but his speech seemed gibberish. She slept and woke and slept more. When she roused at last, a chamber maid with gentle hands propped her in bed. Outside the windows, rain clouds scuttled across a gray sky and pale light washed the eastern horizon. It must be morning.

"Tell me your name." Aewen addressed the servant in a voice that croaked.

The maid smiled and curtsied. "I am Sylder, Lof Raelein."

"Well, Sylder, I am worried about Murial, my maid. Can you tell me anything of her?"

"And what would be you wanting to know?" Murial's familiar voice carried from her outer chamber.

She turned her head. Murial's familiar figure stood in the doorway. Aewen smiled as tears gathered. "Are you well?"

Murial drew near to clasp her hand, her wrinkled face wreathed in smiles. "That's a question I might ask of you."

"But you were…did not Benisch—"

Murial waved a hand. "He pushed me into some sort of passageway in the dark but I groped about until I found a lever that opened the door again. It took some time because it was well hidden, but it seemed a better idea than casting about in pitch black tunnels with no light. Benisch must not have believed I'd discover it, or I might not now draw breath."

As memory returned her to the dark place of despair she'd just escaped, Aewen frowned. "I'd like to know how you did it. I couldn't find any lever to open the door he pushed me through, although I tried and tried." An image of Benisch smiling his genial smile as he shut her away intruded, and she shuddered.

Murial *tskd*, and a gentle hand touched her brow. "Stop getting yourself in a state. It won't do you nor the babe any good. Benisch can't harm you now."

"What happened to him?"

Murial settled in a chair beside the bed. "He saved his own life by telling where he put you, but he'll not trouble you again."

"They banished him?"

She shook her head. "Where could they send him? He's here still, in the dungeon."

"How horrible."

Murial glinted a look at her. "He deserved worse. You could have died, and it's a wonder the ordeal didn't bring your babe into this world early." She shook her head as if disagreeing with someone. "There, now. Let's put the whole thing behind us." Murial hummed a familiar melody. Weary once more, Aewen rested her head on her pillow and allowed Murial's melody to carry her back to childhood.

By the time Aewen pulled again into wakefulness, the fledgling sun had strengthened. She started and sat up. Murial, snoring gently, slept in a chair beside the bed. Aewen's lips curved in a smile, and tears stood in her eyes.

"Well then, wife, do I find you asleep at midday?" Elcon, far more rumpled than she'd ever seen him, smiled at her from the doorway.

Murial snorted and stirred, and Aewen put a finger to her lips before holding her arms out for her husband. He went into them with a groan, holding her so tightly she begged him to let her breathe. Standing back from her, he kept hold of her hand. "I thought I'd lost you."

She smiled at him. "I'm with you still, Elcon, by Lof Yuel's will, if not that of the steward Benisch."

Elcon's jaw firmed, his eyes as turbulent as a stormy sea. "Pray do not bear that name again upon your lips."

Aewen shuddered at the thought of Benisch's fate.

Elcon sat on the edge of the bed. "I blame myself. In my uncertainty and because of our kinship, I allowed Benisch sway. Had I listened to my instincts about him, I might have prevented what happened."

"Hindsight is always clearest, but Elcon, you must not reproach yourself for the actions of a madman."

He straightened and drew back. "I wish I could stay, but we prepare for war." He took a breath. "Rest well this day, my love. Tomorrow will mean a journey."

"Please don't send me away from you."

"I will protect my own. Freaer's armies camp only a breath away, but there is still time for your escape. Kai prepares now to accompany you and Murial to Westerland, back to Cobbleford, where you may bear our child without threat."

"I'm not certain of my reception there."

"Surely your parents would not turn you away at such a time."

Her mother's pinched face the last time they'd spoken came forcefully to mind. "I hope you are right."

"If nothing else, stay at the White Feather Inn until I send for you."

"They may not receive me."

"Aewen, I will not have you face armies here with me."

She blinked, for he'd delivered his decision in a voice that brooked no argument.

His face softened. "When all is clear, I will send for you."

She opened her mouth to speak but closed it again at the anguish on his face. She would not add to his burdens, for he clearly expected Torindan to fall.

He caught her hand and pressed it to his lips.

She would rather remain with Elcon, even if it meant death, but the stirring of the babe inside her womb reminded her that the choice did not touch her alone. She glanced away from him to help her say the words. "I will go."

17

Escape

Aewen lay in Elcon's arms through the long, wakeful night until pale light edged the eastern horizon and the first rays of morning gilded sleeping fields and mountains. How could such peace birth a day of sorrow? Today she would leave the husband she might never see again. She summoned Murial but cautioned her to make as little noise as possible as they prepared for the journey. Elcon would need his wits this day.

Elcon moaned in his sleep and thrashed in the bed. She ran to him. "Wake, Elcon. You dream."

His eyes opened wide. "Aewen!" He called to her as if she were not before him.

She touched his chest. "What's wrong?"

His eyes focused on her, and he touched her face. "Don't worry. This has happened before and I withstood it."

She caught his hand and kissed it. "What do you mean?"

"Freaer seeks to crush me through the shil shael."

"If he uses the soul touch he must draw near. It might not be safe now for me to leave."

"I'm reluctant to send you away, even for your safety, but there's time for your escape. Freaer uses the soul touch from a distance. If he were nearer, it would be stronger." He pulled her down for his kiss, and then touched her damp cheek. "You must be strong, for my sake." His voice broke, and she wound her arms around his neck as they wept together.

Kai arrived, too soon.

She touched Elcon's face a last time. "Fight well."

He kissed her hands. "Safe travels, my love." She would drown in the deep pools that were Elcon's eyes.

Their hands parted, and she turned away with tears blurring her vision, and stumbled with Murial after Kai. They hurried down the vaulted passageway, their footsteps loud in the quiet, and entered the allerstaed by the side door. How different it looked now than on the day of her wedding and coronation. She could almost hear the cheers the throng had raised then, but silence reigned here now.

Kai felt behind a tapestry hanging at the rear of the allerstaed, and then pushed on the paneling, which creaked open to reveal a dark passageway emanating the cool scent of water on stone. Kai lifted a lanthorn to illumine uneven steps hewn in the rough wall of a natural cavern. Beyond the circle of light, a black void crouched.

Murial crowded against Aewen and put a steadying hand to her elbow. Here and there her small *tsk* carried above the echo of footsteps. The cave, itself, seemed to hold its breath. As if in a waking dream, Aewen descended flight after flight behind Kai with Murial at her back.

Kai paused at last and, with a screech and clang, swung open a door. They emerged from the mouth of a hidden cave above the water gate and stood, blinking in the full light of morning. A stiff wind blew in from

Weild Aenor and snarled in Aewen's cloak. As they descended to an earthen path, loose rocks slid underfoot. Water shone in pools from a storm in the night and steam rose from the damp ground.

Two wearing guardian garb waited on one of the twin postern platforms built for defense. Three shadows moving on the other platform resolved into wingabeasts. The darkest of them fluttered its wings, and a chill ran over Aewen. She stepped onto the platform and put her hand on Raeld's warm neck. Elcon could not have told her more clearly he did not expect to live than to give her his wingabeast. Kai gave a low whistle and two silvers, one smaller than the other, stepped toward him. He placed the reins of the smaller silver in Murial's hands. "You've not ridden alone before this, but if you can manage it with my instruction, that will be better for all."

Murial huffed a little when he helped her into the saddle but sat with quiet resolve despite the look of discomfort on her face.

Kai smiled. "Her name is Ruescht, Kindren for the sound made by the rushing wind. She will respond to hands or voice, and she knows the command, 'Follow.'"

Aewen smiled a little. As she recalled, her mother had reacted with much less calm when seated upon a wingabeast. When Kai turned to help her onto Raeld's back, she mustered her courage. He seemed to think she'd ridden alone before for he did not instruct her as he had Murial, nor did he reassure her. She took the reins and waited in silence, determined to show as much dignity as her servant.

The two guardians joined them on the platform. Aewen recognized Eathnor and the tall archer, Aerlic.

Eathnor and Kai clasped arms. As the two stepped apart Eathnor handed Kai the hilt of a hunting knife. "Journey well."

The blade gleamed as Kai examined it. "You may need this more than I will."

Eathnor flashed a rakish smile. "I'm well supplied."

Aerlic inclined his head to Kai. "Keep the wind to your heels." They clasped forearms.

Kai mounted the largest silver. "Stay safe." Without waiting for a reply, he launched his wingabeast into flight.

Aewen pressed forward and urged Raeld to follow. The wingabeast reared and its black wings rose about her. The great wings beat down with a lurch and a rush of air, and Raeld lifted into flight. Aewen glanced back at Murial, glad to find her keeping pace on Ruescht's back. At sight of the vast landscape below, she gasped. Kai had said they would fly low, but they were high in the air.

Rather than heading due west over the trackless kaba forest, they set off northward, taking the longer but more traveled route that led through the mountain passes to Norwood. After that they would bend south and west to pass over farmlands and meadows into Westerland. Since Praectal Daelic had insisted, due to her condition, that she dismount and walk about often, Elcon had been reluctant for her to cross the wild lands. Aewen had yielded to his wishes although it added two days to their journey.

They seemed barely to have taken flight when Kai landed again. Delaying even at the edge of the wilderness seemed ill advised, although Aewen could not deny its beauty. The forest canopy stirred with life as flitlings glided from tree to tree, and the blue of crobok wings flicked at the edges of waterways. Weild Aenor cut a swath through the trees to later join the Whitefeather as it flowed to Maer Ibris, glimmering in blue tides which frothed against the distant shore. Aewen slid from the saddle without waiting for assistance, anxious to walk about and ease her back.

"Have a care!" Murial cried, her forehead creased with worry. "You'll injure yourself or the babe."

Aewen's conscience smote her. "I've taken no harm, but I'm sorry to worry you." When she mounted again, she allowed Kai to help her.

Even with frequent breaks, as the day progressed Aewen found it difficult to sit still. Her back pained her off and on, but not enough for alarm. She'd never borne a child before, so she did not know what to expect, but childbirth had to be forceful, not this odd unsettled feeling. No. This ache must come from so much time in the saddle.

As the journey lengthened, her discomfort increased into grabbing pain that squeezed her in an iron grip until it finally eased, only to return. She ground her teeth against each fresh onslaught.

Murial, riding nearby, turned a troubled face toward her. "Are you well?"

Aewen had hoped to keep the matter to herself until they stopped for the night in Norwood. It was too late to turn back to Torindan even if they could, and she hated to alarm the others. But a fresh spasm cut through her, and she could not keep her face from contorting.

Murial's eyes widened. "The babe comes!"

Kai dropped back to ride beside Aewen and waited in silence until the tide of pain engulfing her ebbed. "We're more than halfway to Norwood." He called across the space between them. "Try and hold on until we reach the inn."

She nodded and did not voice her fear. By the wrinkling of Kai's forehead, he'd read it all the same.

On another day, she'd have reveled in the splendor of the mountainous wilderness where sunlit valleys gleamed beneath purpled peaks seamed by countless waterfalls. Behind them to the south watered canyons bent, mysterious in the distance. Northward, jagged shafts of ice-encrusted stone thrust upward. She knew without being told that these were the Maegrad Ceid of the Kindren, peaks her own people called the Crystal Mountains. The sight of the unforgiving landscape ahead made her blood run cold. Sharp rocks jutted from the snow in the passes, waiting like so many fangs to devour her. If she must give birth along the wayside, let it not be here.

But, as they fought the wind that buffeted, waves of pain swept over her in rapid succession. She moaned and leaned over to vomit. Blackness edged her vision, and she swayed sideways. Murial's scream recalled her, and with an effort she pulled herself upright. "I can't go on!" Her cry ended in a plaintive wail.

Kai brought Fletch close and commanded Raeld in a strong voice.

Aewen no longer held the reins, although she didn't remember dropping them. Raeld followed Kai's silver into a downward spiral and sank to the knees in a carpet of snow.

Kai raised his arms to help her out of the saddle. As another spasm seized her, she clung to him. Warmth flooded her from the waist down followed by the chill of wet garments. Kai spread his cloak on the snow. She wanted to protest such a sacrifice but could not speak. Together, her companions lowered and held her as she thrashed in pain. Cramps drove across her belly, and she ceased to exist as more than a point of pain. The need to push wrenched a scream from her. Murial thrust a cloth between her teeth and warned her to hold back. Aewen bit down upon the cloth and gripped Kai's hands until her own turned white. She could endure no longer.

"Push!" Murial called.

She obeyed. When the iron band around her eased, she gasped in air.

Murial lifted a tense face. "Harder!"

She rode the next wave, and then fell back in exhaustion.

"Again!"

She groaned, but pushed with all her might. This time the pressure eased.

"Once more."

She groaned again, and Murial held up the bloodied baby as she cleared its mouth and nose. The babe's skin went from blue to red, and it brought forth a robust wail. Murial wrapped the infant in her own cloak and laid the small bundle in her arms. "You have a daughter."

A daughter? She'd hoped for a son and heir. Aewen gazed into the tiny face, which bore Elcon's stamp, although the child's eyes were rounded and a fuzz of black covered her head. "I shall call her Syl Marinda."

Murial smoothed her brow. "You've given her a Kindren name. What does it mean?"

"Snow Daughter." Kai spoke for her, and she

smiled at him, grateful to be spared the effort.

❧❧

Elcon peered through the embrasure and into the distance. The view from the parapet above the barbican did not comfort him. He met Craelin's grave regard. "How many?"

"Too many to count. That the armies would bear the banners of Glindenn, Selfred and Morgorad we knew. But Tallyrand and Merboth now join the rebels. Faeraven has split in two." Craelin's eyes flashed blue fire. "And above them all flies the ancient flag of Rivenn."

Elcon shook his head. "Freaer mocks me. Have we news from the loyal shraens? Can we stand?"

Craelin hesitated. "Chaeradon, Whellein, Graelinn, and Daeramor all gather to join Rivenn in defense of Torindan, but late snows block the passes."

"Will they reach us in time?"

"There's a chance."

Elcon shut his eyes. Images passed before him, the familiar faces of shraens who now followed Freaer into battle against Torindan—against *him*. His stomach turned at the thought of fighting even one of the hostile ravens. He wanted to weep, to curse, to implore Lof Yuel but instead straightened his spine. He had little choice but to battle his own people.

He had worsened the situation by bringing home an Elder bride. He should have known his people would not accept her. He turned away from the sight of the advancing armies. He had caused this, in his pride and ignorance, when he rejected Shraen Brael. He could admit it now. He'd suspected all along, *known* somehow, that Emmerich was who he claimed to be—a king come to free them all. He had known but still rejected Emmerich. He'd listened to Benisch's whispers and let fear rule him. He'd worried that Emmerich would grow more important, more powerful than him, and that he would lose control of Faeraven. Out of fear, he'd sent away the very help Lof Yuel had provided and brought his worst fear upon himself. Despite Shae's sacrifice, salvation would not come to Elderland. Instead terror would reign, many would die, and Elderland would fall into darkness, because of him.

A foul stench of decay suffocated him as an evil touch gripped his mind. Despair flooded him, and he dropped to his knees.

Craelin called to him but he couldn't answer. Freaer's touch was nearer and stronger than it had been.

Lof Yuel! In his mind he screamed the name, and the waves battering him ebbed away.

Hands gripped and hoisted him to his feet. He opened his eyes.

Craelin's anxious face stared back at him. "Lof Shraen, are you ill?"

"Freaer." He choked out the name.

Understanding dawned on Craelin's face. He had watched Elcon endure Freaer's mental assaults through the siege of Torindan.

Elcon walked away from the battlements, his shoulders slumping. He would go to the allerstaed and wait for the release of death, but he would not pray. He did not deserve absolution.

Kai cast a glance at Aewen, who lolled backwards against Murial, the babe tied across her front. Her eyelids fluttered as if she tried to open them but could not. Murial met his glance with a worried look. They had bundled Aewen and her child as best they could, but her skin glowed pale in the fading light. The sooner they reached shelter, the better.

He sent Fletch into a spiral. Ruescht followed suit, although riderless. He'd given Ruescht her freedom with nothing more than the command to 'follow,' and the small wingabeast had remained true to her training. Raeld landed beside Fletch. Kai dismounted and hurried to Aewen. As she surrendered Aewen to Kai, Murial took the babe in her arms.

"A groom comes to help you dismount, Murial." As he stomped up the steps to the porch, the sound of merriment increased. He threw open the scarred and weathered door, and it crashed against the wall. All eyes in the common room turned toward him. Silence fell.

He scanned the room and located a tall, muscular man with hair of black, a man he knew well. Quinn the innkeeper crossed the room to pause before him, concern written in his face. "Come with me." He climbed the stair and called down into the room from the landing. "Brynn! Send Heddwyn up, and make it quick!"

Brynn pierced Kai with a look and tossed her head, making her red hair fly about her. Too involved with Aewen's plight, he couldn't bring himself to care about Brynn's continued dislike of him. The last time he'd visited this inn, he and Shae had slept in the stable loft as a precaution against the very prejudice he saw on Brynn's face now. Quinn and Heddwyn had remained his faithful friends even when feelings ran high against the Kindren, but Heddwyn's sister, Brynn, had only added to the general outcry.

Quinn led them down a short hall and opened the door at its end. Kai swept past him into the room and laid Aewen on the simple bed with care. Murial pressed the child into Kai's arms as Heddwyn entered behind them, and he stepped back to let them tend Aewen. Quinn clasped him about the shoulders. "Come, Kai. That's women's work." They reached the hall, and Quinn lowered his voice. "Who be she? Yours?"

Kai stared at Quinn and felt his face flush. "Mine? No, she's Elcon's."

Quinn's eyes widened. "*Not* Princess Aewen? Begging your pardon, she's Lof Raelein Aewen now. Why comes she here?"

"War brings her."

Quinn looked hard at him, and then nodded. "Aye."

"She needs a doctor. Can you summon one?"

"I'll send for Doctor Jorris, but he lives farther north and we may not find him to home."

"Summon him."

But the messenger Quinn sent returned with word that Doctor Jorris waited at the side of a fevered child and would not come. He sent an infusion to ease Aewen's pain and promised to follow soon. Kai approached the door at the end of the hall with a sense of foreboding. Murial answered his knock, the babe in her arms. Her tear-streaked face told its own story. He cleared his throat. "Is she—is Aewen..."

Murial said nothing but stood back for him to

enter. In the bed Aewen lay with her open eyes very blue in a white face. If he had not seen her chest lift as she breathed, he would have thought her a corpse. He drew near her side.

"Come close," Aewen croaked.

Kai bent near her and waited as she took a few shallow, rapid breaths. "Tell Elcon I love him and—I do not blame him." She made a grimace he understood she meant as a smile. "I know Elcon well."

He smiled at her. She did, indeed, understand her husband.

"Let me hold my daughter."

Kai nodded to Murial, who moved forward to lay the babe in her arms. Aewen said something Kai did not catch, but when Murial motioned for him to draw near, he bent over Aewen again.

"Promise me..." She paused to breathe, and he saw just how much the effort to speak cost her. "...return...Syl Marinda...to her father."

"I promise."

Her expression smoothing, Aewen closed her eyes and breathed her last.

❧❦

Elcon woke on the cold stone floor of the allerstaed to a blast of trumpets, Torindan's call to arms, followed by the crash of the first volley from the besieger's catapults. An unholy uproar commenced—the sound of war. He pushed upright, his heart pounding in his chest like a caged bird. His knees shook. With a trembling hand, he pushed the hair from his eyes as he swallowed against the taste of shame. He'd not known the full extent of his cowardice until now.

"Elcon..." His name carried as if borne on a breeze. Indeed a strange current stirred the air. He lifted his head, blinked in sudden light, and gasped.

Shae stood before him. Shae and not Shae, for her face and form were the same as he remembered but somehow inconsequential, a vision he could not touch. She wore a simple tunic of blue and her hair cascaded in a river of golden fire to her waist. She watched him with sad eyes.

He gaped at her. "Have I lost my reason?"

Shae's laugh carried the upward lilt he remembered, although it sounded far away. "Brother, take courage."

"How can a coward take courage?"

"We all feel the bite of fear, Elcon. You must not let it devour you."

"How do you suggest I avoid that? Fear clads itself in armor and marches now on Torindan."

"You must stand, Elcon, and wield Sword Rivenn. If you do not, your armies will lose heart, and Torindan will fall." She faded as she spoke.

He lurched forward. "Wait, don't go!"

"My strength fails. I must leave the gateway." But she lingered, growing fainter.

"What is this of a gateway? Can you not return to us through it? Or do you speak of the veil of death?"

She shook her head. "I have not crossed beyond that veil yet." Her words sighed, just above a whisper. "There are many gateways, Elcon, and many worlds."

Her form shifted and vanished. But her words remained, seeded inside him, sprouting to bear fruit.

We all feel the bite of fear, Elcon. You must not let it devour you.

He steadied himself and turned away from the

place of refuge. It was too late to right the many mistakes he'd made, but he would not allow the manner of his death to further shame the House of Rivenn. Despite all his sins, he would stand before his people as Lof Shraen of Faeraven.

18

Journey Home

Quinn closed the coffin lid, shutting Aewen from Kai's sight.

At his side Murial swayed in grief. "Sleep well, little flitling. May you find the peace denied you in this life." After combing her mistress's dark hair and plaiting it with deft fingers, Murial had watched over Aewen's body until Quinn and Kai placed her in a strongwood box normally used for carrying grain. The makeshift coffin sat upon trestles in the small room where Aewen had died.

"On the morrow I'll take her to Cobbleford for burial." The words tasted bitter in Kai's mouth. With Torindan under siege, he couldn't bring her body to Elcon, and she shouldn't be laid to rest here among strangers.

"You must leave now." Quinn informed him in an apologetic tone.

"But it's yet night."

"I'm sorry, but the other guests won't welcome death in their midst."

Murial dashed away tears. "I can't abide with you to Cobbleford. Without Aewen to shield me, Queen Inydde will turn me away."

Kai had heard and seen enough at Cobbleford

Castle to know she spoke the truth. "You must remain here, with the babe, if they have room for you to stay."

"I would take her to my sister's homefarm in the north, but I doubt she'd allow a baby in the house. She's lived alone so long it's made her into a curmudgeon, I'm afraid."

"That is well. Syl Marinda is too young to make the journey to Westerland now, and perhaps there will be no need. Torindan may stand against Freaer. If that happens, she can go into her father's care as Aewen wished." He did not pretend to know what would happen if Torindan fell.

They loaded Aewen's coffin on a rough cart in the stableyard, and Kai set out by land. Fletch pulled the cart into the mountain heights and crunched through the thinning snow of early spring. Although rutted from the wheels of the carts which journeyed this way, the common road still provided the quickest route across the hilly farm country that bounded Norwood on the south and east. The road followed the contours of the hills and traveled around obstacles, bending in sudden turns with dizzying frequency. He made slow progress, obliged to pause often to steady the coffin. He traveled through the night and day, but at the next nightfall sought shelter in an abandoned barn just where the road curved into the kaba forest. Although the northern part of the forest could not be called wilderness, he would not enter it until morning. Bruins and shaycats might still roam by night despite the scattering of homefarms located there. Besides, he needed rest.

He set off again as the first rays of sunlight searched the morning mists. The predators of the night would lie down now, but as the forest closed about him, he kept his eyes and ears open and his weapons ready. Although the cold and Murial's anointing herbs would preserve Aewen's body, he still carried with him the scent of death.

The road climbed all morning before leveling at a low pass. He dismounted and rested on a flat-topped boulder, averting his face against the nip of the steady west wind. From here he could see as far as the mists curling above the lands of Darksea and Whistledown to the gleaming waters of Maer Ibris. To the north and west a barren salt marsh edged Muer Maeread, the Coast of Bones where his brother, Daeven, was said to have met his end in a shipwreck.

Gazing now upon the long coastline where foaming surf wreathed dark rocks that stood in sharp warning, he longed to search for the truth of Daeven's end. If, as his father believed, wreckers had by night lured Daeven's ship onto the rocks and lain in wait for survivors to emerge from the shipwreck, his brother had been murdered. Because Kai had been needed to protect Shae on her journey to Gilead Riann, he'd denied himself the chance to learn the truth, and, if he admitted it, avenge his brother's blood. Now duty to Elcon and Elderland held him fast.

He returned to the cart. He had made his choices and would not sway from them. He could hope, however, for the day he might walk in freedom upon the shores of Muer Maeread.

The road trended downward, Fletch's hooves striking with renewed fervor. As the road passed through Lancert, it broadened but also congested with traffic. When Elders who drove carts or rode horses and donkeys saw the burden he pulled, however, they yielded. Many gazed upon him in mistrust, for few

Kindren ever ventured this far into the Elder lands, and a winged horse should not pull a common cart. He kept eyes and ears open, but none challenged him. When he left the city with its dust and noise behind, he sighed in relief.

He passed through the heart of Westerland now, with its small hamlets and homefarms carved from virgin forest. The day darkened, casting fields and forest in purpled shadow, for storm clouds gathered. The very air crackled with pent energy.

Kai turned from the main road at Cobbleford. As the cart crossed the bridge over Weild Aenor, known to the Elder as the Cobble River, the roar of the swollen waters nearly drowned the thud of hooves and drum of wheels. The castle loomed ahead, brown and ungainly against the beauty of the weild. Kai stopped at the gatehouse.

"Name yourself and your duty!" The cry came from the battlements above. Kai squinted, for in the dim light he could not well see the figure behind the crenellations. "I am Kai of Whellein, sent to King Euryon in the name of Lof Shraen Elcon of Faeraven."

Silence fell, followed by the hiss of whispering. "How do we know you speak truth?"

He sighed. His body ached from the journey, he hungered, and he had little patience remaining. "The matter is urgent."

Silence, followed by more whispering. He could just see the guard's face peer from one of the embrasures. "What is in that box?"

"I bring the body of one dear to the king."

"Hold there."

Kai sighed again. The shadows lengthened, and a crack of thunder preceded rain, which rolled off the thick perse of his cloak to soak his woolen leggings. Fletch picked up his feet and put them down again, flicking his ears.

"You there!"

Kai squinted upward. He thought he recognized the captain of the guard.

"What brings you here?"

"I would rather speak that to King Euryon in private, for it's a tale of sorrow."

"Sorrow, you say?"

He shifted to ease his cramping muscles. "I will tell you, since it seems the only way to gain admittance. I bring the body of Aewen of Westerland home."

At last the portcullis rose, screeching, and the wooden doors opened. He rode into the gatehouse, where the captain met him. "I will alert the king to your presence."

The wooden doors thudded and chains clanked as the portcullis lowered again. Now in the gatehouse, Fletch shook his head, water spraying from his mane. Rain hammered the ground outside the gatehouse and shimmered silver beyond the arrow slits.

Kai kept his eyes and ears alert, a habit formed during his early training as a guardian of Rivenn. He did not allow his mind to think ahead to his audience with King Euryon or to wonder what happened at Torindan.

The captain returned. Euryon, flanked by two guards, followed him. The king wore such a wild look Kai knew at once the captain must have broken the news to him. Kai dismounted and bowed. Euryon paid him no heed but went straight to the cart and placed his hands upon the coffin. "Open it!"

The captain signaled one of the guards, who hurried from the gatehouse but came back almost at once with a pry bar.

Kai flinched. He'd not considered the possibility that the king would want to open the coffin. Nor had he steeled himself to see the raw pain on Euryon's face as he gazed upon his dead child. Euryon did not weep but reached as if to touch her, only to draw his hand back again. With a curt nod he turned away, his shoulders slumped. "Put the lid in place but do not nail the coffin shut, for Inydde may want to look upon her daughter. Take Aewen to the chapel and advise Brother Robb."

The coffin lid clunked back into place. Euryon faced Kai. "How came this?"

"She died after giving birth. The doctor arrived too late."

Euryon's eyes widened. "Doctor? Not praectal? How came she to dwell among the Elder? Why do you bring her to me rather than bury her at Torindan? Has Elcon cast her off?"

Kai waved a hand to quiet him, for Euryon's last words came out near a bellow. "Nay, Elcon did not cast her off but sent her away for safety's sake. Torindan is at war."

Comprehension crossed Euryon's face. "Freaer!"

"Freaer's armies lay siege to Torindan. He sways half of Faeraven. Elcon thought to spare Aewen, but she went into labor and gave birth along the wayside. We brought her with all care to an inn in Norwood, but she died there."

Euryon shook his head. "I cannot bear the thought of my daughter birthing on the wayside and dying in a common inn." His face crumpled. "I refused Elcon my help against Freaer when he asked it. Had I given it, Aewen might yet live." Grief bent him double, and the captain offered his arm to escort him from the gatehouse.

The two guards who had flanked Euryon bore Aewen's coffin past Kai, on its way to the chapel. He stood alone.

A voice called from above. "Hold there." A guard's face looked through one of the murder holes in the ceiling overhead. The face withdrew and the trapdoor closed. It seemed an interminable wait amid the steady patter of rain.

At last the captain of the guard reappeared. "You there, follow me. Leave your beast. The groom is already on his way to tend it."

Kai followed the captain into Cobbleford Castle and down the long corridor he remembered to Euryon's outer chambers. Euryon stood with Inydde in the midst of the room's red and gilt splendor, shivering like a pauper in a blast of winter wind. Kai made another bow.

Inydde's face gave little emotion away. She might have met him on any social occasion, save for the whiteness of her skin. "You were with Aewen when she died?" She held herself straight and tall as she addressed him.

"Yes."

Tears glinted in Inydde's deep blue eyes. "Did she suffer?"

He hesitated. "All women suffer in childbirth, but Aewen found rest and comfort at the end."

"That is well."

Kai looked to Euryon, who listened with tears coursing down his cheeks. He waited, but neither

Euryon nor Inydde asked about Aewen's babe. Perhaps they assumed the child had died.

Inydde stepped toward Kai. "We will bury her in the morning. You are welcome to attend. After that, you will want to be on your way."

"Yes, that is best. You should know that Aewen's daughter remains in Norwood, under the care of a nurse, until she can join her father in Torindan."

Euryon's eyes widened. "Let us hope he, and Torindan, remain standing."

Inydde raised perfect eyebrows. "If not, you will have to make other arrangements for the child. I'll not harbor a half breed."

❧

In the aftermath of rain, morning dawned with the promise of new life. Trees budded. Early flowers broke through the warming soil. Flitlings hopped from branch to branch. Birdsong filled the garden.

Kai entered the chapel through the open doorway. Aewen's body waited before the altar, her coffin nailed shut a final time. None had gathered yet. With its vaulted ceiling, gilt trim and golden implements upon the altar, the small chapel gave an impression of opulence. As Kai walked to the bier, his footsteps echoed hollowly. A red velvet covering bedecked with gilded early flowers draped Aewen's coffin. He fingered the rough wood that showed at the edges and smiled to himself. Aewen, daughter of the kings of Wester, would go to the tomb in her humble casket. From what he knew of her, she would have preferred that. At the sound of weeping, he turned. Caerla, unkempt and with an air of bewilderment, wrung her hands in the doorway. Her gaze never wavering from the coffin, she paced the length of the chamber and halted before Kai. Tears ran down her cheeks to drip from her face, but she paid them no heed. "Aewen cannot be dead. She would not leave us, thus, without a goodbye."

Without a response to give her, Kai said nothing.

She sank to her knees, so fragile she appeared little more than a wraith. Resting her arms on the edge of the dais, she lowered her head onto them. Kai barely caught her whispered words. "She would not go without letting me tell her how sorry I am for the words I last spoke to her." Heart wrenching sobs overcame her.

Kai could find nothing of comfort to give her.

Voices carried from the path. Euryon and Inydde leaned toward one another in the open doorway. Euryon's face ran with tears, but Inydde's remained impassive. She seemed to clutch her grief as a treasure. Kai stood to one side, watching and waiting as other mourners came. He had already said his own goodbye to Aewen, in the small, stuffy room at the inn. And yet he remained through the brief invocation for Elcon's sake.

Outside in the sunshine Euryon touched Kai's arm and placed in his hand a leather band with a single sapphire at its center. "Give this to Aewen's daughter when she's older. It was her mother's."

The sapphire band blurred, and Kai heaved a breath. "I will."

Euryon turned to lean again on Inydde. The two moved off along the path to the castle. Kai did not follow. He wanted nothing of the funeral feast that waited in the great hall. A sudden longing seized him for the untainted air of the open road.

❧

As Elcon reached the battlements above the gatehouse, the stair gave a faint but perceptible vibration.

Craelin looked up from his examination of the water pot nearest the eastern tower. As Elcon watched, the shining surface quivered and stilled.

He lifted a brow. "Miners?"

Craelin gave a brief nod. "We're sure they mean to collapse the gatehouse towers. We've already started a counter shaft."

Elcon put a hand on the back of his neck and kneaded the knotted muscles there. The days had settled into a monotonous exchange of missiles from the catapults, the constant threat of arrows from ensconced archers, and the attacking armies' steady infilling of a portion of the moat with stones and rubble. Sheltering beneath a makeshift roof, the foot soldiers made progress despite the arrows, debris, and pots of slaked lime and boiling oil rained down upon them. Elcon pictured the siege tower that waited beyond the reach of Torindan's catapults and heard again the cries of the wounded. "When will our miners break into their tunnel?"

Craelin squinted against the sun's glare. "It's a guess but three days, maybe four. We'll meet them with dragonsfire."

Elcon sucked in a breath. Dragonsfire, a mixture which ignited upon contact with water, burned with such fury it eradicated all life in its path. The guardians had perfected a pump system that spewed water and the volatile mixture from hand held tubes. The resultant blaze flared forth with such intensity it resembled its namesake. "Let us hope we alone possess it."

Catapults twanged anew and a barrage of rounded stones flew over the walls. One of the merlons in the parapet gave an awful crack and exploded into shards. As debris caught the edge of his eye, Elcon put up a hand.

Craelin placed himself between Elcon and the parapet. "Here, let me see." He stepped back. "Just a cut, but Praectal Daelic should treat it."

Elcon stepped back. "Daelic has enough to concern him these days without worrying about a simple cut."

A pained expression flitted across Craelin's face. "True enough." He hesitated. "Lof Shraen, perhaps you should not venture here. Why not let the priests hide you?"

Elcon resisted the temptation Craelin's words stirred. "Don't ask me to shirk battle."

"But if you fall the Kindren will lose heart."

Elcon's sweeping inspection encompassed those positioned to defend walls, barbican and gatehouse. He spoke the truth but not without a pang. "They have no heart *now*." In a sense they had already seen him fall. "If I fight with them, they may rally."

"They stand ready to die for the privilege of preserving your life. Will you cheat them?"

He sighed. "I will fight." He touched the corner of his eye, now sticky with blood, and grimaced. "Inform me of any developments. I'll be in my chambers."

"Of course." Archers approached from farther along the battlements, and Craelin walked toward them. "We're well. The masonry took the worst of it."

Craelin's words followed Elcon onto the stair. "I'll set a guard outside your chambers. You might let Weilton escort you whenever you leave them."

Elcon grimaced and put a hand to Sword Rivenn's hilt in a brief caress but made his way to his chambers—for now. He salved his cut eye and then stretched out, falling at once into the oblivion of sleep.

An almighty roar woke him. He sat up in darkness, but light flared around the edges of the window hangings and sent the shadows on his chamber walls into a macabre dance. He stumbled to the window and fumbled at its coverings.

His dressing room door creaked open. "Let me, Lof Shraen." Weilton, who slept within, stepped forward to complete the task.

Bright fireballs with streaming tails lit the sky as they shot over the walls. The cookhouse's thatched roof already blazed. Screams arose but soon died to nothing.

Torindan waited in quivering silence.

Flames from the cookhouse fire showed the stronghold's catapults rocking in retaliation. Stone missiles launched in the face of the enemy's dragonsfire. Ineffective as the effort seemed, an uproar outside the walls indicated some small success.

Shrieks filled the air. Winged death blackened the fire-lightened sky. Elcon drew a shaky breath.

Welke riders.

More screams. Voices raised in uproar. Weilton shoved him out of the window opening just as an arrow whizzed past his cheek.

Weilton slammed the shutters shut. His voice carried over the rasp of the metal latch. "Forgive me, Lof Shraen. I meant no disrespect."

Elcon scrambled in new darkness to find Sword Rivenn. Near his bedside, his hand encountered its scabbard. He hoisted its weight. "Pray don't concern yourself with such niceties, Weilton."

A tap sounded at the outer door. Anders met them in the outer chamber, a lighted lanthorn in hand.

Weilton approached the door. "Who goes there?"

"It's Eathnor. Craelin sends word to Elcon."

At Elcon's nod, Weilton cracked the door but stepped back as Eathnor burst into the room. "You're well, then?"

Elcon lowered his sword and inclined his head in acknowledgment of Eathnor's belated bow. "Well enough. And Craelin?"

"He's uninjured, but we lost several archers on the wall and three who manned a bastion."

"Can we not return dragonsfire of our own?"

"We have not had time to replenish our supplies, and what we do have is marked for use in the tunnels. But I'll ask your question of Craelin."

Elcon could ask Craelin his own questions. "Give your report." His words snapped out, sharper than intended.

"They've filled in the moat and will soon wheel the siege tower next to the wall. Craelin expects its advance by morning. Our footsoldiers and archers stand ready to meet it. Their masonry sappers work under an iron roof to weaken the wall below the ruined bastion. Its thickness should deter them for a time, at least, but we may need to make a foray to stop them. Progress on the counter tunnel halted when our miners encountered bedstone, but they've rerouted."

"And what of the welke riders?"

"I don't know what Craelin intends to do about

them. They showed themselves just as I ducked into the keep."

Elcon turned away to hide tears. Craelin would send wingabeast riders in response, as he'd done during the previous siege. How many would they lose before the rays of morning banished the welkes to their roosts?

"Craelin suggests you seek the priests' protection at once."

"I'll not hide while my people die." Elcon jerked open the door and ran from the chamber. He took the stairs to the battlements above the guardhouse two at a time.

Craelin descended to block his way. "So. You'll not preserve your life."

Elcon's gaze did not waver from Craelin's. "Not at such a cost. What would I save myself for, anyway? If Torindan falls, I'd subsist by wandering—an exiled shraen without a raven—until they hunt me down. If I stand with my people, there's a chance we can hold the fortress until reinforcements arrive. If not, I'd rather die in battle."

"As would I," Weilton spoke from behind Elcon.

Elcon turned with a smile. "You followed me."

Weilton smiled back. "I'm assigned to protect you."

The steady thumping of the battering ram gave way to a splintering crash.

"They've entered the barbican!" An archer called from his position at the parapet. Craelin took the stairs upward, and Elcon followed to look out from an embrasure.

"We'll give a hearty welcome to all who enter the gates of death." Elcon read the truth in the pained expression that belied Craelin's brave words. They might hold the barbican, with its three gates, for a time. But already the siege tower swayed against the sky as it rolled toward the filled-in moat, pulled by teams of muscular bovines.

Eathnor joined them from farther down the battlements "Foot soldiers now ascend the barbican with grappling hooks and ladders."

"Besides toppling the ladders, we can still greet them with pots of slaked lime, stones, and boiling water." Craelin raised an eyebrow in inquiry. "Provided our stores last."

Eathnor gave a swift nod. "They will hold, for now."

"We must halt the wheeled siege tower." Elcon's brow furrowed as the tower rocked closer to Torindan's outer wall. Once in place, archers behind the siege tower's merlons could shoot their arrows downward, and a ramp would lower to provide the enemy access to Torindan's cleared walls. Craelin moved closer to Elcon. "It advances with such speed terror strikes those on the wall."

Elcon clutched the rough stone at the edges of the embrasure. "Shoot the beasts that draw it. That will at least slow its progress. Craelin's eyes widened and then respect settled across his face. He turned to Eathnor. "Go at once and give the Lof Shraen's instructions to the archers on the outer wall."

Eathnor ducked his head and set off to obey.

Elcon scanned the horizon. "No sign of reinforcements?"

"None."

"Let us hope we can hold out." Fear winged into Elcon's mind and found its roost, talons curving to claw his soul. The smell of death breathed over him. Pain twisted in his mind. Sorrow struck his stomach. He doubled over with a cry.

Hands caught him, preventing his fall. "May Lof Yuel protect you." Craelin breathed.

Elcon gripped the stone of the parapet until Freaer's touch slid away. He stiffened. Distant figures streamed from the canyonlands toward Torindan, and Elcon's heart beat double-time within his chest. He shouted above the renewed thumping of the battering ram. "Garns approach."

The look of horror on Craelin's face told its own story. "We'll never stand against so many." He turned his head. "You may soon fulfill your wish to die in battle."

19

The Ice Witch

Aewen's baby, held in the crook of Murial's arm, stared at Kai with bright eyes as he gave the sapphire band into the old servant's free hand. Even here, in the dim light of the inn's hallway, the stone at its center gleamed. Murial tilted her head in question, and he closed her hand around the ornament. "It's from Euryon—for Syl Marinda. I want you to hold it for her until I return from Torindan. I must go now to find Elcon."

"I'll keep it safe." Murial's hand tightened around the band. He thought she took his meaning. He had no idea what he would find when he arrived at Torindan or whether he would return for Elcon's child.

The babe grasped his finger and drew it toward her mouth. Murial laughed and shifted away. "She's a hungry little thing and keeps me busy. It's well Quinn and Heddwyn keep a goat for the milk it gives." She smiled but her eyes filled with tears.

He touched her shoulder. "Look after her safety."

Her dark eyes gleamed. "Aye, and look to your own as well."

In the common room, Quinn delivered a platter of bread and cheese to a grizzled huntsman and then glanced at Kai. "You'll be on your way, then?"

Kai signaled for Quinn to join him outside. When the door banged shut behind them, he leaned close to Quinn. "Thank you for keeping the babe in comfort and safety."

Quinn gave him a level look. "None besides us need know the truth about her parents."

Kai nodded. "That's well, then. I'll try and return soon."

Quinn's face warmed in a smile. "Don't worry about that. Heddwyn be overjoyed to keep the child. She can't bear offspring of her own, you see. That babe fills her arms and soothes her aching heart."

Kai turned to go but at the touch of a hand on his arm, looked back into the innkeeper's rugged face. Quinn cleared his throat. "Godspeed."

డ్≈త

The last gate splintered and crashed. A shudder went through Elcon as many voices raised a visceral battle cry. The enemy now occupied the barbican. All who had defended it must have fallen. They'd held out against wave after wave of footsoldiers. They'd even managed to light fire to the siege tower as it lurched toward the fortress with garns in the place of the slain oxen. But they could not hold it forever against such numbers.

Craelin squinted at him, his blue eyes nested in lines. "With the enemy so close, only a fool would linger here and risk a stray arrow. Let the archers defend the battlements, and we'll put our heads together in the guardroom."

At first Elcon stared at him without comprehension, his thoughts centered on Eathnor, whom he'd ordered to carry a message to the archers. Had he sent him to his death? He could only hope the young tracker had already returned across the drawbridge, now lifted, that spanned a deep channel of the moat between the barbican and gatehouse.

A small thud followed the hiss of flight feathers. Craelin jerked, then doubled as if he'd taken a stomach punch. Elcon reached him in two steps. Weilton met him at Craelin's side. Together, they pulled him upright. Blood seeped in a spreading patch on the shoulder of his surcoat around the shaft of an arrow that projected there. He groaned.

Elcon threw Craelin's good arm over his own shoulders. Weilton supported him on his injured side. Together, they half-dragged, half-carried him down the stairs. Dorann, just passing, halted. Elcon jerked his head without slowing. "Summon Daelic!"

They laid Craelin on his bed, and Weilton broke the shaft of the arrow with care. Even so, Craelin gritted his teeth and moaned. Already blood stained the sheet. Weilton looked across Craelin to Elcon. "The arrow's gone through his shoulder. Let him grasp your hand so I can push the rest of the shaft out."

Elcon lifted a brow. "Shouldn't we wait for Daelic?"

Weilton glanced up. "There's no telling where Daelic may be right now. I know what I'm doing."

Craelin grasped Elcon's hand as he moaned again. "Don't waste your time on the dying."

"You can't die." Elcon squeezed Craelin's hand to emphasize his words. "I have need of you."

Craelin gave the ghost of a smile. "I'll bear that in mind." Weilton turned him on his side and pushed the broken shaft through in a sudden movement. Craelin cried out as beads of sweat stood on his forehead. His eyes closed and he went limp.

When Craelin's iron grip relaxed Elcon massaged his own hand. "He's unconscious. Let's get his surcoat and chain mail off. The arrow slipped between the plates."

Weilton tore the bed sheets into pieces which he pressed against Craelin's wounds. "We need to staunch the flow of blood. He's lost quite a bit already. If pressure doesn't stop the flow, we'll have to cauterize the wound."

"Weilton, as second in command, you must act in his place. Send another to help tend Craelin."

"I mislike leaving him or you."

"I can look after Craelin and myself, but keep me informed. It's only a matter of time before they breech the wall."

"Don't worry, Lof Shraen. We can shoot fire arrows and use catapults. Of course, the thickness at the base of the walls will deter them, at least for a time. We have enough pots of quicklime, oil, shards, and stones for a good defense."

Elcon asked the question most pressing his mind. "Can we hope to hold them off until our reinforcements arrive?"

Weilton's eyes gleamed. "There's always hope—and prayer."

ॐॐ

The stable boy, emerged from the far end of the stable, pitchfork in hand. Kai had come to know and trust Hael. He was a cheery fellow with apple cheeks and brown hair. Hael knew his way around a horse, whether it had wings or no.

"Help me, will you? I must leave this day and take all the wingabeasts."

Hael gave him a bright look but asked no questions. With measured movements he approached Raeld, while Kai turned to Fletch. Ruescht whinnied in inquiry and the boy laughed. "She's a might concerned about being left behind, I think." He patted her neck.

Once Fletch and Raeld were saddled and bridled, Kai led them outside and left Hael to follow with Ruescht. He squinted in the sunlight, blinded after the dimness. Beyond the stableyard, cleared pasture land sloped to the White Feather River, which roared and boomed against its banks. Kai mounted Fletch as Hael joined him and offered him Ruescht's lead rope. Kai shook his head. "Tie it to her saddle horn, as I've done with Raeld." He laughed at Hael's look of surprise. "They'll not stray."

"I didn't know the wingabeasts obeyed so well."

"They are trained to it."

Hael stepped away but waited. Kai smiled and nodded a farewell. Hael never seemed to tire of watching wingabeasts lift into flight. After commanding the other two wingabeasts to follow, Kai signaled Fletch. Powerful wings lifted and then beat downward as the wingabeast sprang upward. Raeld and Ruescht arched into flight over the White Feather River, which roared and foamed below. The peaks of Maegrad Ceid jutted skyward before him as Fletch climbed toward the passes. They needed to gain height to cross in safety, for wingabeasts flying over the Maegrad could encounter wind shears and vagrant currents. Kai was used to navigating them whenever he returned for visits home to Whellein, but he never quite relaxed until he'd cleared the passes.

He smiled at the sudden memory of teasing Shae about the Ice Witch. In truth, an ancient legend about Erdrich Ceid warned of the arts she employed to freeze solid those who strayed into her icy domain. His smile widened. Shae had believed the tale. How strange that thoughts of Shae brought him only joy now. He would always love and miss her, but somehow the pain of his loss had eased.

He crossed over foothills clad in kabas and seamed with silver waterfalls. The trees grew smaller and finally fell away in lieu of banks of snowflowers and penstemons. These, in turn, yielded before the silent tumbled boulders of glacial moraines. The snow in the passes sparkled like diamonds. A particular patch drew his attention—the place Aewen had given birth. Fresh snow already erased any marks of disturbance.

Fletch lurched and tilted in a crosswind, batting his wings to correct his flight. Raeld and Ruescht recovered as well. Kai turned his attention wholly to flight. They entered turbulent currents, and then a sudden pocket of calm. Although Fletch's wings beat the air, they plummeted. Kai fought to bring his wingabeast out of the downdraft he'd sunk into, for the shoulders of the passes loomed near. Fletch tilted, and Kai cried out as the mountain seemed to heave toward him.

శ్రా

A figure blocked the light in the doorway, and Elcon looked up in expectation. "Did Weilton send you?" He shifted to ease the ache in his shoulders from half-bending over Craelin to press the cloths over his wounds.

Dorann looked surprised "Nay. I came back when I couldn't find Daelic. I left word for him and now offer myself in his place."

"That's right. You know something of healing."

Dorann moved to the bedside, his attention on Craelin's prostrate form. "I know the old ways."

Elcon straightened. "They'll do."

Dorann pulled the bloody cloths aside and shook his head. "We'll need a fire. I can light one soon enough."

"Weilton suggested cauterizing the wounds."

Dorann already squatted before the cold hearth. "We can hope he'll recover. He's lost a lot of blood. Has Weilton gone, then? Why do I find you alone at Craelin's side?"

"Weilton left for the guardroom to assume Craelin's duties in his absence. I took you for the help he promised to send."

"So, another will arrive soon? That's well, then. An extra pair of hands won't go amiss should Craelin rouse."

Elcon took his meaning. He'd not seen wounds cauterized before, but he understood it as a grim business. A memory stirred. "Where were you headed earlier?"

Dorann blew on the small flame that sputtered in the hearth. "I came in search of Eathnor."

Elcon hesitated. "He may have been on the barbican's battlements when it fell."

Dorann's amber eyes were bright. "He was there, as was I."

"I thought none escaped."

"Some did." He turned back to the fire. "Most did

not. When Freaer's footsoldiers intercepted us I lost sight of Eathnor in the fight. I don't know if he made it across the drawbridge. If he did, I thought to find him, or at least word of him, in the guardroom."

A shadow fell across the doorway. A figure moved into the chamber. "I can give you word of your brother, who has worn out the pathways looking for you."

Dorann sprang to his feet and met Eathnor's embrace.

A roar separated them as a fireball landed nearby. Vibrations rose through the stone floor.

"More dragonsfire!" Elcon found his voice.

Dorann staggered to the open door. "That was in the bailey, just beyond the gatehouse arch!" Across the moat an eerie battle cry rose and fell. A grim expression crossed Eathnor's face. "They'll rush the walls soon."

Dorann laid an iron poker in the fire. "Meanwhile, let's tend Craelin."

When the poker glowed red, they worked with speed. At the first hiss and stench of burnt flesh, Craelin roused with a shriek, but Elcon and Eathnor held him fast. At the second hiss, he fainted dead away.

Dorann stood back. Sweat beaded his forehead. "If he lives through the night, we can place him among the other wounded in the care of the priests."

Eathnor gave a swift nod. "I'll watch over him until then."

Dorann cleared his throat. "*I'll* watch over him, you mean. What of your other duties as a messenger of the guardians?"

Eathnor smiled. "Few know I've cheated death. I'll

report to Weilton soon enough."

Elcon lifted a brow. "I'll tell Weilton you live, Eathnor, but I prefer you to remain at Craelin's side for now. If any of us lives through this night, we'll need to stand and fight."

Eathnor smiled. "What say you, brother? Shall we cheat death a second time?"

∽≪⊚

Dead air hung in a pall before him. An orange sky glowed overhead. Trees flamed red. Kai slid from Fletch's back. He dug his hands into black snow that stretched in all directions. It numbed his flesh. He stood and looked about. He could see nothing beyond this strange hollow.

Was this death, then—a place of nothing more?

At a thin whistling exhalation, he turned. Fletch, frozen in place, breathed no more.

Terrible cold blasted Kai as the Ice Witch claimed him too.

∽≪⊚

Dragonsfire worried the sky late into the night, but now its absence troubled Elcon's scant sleep. He rolled from bed to his feet. He'd borrowed Kai's guardhouse chamber for the night because of its proximity to Craelin's and to remain close to the battle. The rampant gryphon carved into the strongwood door to Craelin's chamber loomed out of the semi-darkness. He heard no sound from within.

The cool metal of Sword Rivenn weighted his hand as he passed beneath guttering torches and climbed the silent stair to the guardhouse tower. At an arrow embrasure near the top, he paused and looked out. Shreds of cloud obscured the pale moon, which picked out the high peaks in outline. The land below lay in darkness. As he watched, blackness blotted out even the moon's feeble light.

He stepped back, his heart pounding. The sword in his hand came alive with light. A scuffling sounded overhead. He withdrew into shadow, every muscle tensed.

A stench permeated the heavy air, so rotten he gagged. He had cause, it seemed, to regret releasing Weilton from his service. He'd never smelled garns before, but he'd heard of their foul odor. How many descended?

His knees shook but held. The wall's rough stone pressed his back. The shuffling neared. A shadow stretched long in the wavering light. The time for escape had fled. He thought to hide but that required he sheath his sword to conceal its light. Sweat beaded his brow. Words from the past crowded his mind.

My son, you shall make your own history. We all feel the bite of fear, Elcon. You must not let it devour you.

I receive and will keep the Alliance of Faeraven with all my heart.

He breathed a prayer and swung out to meet the dark shape on the stair, a welke and its hideous rider. The welke screeched. The muscular garn on its back, hair sprouting from places not covered by the befouled hides it wore, grunted. The welke responded, pecking at Elcon's hand. He cried out and as blood ran down his forearm the great sword fell from his nerveless fingers.

The garn grunted again and bared fangs as it

raised a barbed sword. Elcon flung himself backward but the welke advanced. He shot a glance at Sword Rivenn, its light flaring just treads below. He'd never reach it in time. He fetched against the cold wall, sorrow washing over him. Why had he rushed out alone and without his dagger? His foolishness, this time, would cost him his life.

20

Sword and Lance

The travesty of a smile stretched the garn's flat features. The sword whipped downward as Elcon jumped out of harm's way. Metal pinged against stone. The garn grunted. Elcon crept sideways along the wall. The welke followed.

A blade sang past Elcon to land with a thud. The welke fell with a hissing breath, a knife embedded in its throat. Elcon flicked a glance down the stair but saw nothing. The garn arose from the welke's carcass, unfolding itself a long way upward to stand heads taller than him. Elcon fought to control his breathing. The barbed sword lifted, and the ugly face twisted in rage.

Torchlight died but revived and shadows swung wide. Sword Rivenn glowed, just out of reach, but hope still flickered within Elcon. Like Eathnor and Dorann, he would cheat death, although he had only his wit to pit against the garn's strength. On impulse, he shifted to run down the stair but backed upward instead. The blade struck the wall where he would have been, scattering bits of stone. The garn bellowed and swung toward him, but paused to scan the shadows, now at its back, from which the knife had come.

Elcon pushed away from the wall. He couldn't count on rescue, and his maneuvers had only taken him farther from his sword. He backed upward on the stair. If he lured the foul creature to the top of the tower he might cause its fall.

A stone thudded into the garn from behind. Although the stone clattered away without any apparent effect on its target, the garn turned toward the shadows.

A figure Elcon recognized sprang from the shadows. Dorann crouched before the beast, a hunting knife in his hand.

The garn roared, lunging as the barbed sword sliced air.

Dorann danced away.

The creature tracked him in grim silence. Again the barbed sword whipped through empty air. The garn roared as Dorann's blade dripped blood.

The combatants faced one another, panting.

Raising its sword with both hands as blood ran down one arm, the beast uttered a bloodcurdling battle cry as it made a run at Dorann. The tracker whirled sideways and away but his opponent stumbled and pitched headlong down the stair. Dorann followed. Elcon caught up his sword, but by the time he reached Dorann, the garn lay still.

"Eathnor heard you at the door." Dorann told him between breaths. "I decided you needed looking after."

Elcon sought his voice. "Thank you."

The tracker gave a curt nod and looked back to the dead garn. "Bruins fight harder."

Elcon stood at one of the arrow embrasures in the gatehouse tower. The garn and welke no longer threatened, but dawn's light revealed a tide of the foul beasts surging past the barbican and spreading out through the township of Torindan. Countless rafts sliced through the murky waters of the moat toward the fortress walls.

Elcon turned his head. "Can we hold them?"

Weilton's expression was grave. "We expended the last of our dragonsfire to win and collapse the tunnels. As for the rest of our supplies, well, they can't go on forever. Perhaps we should seek surrender."

Elcon thrust away from the embrasure. "We can't give up."

The lines in Weilton's face seemed to deepen in the feeble light streaming in from the arrow slit before him. "You should save yourself, Lof Shraen. Why not escape through the priests' passageway? Don't let Torindan fall in vain. As long as you breathe, hope lives for Faeraven."

"My father would not flee like a coward!"

"He didn't face this evil."

Elcon shook his head. "No. I'll stand before I die. I plan to lead a force of hand-picked wingabeast riders in a foray against the garns."

Weilton stared at him. "Their numbers are too great. You speak of suicide."

He raised an eyebrow. "I will bring honor to the House of Rivenn, even at the cost of my life. If I lay it down, I may win one more day for Torindan's reinforcements to arrive. If we do nothing, all our lives are forfeit. Don't deceive yourself. Surrender will bring no mercy."

Weilton's face flushed. "Your plan has merit. Only

let me go in your place."

Elcon put a hand on Weilton's shoulder. "I count on you to hold the fortress in Craelin's absence. Come, no more talk of surrender."

A determined look crossed Weilton's face. "Agreed."

Light footfalls set up small echoes to meet them in the stairway. Eathnor ran toward them from below, passing in and out of shadow. He spoke before they met. "The garns run on the walls."

"They waste no time." Weilton swung toward an arrow embrasure in the wall.

Elcon took Eathnor's arm. "Ride with me against them."

Eathnor's eyes widened, but then he squared his shoulders. "Aye."

Elcon nodded to Weilton. "Send five of our best riders to the stables without delay. We'll defend the wall."

Weilton joined them. "As you say, only let the archers and foot soldiers guard the wall. Flying between them, the wingabeasts would get in the way, and you could be injured. But cut off the second wave of boats if you can." He started back up the stairs. "I'll send riders." Elcon and Eathnor ran down the stairs together and found Dorann in the bailey. He bobbed his head at Elcon's approach. "Craelin's settled with the priests. Time will tell whether he lives or dies."

Elcon and Eathnor did not slow as they took the path to the stables. "That's true for us all." Eathnor called to his brother.

"Tell me what's happened." Doran kept pace.

"Have you gone deaf, my brother? Can't you hear the garn's battle cries?"

"Of course. That's why I left the wounded to fight alongside the footsoldiers."

As they reached the stable door a ball catapulted through the air to thud into the path behind Dorann. Shards flew as Elcon ducked into the stable and Eathnor pulled his brother inside. "Watch yourself. It would be well if one of our parents' sons lived through the day."

Dorann pushed away from his brother. "You ride against garns without me, don't you?"

Elcon left the brothers to their goodbyes.

"Lof Shraen!" A stableboy bowed.

Elcon waved a hand. "No time for that. Saddle seven wingabeasts. Lives depend on your speed."

The stableboy stared at him, but then hurried toward the wingabeasts as he called out. Two other stableboys joined him at the task, and finally, Guaron himself. At last the beasts stood ready but only three riders had appeared, Demeric of Chaeradon, Pelsney of Daeramor, and Oalram of Rivenn.

Elcon paced to where Eathnor waited beside Dorann near the door. "Do any others approach?"

Eathnor shook his head. "Nay."

"We'll ride ahead without them then. There's no time to wait."

Dorann stirred. "I'll ride with you."

"Dorann, you've little experience on a wingabeast and none in battle.

Dorann gave him a quelling look. "I rode to Maeg Waer and back, did I not?"

Elcon raised a hand to still Eathnor's response. "Ride, then."

They mounted and rode into the bailey at once. Two more guardians appeared on the path from the gatehouse, and Elcon nodded them toward the stables. They could follow to replace those who fell.

With a touch Saethril, the black he rode in place of Raeld, spiraled into flight. They lifted above the meager security afforded by the curtain walls. He pressed Saethril upward, out of the range of missiles, passed over the gatehouse, and hovered above the moat.

A sudden gust rushed against his ears and caught the edge of his cloak. Not far overhead, gray clouds scuttled across a pale sky. Distorted shadows raced over dark figures below. Six rafts of lashed-together logs bumped the walls between towers. The garns aboard them huddled beneath shields lifted to form a roof above their heads. More rafts entered the waters to cut through floating corpses.

Nearby, the bridge made of rubble acted as a causeway for masses of garns streaming through the barbican. A volley of arrows, stones, and pots of quicklime hurtled downward. He shook his head at the futility of such efforts, for as soon as one garn fell another took its place.

Lightning flashed overhead and thunder shook the air. His pulse surged in his ears. There it came again— a distant trumpet blast. On the horizon to the north and south armies approached. He met Eathnor's vivid gaze. Dorann, hovering on Sharten beside Eathnor's wingabeast, Roaem, looked ready for anything, as did the other riders. Elcon took a breath to steady himself before raising his lance. At his signal Saethril plunged toward the second wave of rafts as Elcon voiced the ancient battle cry of his people.

Arrows whizzed past, launched by hostile archers in the barbican's battlements. At their approach, the garns stopped rowing. A shield deflected Elcon's first thrust and a barbed spear followed him upward. Another volley of arrows zinged through the air. A wingabeast shrilled. Elcon lifted out of range. The other riders fell in rank behind him, all save one. Dorann pushed away from Sharten's limp body, heaved a breath and dove under the water. Arrows pricked the surface where he had been.

Elcon turned Saethril with the speed of thought and dove toward the garns, Eathnor on Roaem beside him. As they neared, the raft beside the dead wingabeast rocked and two garns fell into the water as the others fought to remain standing. Elcon frowned in puzzlement, but then Dorann push away from the edge of the raft. Eathnor dipped low on his wingabeast and reached for his brother. Dorann's eyes widened and he slipped beneath the water.

"Dorann!" Eathnor's shout pierced Elcon.

Arrows sang through the air, forcing Elcon and Eathnor to lift above them. One of the garns Dorann had tipped into the water cried out, and then stretched in a dead man's float, arrows bristling from his back. Elcon scanned the surface. "There!" As he pointed, Roaem hurtled downward. Eathnor must have already seen Dorann rolling in the water, locked in a deadly embrace with the second garn that had fallen from the raft.

Saethril dove through the air behind Roaem, and Elcon's lance found its mark as a garn grunted. The rest of the wingabeast riders descended, and more garns fell. Wingabeasts shrilled. Foul water splattered upward, and Elcon no longer saw Dorann. When Saethril lifted away two wingabeasts floated motionless in the moat, their riders face-down nearby.

Shadows winged overhead, black against the sun-welke riders. Saethril shuddered. Elcon put a steadying hand on the wingabeast's shoulder and checked the riders he led. Only Eathnor and Pelsney remained. He glanced toward Torindan, but no other wingabeasts lifted into the air. Had the other two decided not to ride?

Death rode over him, delivering an unseen blow that sent him reeling in pain. Despair smote his mind with force, and the world went dark. He listed in the saddle, clinging to the pommel. "Steady!" he called to Saethril. If his wingabeast shifted, he would fall. As wave after wave of power lashed his mind there was nothing he could do but grit his teeth and endure.

Another, gentle touch whispered across his mind to shield him. Shae. Somehow his sister had found a way to protect him, even from the world between. He pulled upright in the saddle, and his vision cleared.

He gave again the battlecry and turned to meet the welke riders. A ragged raptor fell upon him with claws extended. He pulled Saethril upward and rolled sideways to catch the creature and its rider by surprise. The lances met, the first shock jolting through him. Saethril screamed and showed the whites of his eyes but at Elcon's command spun back toward the welke. The lance's second impact nearly unseated Elcon. At the third his lance fell from his already wounded fingers. Drawing Sword Rivenn, he reined Saethril about.

A shadow rode in from the side. The hair on Elcon's arms rose, and he fought the rise of panic. Saethril shuddered and arched his neck, but held steady even as raptors neared on either side.

Elcon gave the signal that sent Saethril upward.

Screeching, the welkes collided and plummeted together.

Shrieks rent the air. A welke tore into the wingabeast Pelsney rode even as the garn rider's barbed lance penetrated his chain mail. Pelsney and his wingabeast hurtled downward as welke and garn screeched in triumph. The welke wheeled about and glided toward Elcon. He had time to register a vicious battle between Eathnor and two welke riders before the garn reached him.

One of the garn rider's eyes carried the opacity of blindness, but the other fixed unwaveringly on Elcon. The welke the garn rode neared with claws at the ready, perhaps emboldened by its taste of blood. Saethril shrilled and shuddered but held. If they lived, he would give Saethril carrots every day. Elcon waited until he swore he felt the welke's hot breath, longer than his own nerves could stand. At last he signaled Saethril. As the welke screeched and the garn grunted, the wingabeast dropped into a rolling spin that leveled just above the ground.

Elcon touched Saethril's quivering shoulder, and his hand came away damp with sweat. Arrows shot past. He signaled a rapid climb. As Saethril spiraled upward, air cooled Elcon's face. The one-eyed garn already pursued. In the small space of time he'd gained, Elcon looked about. All had fallen save Eathnor and himself. Only one welke rider dogged Eathnor now. Elcon frowned. Eathnor's movements slowed and his lance wavered.

With renewed strength, he lifted his sword and raised the Kindren battlecry as he launched Saethril toward the one-eyed welke rider. A startled look crossed his pursuer's face, but smugness soon chased away surprise. The garn turned his welke to approach Elcon from an angle that favored his good eye. Elcon again waited until impact seemed certain before signaling Saethril. His wingabeast bumped upward, just out of reach, and the welke's claws clicked together below.

He came up on the garn's blind side, close enough to hear him grunt. Elcon acted with speed before the foul creature could turn. He thrust his sword into the vulnerable spot below the garn's helmet. Blood spurted. The garn went limp and fell from its seat as Saethril lifted away.

The welke screeched and circled toward Elcon.

His chest heaved. His ears rang. The edges of his vision flamed red. He gathered his remaining reserves of strength to point Saethril's head toward the welke at all times. The foul creature's circling narrowed. If he tried to break free the welke would attack.

A horn sounded and a battlecry Elcon knew thrummed through the air. As the two belated wingabeast riders approached, the welke abandoned Elcon and soared away. Eathnor's attacker flapped past, ignoring him. Countless dark bodies streamed back through the barbican and broke formation as Freaer's armies fled into the eastern desert, pursued by the armies of Chaeradon.

One man, bruised and bloody, stumbled toward the hold. Elcon squinted. Could it be? And then he was certain.

Dorann.

He had cheated death after all.

Part Three:Sojourn

21

Conviction

"And so you steal my daughter from me again."

Elcon took Euryon's measure. The Elder king looked older and gaunter than Elcon remembered, dwarfed by the lofty presence chamber where he huddled upon his throne. "I beg you—" He waited to speak again until he could soften his voice. "Let me take her home to Torindan, where I can hope one day to join her in the tomb."

Euryon's eyes, pale blue like Aewen's, shone with tears. "She embraced you in life. I will not withhold her in death. Take her."

Elcon swallowed back his own tears. "And the babe?"

"I don't have Aewen's child. Kai keeps her somewhere with a nurse, he said, although he did not tell us where. Did he not mention this?"

"No. Two of the wingabeasts in Kai's care landed outside Torindan's barbican, saddled and bridled, with the reins tied to their saddle horns. Both Kai and his wingabeast vanished. We suspect Kai met with an accident. Trackers now search for him."

Euryon's expression grew meditative. "If Kai did not come back to you, how did you find Aewen?"

"After the riderless wingabeasts returned, our guardians made inquiries. The owners of the inn on the White Feather River knew of Aewen's death, and of our child." He kept his words curt to curtail their pain. He did not want to dwell on what Aewen had suffered. He clenched his jaw, clamping down upon such thoughts. He could not allow painful memories to birth despair and bleed his strength.

Euryon's face took on a look of penance. "I should have given you the aid you asked against Freaer. If I had, Aewen might yet live."

The words settled between them like stone weights. Elcon shook his head. "I should not have forced her to travel so near childbirth. In my zeal to preserve her life I ended it." His voice broke. "The fault ever remains mine."

Twin tracks of moisture ran down seams in Euryon's cheeks. "We must each bear our own burden."

࿐

A wheel dropped into a pothole, and as the wagon tilted, the coffin edged sideways. The Anusians pulling it tossed their manes and whinnied. Elcon pushed to his feet and readied himself to jump, but the wagon shuddered and righted itself again. He settled onto the rough wooden seat, and expelled a relieved breath as he gathered the reins again. The wagon trundled onward.

Eathnor rode forward. "Will you not allow me to drive?"

Elcon gritted his jaw. Eathnor would no doubt manage the cart better but he wanted—needed—to bring his own wife home. He shook his head but spared Eathnor an attempt at a smile.

"I must go to my child."

Light eyes pierced his. Eathnor seemed about to speak but instead dipped his head, nodded, and fell back to join Weilton as part of his rear guard. They must all think him mad. He'd not heeded Craelin's warning against travel at such a time of unrest. He gripped the reins and scanned the rutted road. He had promised Aewen he would come for her. He'd kept his promise.

Aerlic rode Argalent, his silver wingabeast, as part of the advance contingent. Dorann traveled beside Aerlic on one of the golds. Since Sharten's death, the tracker had formed a bond with Destrill, the wingabeast whose name described the sound of thunder. Dorann's rough hide jerkin contrasted with the green and gold of Aerlic's surcoat. Although willing enough to serve his Lof Shraen, the tracker refused the colors of the guardians. The two searched the green shadows of the kaba forest and tilted their heads to scan the thick branches knitting together overhead. They watched for beasts and for bandits. Elcon could not prevent himself from doing the same. Every flicker of movement caught his eye. This great forest of shaggy-barked trees seemed to go on forever, but when light broke across the road in the distance, he sighed in relief.

They emerged from the forest into rolling hill country covered in brush and dotted with homefarms. The wagon groaned and shook and bumped along. As the Anusians mounted the next hillock, muscles bunched, hooves clomped, and manes flew. Elcon struggled to remain seated. The wagon pitched and sometimes halted without warning as one wheel or another sank into soggy low places gouged by rainwater.

By the time they pulled off the road along the banks of the White Feather River, purple stained the horizon. The water tumbled over stones here before spreading wide and shallow to comb through glistening rocks. Elcon braked the wagon and stretched to ease aching muscles. Weilton brought him water, and he ate waybread and cheese. He made for himself a bed of furs beneath the wagon so that he might sleep near Aewen this final time. A willet hooted somewhere in the weilos as the camp faded to a palette of gray across which moved the darker shadow of Eathnor, first to take watch duty. And then the light leached away altogether and he saw shadows no more.

He opened his eyes in the night to watch the stars wink on as clouds sailed before the wind. Aewen came to him then, although at first he thought her whisper that of the wind. Her touch brushed his face and hair. Her mouth caressed his in the briefest of kisses. She smiled, her face and hair aglow, but a tear glistened on her cheek. He brushed it away. "Peace, now…"

She caught his hand and kissed it. "I'll always love you, Elcon."

He smiled even as tears wet his own cheeks. "I love you, Aewen."

She squeezed his hand. "Promise me you will find our child."

He reached to cradle her cheek but met only air. "Be still, my flower. How can I not seek my own flesh?"

He sat up, for he could see Aewen no longer, although her weeping rode the wind. Then, even that was gone. He peered into the blackness and struggled to free himself from the furs, which twisted about to constrain him. "Aewen, wait! Come back!"

"Are you well?" Weilton asked out of the moonlit darkness.

"Aewen." He gulped in air. "I—I must have dreamed of her." He wept then, tears of sorrow. Aewen would come to him no more.

"Try and rest, Lof Shraen." Weilton's whisper reached him.

"Wait!" Elcon rolled from beneath the wagon and stood.

Weilton turned back to him. "What troubles you?"

"She spoke—she spoke of our babe."

"The innkeeper at the White Feather will know the child's whereabouts. We should arrive there after midday on the morrow."

Elcon drew a ragged breath. "If only I'd taken time to stop there on our way to Cobbleford. I might have found my child the sooner."

"Only a little time remains before dawn. Try and spend it in peace, Lof Shraen. We'll set out at once by daylight."

After Weilton left him, Elcon settled into his furs, but sleep eluded him. He lay still as the river rushed on. He had not lain down in peace for far too long.

❧❦

A distant rooster crowed, and Elcon jerked awake. Mist sparkled in a dance above the river and dazzled his eyes. He blinked to ease their aching and crawled from beneath the wagon to stand on stiff legs. His companions already moved about, his own weariness reflected in their faces. This sorrowful journey had taken its toll on them all. A night at the inn would come as welcome.

They spared scant time to gnaw hard cheese with dry bread before setting out. The passage of night had improved the road not at all. They did not pause for a midday meal but pressed onward as they neared the inn. The road eased onto a flat to run through rich farmland, winding near the river's edge. The White Feather ran deeper here and at times undercut its banks. At one such place the road had washed out. Despite this difficulty, they arrived at the Whitefeather Inn not far past midday and gave over the wagon with its contents, the Anusians, and wingabeasts to the bright-eyed young stable hand who greeted them. Elcon gave the apple-cheeked youth a nod. "Our beasts will find safety and comfort in your hands. What is your name?"

The youth gave a quick smile and ducked his head. "I'm Hael and pleased to tend your creatures, good Kindren. I've cared for wingabeasts before."

Elcon frowned. "What do you mean? How came you to tend wingabeasts before this?"

"Kai, one of your guardians stopped here often when he traveled to his homeland of Whellein." His brows drew together in a frown. "I hear Kai has disappeared."

"He has, but we've found no body."

"I hope he lives."

The inn was smaller than Elcon had expected but warm and clean. A black-haired Elder with eyes of brown greeted them when they entered the common room. "I am Quinn of Norwood, the keeper of this Inn. Do you seek a meal only or plan to stay?"

Quinn spoke to Elcon, but Weilton answered. "You address Elcon, Lof Shraen of Faeraven."

Quinn's eyes widened. "Lof Shraen! You honor my inn with your presence."

Elcon inclined his head to acknowledge Quinn's bow.

Weilton spoke again. "We'll tarry the night should you have space for us."

Quinn lifted an eyebrow. "We'll manage, if you can sleep double."

"You can't expect the Lof Shraen—"

Elcon cut across Weilton's protest. "After sleeping on the hard ground we'll count it joy."

Quinn led them up a flight of scarred but scoured wooden stairs. He paused along the short corridor to throw doors open in invitation. Their company dwindled until only Elcon and Weilton remained with Quinn. At the end of the corridor he led them into a small but comfortable room. "You'll rest well here, I think. It's not large but there's a bed for your servant in an adjoining room. I'll send water for washing." With a final bow he withdrew.

Elcon sought his voice. "Wait."

Quinn turned back with a raised brow.

"I have questions to ask of you. My wife, Aewen, died here."

Quinn's expression grew sad. "She did."

"What became of our babe?"

Quinn's glance shifted away and then back to Elcon. "I thought you knew. The nurse left to take the child to her sister's homefarm in the north but along the way she wandered into a bog and, well…"

The small chamber closed in on Elcon. "What's this you say?"

"She set off soon's he left for Torindan. Bog cutters brought her back."

"What do you mean?" Elcon passed a hand before his eyes, afraid he already knew the answer.

Quinn blew out his cheeks. "I'm sorry to have to tell you this, but both the nurse and child drowned. Their bodies were torn apart by wild animals, but what remained of them we buried."

Promise me you will find our child.

"I would visit her grave."

"Only rest a bit and I will show it to you, Lof Shraen."

"Take me now."

"As you wish. Come with me."

Weilton followed Elcon behind Quinn back down the creaking stairway.

Quinn led them out of the inn. At the edges of the stableyard a path cut into the kabas. As it skirted the banks of the river, a freshet lifted Elcon's cloak and rushed through the leaves overhead. The path soon bent away from the river and faded to a thin track that ended at a gate. Shadows weaved across the graveyard embraced by a wrought iron enclosure.

The hinges gave a rusty screech as the gate gaped enough to let them pass. Quinn went at once to a newly-turned grave and gestured to the single flat headstone barren of engraving that marked them both. "We didn't know what we should write. It seemed best to leave it blank."

Elcon hung back near the gate with Weilton silent beside him. He swallowed around a lump in his throat. "I'll take my child home and lay her to rest with her mother."

Quinn's eyes glinted with an odd light, and he seemed about to say something but only twisted his hands and stepped away from the graves.

Elcon knelt beside the small plot where the daughter he would never know lay. Poor child. She hadn't deserved this, nor had Aewen's faithful servant. He bowed his head as tears bathed his cheeks. This was his fault, too.

∽∾

Elcon joined his contingent in the stableyard and climbed into the wagon now bearing two coffins. The stableboy he'd met yesterday stood back and folded his hat in his hands. The advance guard set out, and Elcon slapped the reins against the Anusian's sturdy necks. The wagon lurched and swayed as the inn fell behind. The road to the passes of Maegrad Ceid climbed and narrowed until it became nothing more than a steep footpath little suited for the wagon bumping over it.

Finally, Elcon climbed out of the wagon and led the sweating Anusians. Their hooves slid in the wet snow as they forged ahead. Spring had not yet claimed the high places of Maegrad Ceid. A wintery sky glowered, dismal and gray. As they reached the pass, the advance contingent halted, and the Anusians slid to a stop. Elcon frowned. A thick blanket of new snow lay over all. Eathnor rode into the lead, scouting for any signs of ambush from vagrant road agents. His whistle signaled that all was well, and Elcon returned to his seat on the wagon box. He set off behind the advance contingent with wheels slicing through the bed of snow and Weilton bringing up the rear. So as not to disturb great drifts piled against the up-thrust peaks, the group kept silent. Elcon, his face stinging as wind tore at him with icy fingers, huddled in his wool cloak. The Anusians never wavered, tossing dark manes as they kept to the road.

Descending from the passes posed a new challenge. Elcon braked the wagon often to prevent it from running away. His muscles ached long before the road leveled to relieve them. A valley of surpassing beauty rewarded his efforts, a place where silvery waterfalls threaded sheer cliffs, grasses waved, and bright streams wended.

The road pitched upward and bent around the shoulder of a peak. Elcon's spirits lifted, but sorrow also gripped him at the first glimpse of Torindan floating above distant mists.

ॐ∽ॐ

"Lof Shraen, I think this search of yours ill-advised."

Sword Rivenn, its edges honed to sharpness, glinted in the light from the window of Elcon's outer chamber. He lowered the ancient blade and faced Craelin, who sat before the fire. Craelin's head tilted in an uncompromising manner but weariness lined his face. Elcon spoke in quiet tones. "So it may prove, but I will not sit by and do nothing while Freaer rebuilds his strength."

"Send another."

"*I* must go. I'm the one who sent Emmerich away. I'll ask him to return."

A look of reservation settled over Craelin's face.

"Then allow me to accompany you."

"The guardians need your guidance. I will be safe enough with Weilton. Eathnor accompanies me as well."

"Lof Shraen, will you not take Guaron to tend your mounts?"

"The wingabeast keeper must remain at Torindan. Freaer will soon return and, when injured in battle, wingabeasts respond best to Guaron's care."

Craelin cast a doubtful look at Elcon. "I cannot hide my mislike of this quest. You're not even certain where to find Emmerich. The rumors that he dwells within the kaba wilderness could be wrong. You might endure the Vale of Shadows for nothing."

"I have to try."

"You could be sighted by welke riders in the skies near Torindan."

"I'll travel at first by land. I must go, Craelin. This may be a fool's errand, but I can't do nothing. Unless the DawnKing fulfills prophecy, Torindan will fall."

Craelin's eyes lit. "You claim him as DawnKing after all?"

"I claim him."

"You've had a change of heart."

Elcon sheathed Sword Rivenn. "I must have guessed it all along. Who else can he be? But he frightened me, for he read my heart and mind. And so I ignored the truth and banished him out of cowardice. I need to find him and ask forgiveness if it is not too late."

Craelin's face softened. "I'll tell Weilton and Eathnor to ready themselves. When do you depart?"

"I see no reason to delay." Craelin rose and bowed before leaving. Outside the window in the inner garden flitlings chased through early flower bushes where once he'd walked with Aewen.

He swept a glance about his outer chamber with its blue velvet, carven wood, and gilt edgings. He'd abandon such finery for the dim kaba forest, eat waybread, and drink stale water. He'd even given up his feather tick for a bed of forest duff and count it all gain if he could but find Emmerich. His pride and fear had kept him from admitting until now that even the Lof Shraen of Faeraven and son of Rivenn, could not save Elderland, Faeraven or even himself without the DawnKing of prophecy.

22

Grace

Weilton turned in the saddle. "Eathnor suggests we make camp in the meadow ahead, Lof Shraen."

Since venturing into the kaba forest, they'd spent each night in a place clear of tree branches and other perches where a jaggercat might wait to spring. At the thought, Elcon tilted his head and scanned the canopy arching overhead. Nothing lurked there. He forced his attention back to the matter at hand. "As Eathnor wishes. I'll not question the guidance of one who grew up tracking in these woods." If Eathnor wanted to stop for the night although much remained of daylight, he had a sound reason.

"We should reach the Vale of Shadows on the morrow. Let us rest this night as much as we can." Elcon's pulse tripped, but he kept his voice calm.

Weilton stiffened. "Did something move?" He pointed. "Just there!"

Elcon stared into the forest shadows. "I don't see anything."

Weilton shook his head with a faint smile. "This forest unnerves me." Elcon made no argument. It bothered him, too.

They broke free of the trees into lowering mists that splintered the feeble light into shafts. A breeze stirred seeding grasses and ruffled wildflowers. A rill tumbled over rocks—a glimpse of silver soon hidden by forest darkness. The shadow of a nameless peak towering above the canopy already crept into the meadow.

Weilton unsaddled and groomed the wingabeasts, then turned them loose to graze and drink clear water. Eathnor netted for gillyfish, tender-fleshed morsels peculiar to these western streams. Elcon joined Eathnor on the banks of the rill. Trees *shushed* in the background and the rushing water sang its own melody. Small white fish flicked through the clear water but didn't often escape Eathnor's net.

The Vale of Shadows lay in the heart of the kaba forest on the border of Rivenn and Westerland. Elcon had seen it far below, mist-shrouded and mysterious, on his few journeys to Westerland. Tales warned madness would take those who wandered under the boughs of its ancient forest, for it lay under an enchantment. Even so, rumor held that Shraen Brael dwelt within the vale on the banks of Weild Aenor.

They ate fish and greenings with waybread, a warm meal taken with good companions around a campfire. The tension in Elcon's shoulders eased and his eyelids drooped. When a dark shape moved into the meadow, only Eathnor's sudden stillness alerted him to danger.

Eathnor held up a hand in warning, his face tense. The wingabeasts had stopped grazing and held in stillness. A large bruin, its nose quivering, lumbered out of the forest and across the rill. Eathnor snatched his hunting knife from its sheath. Weilton notched an arrow to his bow. The bruin halted short of the fire circle, raised a heavy head, and scented the air.

"Stay down. Back away. Move with care." Eathnor's low voice steadied Elcon. "Perhaps the beast will feed on our scraps and leave."

Elcon shifted toward his sword, which rested against Raeld's saddle. Why hadn't he kept his weapon closer? Weilton crept toward Elcon, his sword drawn. Eathnor retreated also, taking short steps. The bruin bawled at them and swung toward the remains of their meal. The wind shifted, and smoke swirled toward the bruin. The beast halted, and then started toward the wingabeasts.

Eathnor's Roaem shrilled and reared. More wingabeasts screamed. Wings unfurled. Hooves thudded. Bawling, the bruin rose to its full height. Elcon held his breath as the brawny creature swayed, claws distended. At last the bruin dropped and swung to snatch a morsel of fish. Eathnor whistled, and Roaem settled onto four legs. The wingabeasts still pranced with nostrils flared and flexed their wings but did not lift into the air.

The bruin swallowed the last portion of fish and snuffled about in the dirt. Finding no more scraps, it loped across the meadow with coat rippling, to disappear beneath the understory.

Eathnor cut through the grass to the place the bruin had vanished, and Weilton moved in front of Elcon.

Remembering to breathe, Elcon took another step, and his hand closed on Sword Rivenn's hilt. He drew the blade from its sheath and waited in silence. Although he strained to hear, the bruin seemed to have vanished.

Weilton relaxed his posture, and Elcon placed his sword once more in its sheath but kept the weapon at his side.

Eathnor joined them. "Sleep near the fire this night for safety's sake." He moved off toward the wingabeasts.

Elcon took him at his word, making his bed as close to the fire as smoke and heat allowed. After the day's events, he thought he'd not slumber but the flames blurred before his eyes and he wandered into uneasy dreams. At intervals he started awake but eased at the sight of a dim outline waiting and watching at fire's edge with weapon drawn.

He woke to birdsong and a dew-drenched meadow bathed in early light. It seemed impossible that danger could lurk in such a place, at least until high branches shook at the edge of the forest. Elcon's heart thumped. In a flurry of feathers a pair of white birds burst from the trees to weave across the meadow in ungainly flight, their long tail feathers streaming behind.

"Kairocs." Eathnor's voice, close at hand, made Elcon jump. "They nest in tall trees."

"I've heard of such creatures and even watched their flight from Raeld's back, but I've never seen them so close before."

"They're magnificent."

"Mother refused to eat them, saying they were too beautiful to sacrifice."

Eathnor smiled. "Crobok tastes better anyway."

They broke camp and scaled a long ridge as the trees shrank and finally disappeared altogether. Elcon rode single-file between Eathnor and Weilton along a rotting spine of rock that plummeted on either side but gave views across Elderland in all directions. Northward, the kabas yielded to hills rolling through cleared farmland. The White Feather wound through green grass as it flowed toward Maer Ibris. Farther east the ice-clad peaks of Maegrad Ceid pushed upward, and then rank upon rank of hills covered in kabas unfolded toward Torindan. The stronghold of Rivenn lifted out of the forest to stand in relief against its encircling peaks. The bright ribbon that was the south branch of Weild Aenor unfurled through the kaba forest to mark the border of Sloewood and Merboth where grass-covered plateaus thrust above the trees. Due west the forest canopy stretched in patterns of green and smoke gray all the way to the tidelands. The distant luster of stone in the direction of Cobbleford Castle stirred an ache within Elcon.

At the top of the ridge Eathnor waited for Elcon and Weilton to reach him. "Trackers keep the path clear to this point, but we'll not find the way easy from here on." He tilted his head. "Have we traveled far enough from Torindan to avoid being sighted by welke riders? It would be easiest to fly." He shrugged. "There's no way to avoid a chance discovery if we fly, but that's less likely this far from Torindan. It's worth the risk." He dismounted and peered from the edge downward into a sea of mist. "I don't know if we will find Emmerich below, but I have to seek him even into the Vale of Shadows."

Elcon moved away from the edge. He and his companions ate waybread and cheese in haste while the wingabeasts plucked at the scant grass bold enough to seed in such thin soil.

Elcon launched Raeld into a glide above the misty valley, and the wingabeast descended into a broad spiral. The wind of their passing buffeted Elcon, and he turned his face aside to breathe. The mists that clung shredded away as the kaba canopy closed them in. The shaggy bark of looming trees gleamed purple-red against their emerald leaves and the pale fronds of dragon-tongue ferns beneath them. Raeld's hooves touched the humus in a soft landing. Weilton landed Baeltor, and Eathnor brought down Roaem. As they searched around and above them for possible threats none spoke.

At Weilton's nod, Eathnor led them toward a lighter patch of forest to the west. Elcon strained to see in the dimness, although it was near midday. They emerged onto moss-covered rocks that narrowed and deepened the river channel. Wavery light reflecting from the sliding water blinded Elcon in unexpected radiance.

No sign of animal life imprinted itself here. No fish broke the surface. Birds did not flit through the trees. But insects crawled about and swarms of biting flies drove them back from the water's edge.

Eathnor waited for them on Roaem, his eyes shining pale in the forest shadows. "Since Emmerich is said to live along the banks of Weild Aenor, we should fly its length."

"Let us do so, then." Elcon's voice sounded sharp to his own ears. "I mislike lingering in this dreary place." He did not add that a heavy cloud of sorrow hung over him or that he sensed something watching them from the shadows.

Without a word, Weilton dismounted and moved farther into the forest, leaving Baeltor to follow.

"What are you doing?" Eathnor called after him, but Weilton made no answer.

Eathnor slid to the ground and grasped Weilton by the shoulders. "Did you not hear me?"

Confusion came over Weilton's face, and he pushed at Eathnor's hands.

"Answer me." Eathnor gave him a small shake.

Weilton broke away from Eathnor. "What are you doing? There's no need to manhandle me."

"I'm sorry." Eathnor stepped back. "I feared for you."

Weilton's brows drew together. "I—I'm not quite certain why. I thought—I thought—are we not to look for Emmerich?"

Elcon nodded. "Yes, we're to look for Emmerich but along Weild Aenor."

Weilton frowned. "I must have misunderstood." He mounted Baeltor and rejoined them as if nothing unusual had happened. Elcon was in no mood to puzzle out the small mystery, not when they could be close to finding Emmerich. He sat taller in the saddle. "Come, let's search before dark."

They circled upward and leveled just above the water. Despite twice flying the river's length, however, they found nothing.

"Maybe we can see more from higher in the air." Elcon reasoned, but even a vantage point just above the trees brought them no success.

Elcon pushed away his disappointment, but it returned to crush him. The longer they remained in this valley, the heavier he felt. Sorrow rode him until he thought he would die of it. A terrible sense of something important lost crept over him, and his heart pounded as his throat went dry.

They gathered on a flat-topped boulder jutting into the river from a small islet. Darkening waters swirled on either side. Elcon heaved a breath. "It's no use. Emmerich is not here. We'll never find him."

Silence met his pronouncement, and Elcon looked into the faces of his companions. All mirrored his own sorrow and hopelessness. A surge of anger tore through him, and he clung to its vibrancy. He fell to his knees. "*Lof Yuel!*" His bellow echoed through the hills that closed in the valley. He bowed his head and wept.

A ray of sunlight lit him, and he raised his head. He stood, squinting across the channel, barely able to credit his own eyes.

Emmerich walked along the bank, a water bag dangling from his hand. He looked across to Elcon. "You've come.

Wait for me." With his eyes fixed on Emmerich, Elcon gave a whistle. Hooves stepped toward him, and he mounted Raeld. He launched above the river, his wingabeast surging into the air, but Elcon brought him down almost at once onto the shore near Emmerich. As he dismounted his boots crunched pebbles. Emmerich waited with his arms folded, an unreadable expression on his face.

Elcon forced air into his lungs. "I've found you."

"You have." Emmerich's lips twitched. "Or perhaps it's the other way around."

Elcon fell to his knees. "Why look with such kindness on one who rejected you? I've been a fool." Had he accepted Emmerich from the beginning Aewen and many others might even now live. Sorrow clouded his mind. He had come all this way, and he could not ask for forgiveness.

"Elcon, lift your head."

He looked up in mute obedience. Even in the dying light, he saw himself reflected in Emmerich's eyes.

"What troubles you?" Emmerich's voice was soft.

Elcon waited for his throat to ease. "My own guilt."

Emmerich gave him a steady look. "You speak of guilt easily but the idea of mercy comes with more difficulty."

Hope sparked within Elcon. "Tell me of mercy."

"It requires more of you than perhaps you will accept."

"Tell me nevertheless."

Emmerich gave him a measuring look. "As you wish, Elcon, son of Timraen, Shraen of Rivenn and Lof Shraen of Faeraven. Forsake your own worth. Mercy cannot be earned by might, nor can it be won by guile. It must be received in the same way a child takes a crust of bread from a parent's hand." This, then, is the noblest challenge—to accept forgiveness by another's merits and not your own."

The hope within Elcon swelled into flame. "I crave mercy more than food or water."

"I have already forgiven you for banishing me." Emmerich offered a hand to him, but Elcon held back.

"How can you offer forgiveness before I've asked it?"

Emmerich frowned. "My forgiveness does not depend upon you."

Elcon fell silent. He had much to ponder.

Emmerich waved to Weilton and Eathnor, who waited beside their wingabeasts on the river bank. "Come if you're hungry. I have food for the willing."

23

Siege

Craelin stepped out of one of the guard rooms in the gatehouse. "Lof Shraen! It's well you've returned. Freaer will soon attack."

Craelin looked from Elcon to Emmerich, who rode with Eathnor on Roaem. Elcon dismounted and handed Raeld's reins to Guaron, who approached from the direction of the stables. "We must have a little time. We saw nothing on our approach. How come you to know of this? How near are his armies?"

"A messenger sent from Shraen Enric of Graelinn warns that armies set forth again from Weithein Faen. The emissary did not spare himself and his horse in reaching us. The armies will not come at such a pace. We may have two days before they arrive, perhaps three."

Elcon inclined his head. "Where do we stand?"

Craelin's face took on a rugged look. "We are as ready as depleted supplies make us."

Elcon slanted a glance to him. "Come to my chambers in a little while."

"As you wish."

Elcon turned to Emmerich, who had dismounted and now joined him. "I pray I have not brought you back to Torindan too late."

Emmerich shook his head. "We may yet save Torindan—and Elderland—but much depends on you."

Elcon caught his breath. "I don't understand."

Emmerich's eyes glinted. "The fate of many rests on your decisions, son of Timraen."

"Then may I be wiser in the future."

Elcon would have liked to ask more questions, but Emmerich turned to help Guaron gather the wingabeasts. His words followed Elcon into the inner garden, where he paused to drink in the solitude. Weilton stood upon the path, waiting for Elcon to return to his chambers. He would go, but first he needed to reflect. Instinct told him that Emmerich had, in a few words, given him the key to unlock victory. Elcon wandered beneath the stunted strongwood trees, their branches dark and twisting, the leaves, edged with gold in the sunlight, curling into a green tunnel. The pattering of water in the fountain carried to him here, where he had once held Arillia and made a faithless promise to her. He remembered with regret the bruised look in her eyes when she'd faced him across the table after Aewen's coronation. She'd handled herself with better grace than he'd deserved. Of all the things she could have done and said that day, she'd kept silence.

Why he thought of Arillia now he did not know, except that her shadow came to him whenever he wandered this green bower. Perhaps he would never be free of Arillia, for she lived in his memory, touching him with guilt each time he thought of her.

Elcon abandoned the garden, for it ceased to comfort him.

☙❧

Craelin entered the meeting chamber, and Elcon glanced up. "Anders, leave us." His servant obeyed, the door clicking shut behind him.

Craelin slid into his customary place beside Elcon and across from Emmerich and Weilton. "I bring ill news. A messenger from Whellein arrived last night to inform us that Daeramor now allies itself with Freaer's forces against you."

"Not Lammert, too." Elcon put his face in his hands. He saw again in memory a laughing youth, his eyes alight with merriment and mischief as he called down to Elcon from one of Torindan's twin guardhouse turrets. Although Lammert had always been the older, whenever he'd visited his zeal in exploring Torindan had bridged the gap in their ages. Would Lammert now use his knowledge of Torindan to usurp his Lof Shraen and friend?

"I am sorry."

Craelin's voice penetrated Elcon's misery. He drew a shuddering breath but lifted his head. "More ravens stand against us than for us now. And yet, we must save the alliance of Faeraven, if we can. Any news of the reinforcing armies?"

Craelin did not meet Elcon's eyes. "They have at best a three-day journey before they reach Torindan."

Weilton's hiss raised Elcon's hackles. What had Craelin said about Freaer's armies? *We may have two days before they arrive, perhaps three.* If Lof Yuel smiled on Torindan, reinforcements and Freaer's armies would arrive together. Elcon pushed away the fear that deliverance from the forces arrayed against them might come too late. "Let's lay out our defenses quickly. We need to set a battle strategy."

During the discussion that followed, Emmerich contributed nothing, but watched them with an odd light in his dark eyes. A frisson of uneasiness shook Elcon. Just where did the Elder youth's loyalties rest?

∂∽∾

A dark line of bodies formed on the horizon, moving with endless precision out of the canyons of Doreinn Ravein toward Torindan. The sound of marching added percussion to the air. The shaking of the ground reached Elcon even through the thick stone of the battlements above the guardhouse where he stood between Craelin and Emmerich. They'd only had two days to prepare and must yet finish reinforcing the outer wall, but their efforts would have to serve. He turned toward Craelin, no longer wanting to look upon the approaching hordes.

"We'd better launch the catapults."

"Stand and hold." Emmerich spoke in so quiet a voice that Elcon did not at first register his words. He gaped at Emmerich. "*What* say you?"

Emmerich's eyes held his. "Do not rush to battle. Wait."

Elcon curled his hands into fists. Everything in him shouted that he should ignore Emmerich's advice. He had to make the right choice. He must not fail again. Craelin's face reflected Elcon's own conflicting emotions. Had he made a mistake in putting his trust in Emmerich? What if Emmerich was not Shraen Brael after all? Elcon would lose everything, including his life. He would be remembered as the Lof Shraen who by folly caused Faeraven and Elderland to fall. His name would become a curse.

Elcon forsook the battlements and sought the inner garden but found little solace among the roses and early flowers. He paced; his mind in a fever of indecision. Should he listen to Emmerich or seek his own counsel? The burden of decision was too great, and he collapsed on the edge of the pool. Wind caught the spray from the fountain, sending droplets to anoint his face. Above the pool, the bronze figure of Talan, gleaming with subdued luster, rode a wild wingabeast. A melody strayed into his mind, bringing with it the words of an ancient ballad, "Talan's Wild Wingabeast Ride."

High in the sky of Daeramor Raven,
High in the sky over mountains fair
The wild wingabeasts pass at twilight.
Echoes of their wingbeats fill the air.

Deep in the heart of the Maegrad Paesad,
Deep in the heart of the ancient lair,
Talan of Kunrat lies in waiting—
Waiting for a wingabeast to snare.

Then comes a thudding hoofbeat sounding,
Then comes a flutter of flittering wing,
Down flies a wingabeast seeking shelter,
Hidden there, Talan waits to spring.

Out cries the beast as Talan takes hold,
Out cries the beast that, frothing and bold,
Drags its ropes and leaps to the air,
Climbing toward the heavens dark and cold.

Up climbs the wingabeast into the sky,
Up climbs the wingabeast and dives and rolls,
Twisting in flight to lose its rider but
Nothing could make Talan break his hold.

High in the sky of Daeramor Raven,
High in the sky over mountains fair,
Talan of Kunrat rides the wild wingabeast,
Taming it with bravery most rare.

The bronze figure of Talan leaped into focus. Struck by a sudden revelation, Elcon stood. How could he, a son of the same Talan who had tamed the first wild wingabeast, let fear rule him? And yet he had. He'd driven Shraen Brael away, sent Aewen on a journey that led to her death, and had almost rejected the very salvation he'd desired—all out of fear. Whether it meant victory or defeat, he would not let fear rule him, not *this* time. He turned away from the fountain and toward the gatehouse.

ह∞6

Craelin stared at Elcon with disbelief written on his face.

"Hold." Elcon repeated, lifting his voice to be heard above the din made by marching warriors as they stormed toward Torindan's guardhouse.

Craelin opened his mouth as if to protest but closed it again. He looked down upon the advancing armies. "This is madness. They will be upon us soon. Will we *give* them Torindan?"

"We will stand and hold." Elcon kept his voice without inflection.

Craelin looked to Emmerich, between them on the battlements, and then back at Elcon. "As you say, Lof Shraen."

Emmerich's lips twitched into a smile. Elcon descended the stair to find Weilton and Eathnor, the two he'd chosen to fight beside him, on their way up. He would fight as long as he could and would only seek escape through the hidden passageways if Torindan fell. If left to himself, he would choose the honor of a death in battle, but he must consider Faeraven. If he escaped to rally again, perhaps all would not be lost.

He put uneasy thoughts of defeat from him. He should not let their whisper stir him to fear and intrude on his judgment. He would look to the needs of his people this day and give way to the voice of a higher Shraen.

The march of the soldiers grew deafening. Elcon returned to the battlements above the guardhouse. Craelin bent an urgent look upon him. "What say you now?"

Elcon fought panic. "Well, then?" His voice was a plea.

"Stand and hold." Emmerich spoke in a firm voice.

Fear seized Elcon by the throat. His new resolve melted like snow in his mouth. He put out his arm in a blind motion and felt fingers close over his wrist.

Emmerich leaned close, his breath touching Elcon's ear. "Courage." He spoke but the one word, but it recalled Elcon from the edge of hysteria.

He pulled upright and answered Craelin's shocked countenance. "Hold." Although he uttered only the one word, that word cost him greatly.

Craelin lifted his head and flared his nostrils, but

he repeated Elcon's command to Weilton, waiting nearby. The first of the foot soldiers reached the outer wall and threw grappling hooks as archers rained a volley of arrows upward to protect their climb. Craelin's face reddened, and following the direction of his stare, Elcon paused, much struck. Standing a little apart, Emmerich raised his arms as if in supplication. His eyes were closed, and his face shone with peace. Elcon stepped toward him but halted, afraid to draw near such radiance.

Darkness fell, so complete not even the moon or stars alleviated it, and in this darkness, Shraen Brael shone in a gathering light. Elcon went to his knees. Outside the walls the cacophony of battle lifted in unholy counterpart, and the smell of death gagged Elcon.

When the sounds came no more, Shraen Brael lowered his arms, the light from him retreating until he became once again the Elder youth, Emmerich, standing in the fitful illumination of the torches of the guardians.

"Lof Shraen!" Shouting above the startled exclamations of the defenders of Torindan, Craelin pulled Elcon to his feet. "We cannot tell all that has happened, but it seems the darkness confused our enemies and after turning their swords upon one another they have fled."

Elcon cast about for words to say to Emmerich but found none.

Emmerich smiled. "You begin to understand grace, I see."

Elcon's smile wavered. "Thank you. I don't understand what happened, but I know you saved us this day."

The torchlight shifted and made of Emmerich's eyes dark pools. "Salvation came from Lof Yuel, son of Talan."

Elcon stood for a time, watching as the stars winked on in the sky, one by one. At last the moon, covered in haze, shone forth with pale light. Tears that blurred his vision made the stars run together.

"Come away, then." Emmerich had gone but now returned to his side as Craelin and most of the others moved toward the stairs. Elcon drew a shuddering breath as the tension eased from him. The battle had been won. He let Emmerich guide him away from the parapet.

24

Decision

Before Elcon could turn aside, Arillia, walking with her maid beneath the budding strongwoods, saw him. He almost did not credit her as more than a memory at first, for she came to him thus in this garden at times, lingering beneath these very strongwoods. But this Arillia looked older, more care worn, and the bounce had left her step.

"Hello, Elcon." Her voice brushed against him, soothing as ever, but her upper lip quivered. He inclined his head to her, and she and her maid bowed. He fell into step, walking beside her past the place where he'd touched his lips to hers and promised to court her. Did she think of it, too? "You have come for the festivities." He stated the obvious in an attempt to drive unwelcome memories from his mind.

"I've come from Chaeradon with my parents." She dimpled, so lovely that he caught his breath. Her skin glistened with health, golden hair cascaded to her waist, and eyes of calm gray regarded him with a hint of sorrow he knew a longing to soothe. Elcon chided himself for his reaction, for only the spring before he'd held Aewen in his arms before she went from him to her death. He could not let himself forget Aewen, and yet he found an odd comfort in the fact that Arillia accompanied her parents rather than a husband.

They spoke of the greening, of course, when the maidens of Torindan decked themselves in Early flowers, and thoughts of courtship filled young hearts. He wished he could ask if Arillia had suitors, for surely she must. He did not know why such a thing should interest him except that Arillia had been a part of his life for so long he'd grown accustomed to thinking of her. In the past, he might have teased her without mercy until he gained her secrets, but now he held his tongue. The constraint between them had not existed before. He had placed it there. He must remember he had abandoned his place in her life, and nothing could ever change that.

He nodded to Arillia and murmured a farewell. But the image of her eyes, overshadowed with sorrow, stayed with him all that day. At night, as he lay abed waiting for sleep, he let his thoughts, for a few wild heartbeats, linger on the memory of Arillia in his arms.

When he slept, he dreamed of Aewen, standing inside the gatehouse of Cobbleford and watching him out of enormous blue eyes, her babe in her arms. He tried to reach her, but the portcullis fell between them. He called to her to wait, but she turned away as the wooden doors thudded to shut her from him.

Elcon woke in a sweat, for the dream had seemed so real. *Find our child.* The words sighed through the chambers of his mind. He wept then for Aewen and for their lost daughter. Anders tapped at the door, peered in at him, and then stepped into the inner chamber. "Are you well?"

Brushing his tears aside, Elcon sat up. He heaved a breath. "Sometimes I dream."

A look of sympathy dawned on Anders' face.

"Your dreams serve you ill."

"They bring Aewen back but take her from me again."

He shuddered. Aewen stood watching him, babe in arms, at least in memory.

"Well then, are you ready to rise?" Anders brisk voice drew him back.

Elcon let go of the dream image and pushed confusion from his mind. "I am ready." He spoke with hesitancy, for these days only an effort of will forced him from his bed to don the robes of Lof Shraen.

It had been three months since Shraen Brael had saved Torindan, sending darkness to confuse the invading armies. The four remaining loyal shraens had arrived in time to discourage the survivors of the rout from regrouping and attacking Torindan again. But Elcon took no joy in the fact that many of the Kindren opposing him had died, slain by their fellows. Blood stained his own hands, for he had given no thought to any but his own desires. His choices had driven a wedge between the Kindren that made them easy prey for one such as Freaer.

Torindan enjoyed a time of peace now, but it would not last forever. Freaer had returned to Pilaer, where he would bide his time and gather strength for another assault. That he would come again, Elcon had no doubt. Sometimes he felt Freaer's soul touch searching to find and cripple him. He knew the hatred Freaer bore him, more so now, since he'd tasted defeat at Elcon's hands.

Anders helped him into the blue and gold ceremonial garb he would wear throughout the feast day. To break his fast, Elcon took a little bread and cheese, washing them down with spiced cider. The tall windows in his outer chamber showed across the bailey to the inner garden. Already, despite the rising mists of morning, a couple flirted on the pathway. In the past, Elcon might have called out encouragement or even joined in friendly competition for a winsome maid, but not today. That part of his life had died forever with Aewen. In truth, he could not remember ever being as light of heart as the two engaged in banter outside his window.

The ceremonies progressed, and Elcon did his part. He attended the twilight wedding which joined all those who decided on this day to marry. Afterwards, he danced with each bride at the reception in the great hall, never betraying by the flicker of an eyelid that he longed to escape such duties. Relinquishing the last bride back to her new husband and stepping away, he looked up to meet Arillia's gaze. The contact caused a jolt to go through him, almost as if she touched him. As he made his way to her side, he chided himself for such fancies. He could not ignore her now she knew he'd seen her. Or perhaps she would prefer he do so. He had no way of knowing and would not take the chance of hurting her further. Standing beside her maid Arillia looked a little forlorn, although her beauty could not be faulted. She wore an overdress of embroidered batiste, kilted at one side to show the fine linen of her underskirt. Her hair fell to her waist, with flowers woven into the golden curls with such skill as to look artless.

"Will you dance?" To save them from conversation he gave the invitation at once.

Arillia started a little, and he realized he'd spoken over loud. He warned himself to calm as she recovered herself and moved to stand opposite him in the line of dancers. As the music began, they drew near with heads toward one another for several heartbeats. They broke apart and he circled her, and then caught her by the waist as they walked together facing outward. And so it went, on and on. As they drew close once more, Elcon berated himself for suggesting they dance. He tried not to let Arillia's eyes snare him, but he could not deny the warmth that ran through him. It would be unnatural for him to feel nothing when gazing at a beautiful maiden in his arms, but he could not help the guilt that flooded him. It seemed disloyal to Aewen and their dead child for him to enjoy such a thing.

When the music ended, he stepped away from Arillia and inclined his head in thanks, grateful to escape. But she touched his arm and looked up at him in appeal. "Will you walk with me in the garden?"

He could not bring himself to refuse her, and so, against his better judgment and with Weilton and her maid trailing behind, Elcon passed through scented shadow beneath strongwood trees to emerge into moonlight at the garden's heart beside Arillia. They strolled toward the fountain, awash in silver and sparkling as it cascaded into the dark pool to spread ripples of light across the silken surface.

As she faced him, Arillia's beauty made him catch his breath. "Elcon, I did not speak this earlier, although I should have. My heart breaks for the sorrow that lies upon your brow." Tears shone in her eyes. "If I could, I would bring Aewen back to you."

Elcon put a hand out to still those she twisted before her. "Peace, now. Your sorrow brings me no comfort, Arillia." He brushed the tears from her cheek. A longing to enfold her in his arms to soothe her and find a comfort of his own gripped him. He released her and turned back toward the fountain. "We've never spoken of it, but I did you a great wrong in marrying Aewen, Arillia. You've no reason to wish for my peace."

Her quiet weeping swept over him. "I cannot help myself, Elcon."

"You should hate me."

"And yet I do not." She gave a weak smile and dried her eyes, her gaze going past him to the fountain. "I was furious at first. Perhaps if we had not been expected to marry from our early days, I might have borne the shame better."

Elcon considered her words. He'd not realized before just how completely he had shamed her, but he understood it now. "I'm sorry."

Her eyelids quivered as fresh tears made a shining path down her face. He did not touch her this time to stop them. Her eyes opened, and she blinked. "Can we not leave this in the past, Elcon? I forgave you long ago and only wish to forget what I suffered."

"I did not mean to make you cry, Arillia. You should laugh instead with an admirer."

Her attempt to smile faltered. "I want no such admirer."

He arched a brow at the vehemence with which she spoke and angled his position to stand before her again. "What's this nonsense?"

She frowned her annoyance.

He smiled as time slipped backward to bring them together as they had once been. "I mean what I say, Elcon. I want none to speak pretty words to lure me."

"I fear you may soon stamp your feet. My words irritate you, but at least they have stopped your tears."

This time her smile succeeded. As they wandered

the garden, Elcon took care to keep it upon her face. They returned to the great hall where warmth and light and life reached out to them. The music was lively but the frenzied gaiety of courtship jarred Elcon's inner disquiet. He needed to escape to a place of solitude where he could regain his composure.

When Gaerlic of Daeramor danced with Arillia, Elcon edged toward the central archway but halted in unease. The way Gaerlic looked at Arillia disturbed him. The time neared for Arillia to marry, she even lingered overlong on its cusp. He knew this, but he did not somehow favor her marrying anyone, and certainly not Gaerlic. He squared his shoulders, as she moved through the dance with slender grace. Gaerlic's possessive hand at her waist and the way he watched her face galled Elcon, although he didn't try to understand why he should feel Arillia belonged to *him* when he planned never again to marry. More than a little disturbed, he strode from the room without grace.

❧❦

Shadows advanced and retreated before the lanthorn Weilton lifted as Elcon entered the allerstaed. Each footstep echoed, awakening for Elcon echoes from the past. Shae knelt beside him in prayer. Kai bowed at his feet and pledged fealty. Aewen stood with him once more, taking him as her husband and protector.

On an impulse, Elcon spread his arms and spun in a circle, tilting his head to gaze into the shadows cloaking the ceiling. *Here I am, Lof Yuel. Take me in death, that I might forget the lives I've destroyed.* He lost his balance and slammed against hard stone.

Weilton rushed to him. "Are you well?"

Elcon pulled air into his lungs. "I seem to be."

A figure moved out of the shadows behind the altar, and Weilton went still, ready to spring, but then he relaxed again.

Emmerich stepped down from the dais. Moonlight from the high windows painted rectangles across the strongwood floor, marking his progress toward them. "You've come at last." He grasped Elcon by the arm and pulled him to his feet.

"Have you been waiting for me?" Elcon asked the question although he already knew the answer.

Emmerich touched his shoulder. "Death does not bring forgetfulness, Elcon."

Elcon swallowed and sought his voice. "Then there is no hope of peace."

"You cannot hope to receive in death what you deny yourself in life."

Elcon frowned. "You speak of grace."

"I do, and of the absolution it gives."

Absolution. The word resounded within Elcon. Emmerich started back toward the dais, and he fell into step beside him. "Tell me more."

"Absolution comes from outside your own worth but not outside your own will."

Elcon considered this. "Since absolution requires another's forgiveness it cannot come from my own worth. But how does it rise from my will?"

"You choose to accept or reject forgiveness. If another forgives you but you cling to guilt, you deny your own absolution and condemn yourself anew."

They reached the prayer altar before the dais and Elcon knelt. "But many of those from which I would seek forgiveness lie dead."

"Lof Yuel offers you forgiveness. You have only to accept it."

A sob caught in his throat, and Elcon bowed his head. "If I thought I could be free of guilt —"

Emmerich knelt beside Elcon as his shoulders shook with sobs and tears washed his eyes. "Make your peace with Lof Yuel, Elcon, and also forgive yourself. Only then can you be free."

⤙⤚

Arillia's laugh carried down the table to Elcon. He paused, mid-sentence, forgetting what he said to Shraen Enric, who waited in expectation. Torchlight bathed Arillia's skin in a rosy light. A spark of amusement lit her eyes as she spoke to Gaerlic of Daeramor, across from her, and his laughter rang out in turn. Elcon sighed. He would have little success in ignoring Arillia with the corner of his eye catching her every movement.

Across the table Enric leaned forward. "You were saying, Lof Shraen?"

Elcon cast back, but could not discover the lost thread of conversation. "I've forgotten." Arillia laughed again, and before he could prevent himself, he turned his head her direction. With an effort he pulled his attention from her.

Enric glanced toward Arillia then gave a smug smile. "More pressing matters claim your thoughts. A rose of Chaeradon may appeal far more than the roses of Torindan."

Elcon could think of no response. If he didn't want rumor to fly, he'd better be careful. Perhaps he should excuse himself. In truth, he longed for this tedious meal to finish so he could abandon his guests to the entertainments Tarrat, his new steward, had arranged. Jugglers, bards, and acrobats waited to regale them. He would not remain in the great hall longer than need be, for spending time near Arillia in the company of her suitors always made him restless. He rejected the idea that he might himself join their ranks. Even if he had not injured Arillia in a way that removed him forever from her consideration, how could he relinquish Aewen in such a way?

He started, for he'd failed to respond to another of Enric's questions, and had forsaken their conversation. Arillia looked his way, and his gaze meshed with hers for several heartbeats before he could bring himself to look away. He stammered an apology to Enric and met a forgiving smile.

"Never mind. Your thoughts are where they should be in this season of new beginnings."

Elcon gave a small smile. "I thank you for your grace, Enric. New beginnings can only come where there are endings."

"That is so, Elcon, but even warm memories bring cold comfort in the dead of winter."

A juggler on stilts drew their attention then, sparing Elcon the need to reply. He slipped away, leaving his guests to their own devices. As he arose, the weight of Arillia's gaze followed him from the chamber. That she read his intent he had no doubt. She had always known him too well.

Weilton stood as if to follow him as well, but Elcon waved for him to remain. He wearied of guardians dogging his steps and refused to live in fear within the walls of Torindan. Besides, he carried a dagger on his belt.

He had meant to return to the quiet of his chambers but the splash of falling water carried him to the moonlit pool at the center of the garden.

A flutter of wings startled him, and a great bird lifted from the pool's edge, its wings pale and gleaming. A passing kairoc, come to drink.

The ceremonial garb he wore was warm enough, but he shivered a little in the night wind, freshened by a lingering hint of winter. Trees tossed silvered heads and the pool's surface rippled. He should not remain here long, not when comfort waited at his fireside.

The wild music of the night struck a responding melody within him. As he had done in the allerstaed, Elcon spread his arms and turned in a circle, his head back. He lowered his arms and breathed deeply of the chill air, which bore the scent of Early flowers. Clouds scuttled across the face of the moon and sent shadows racing over him. Talan and his wingabeast jumped in the changing light, as if they contended still.

He should encourage Arillia to wed. That pompous Gaerlic would offer for her, Elcon did not doubt. Arillia was everything Gaerlic could want in a raelein when he became shraen of Daeramor. She possessed every virtue expected of a maid. Her skill with a needle recommended her, as did the voice she lifted in song and her quiet manner. Arillia's deportment held no lack, for she had long been trained into obedience by her mother, as befitted a daughter of Chaeradon's lineage.

Elcon crossed his arms to warm himself. He did not really want Arillia to wed Gaerlic, but that was from selfishness. Yesterday in this garden with her he'd felt again a thread of attachment stretch between them. He'd felt it, and despite himself rejoiced in its strength. And now Arillia occupied his thoughts. Her face even pushed aside Aewen's in his mind. As the realization struck, pain tore through him and he turned away from the fountain, leaving Talan to tame his wingabeast alone. He would not forget Aewen, nor would he betray the memory of the child they had lost.

Arillia walked toward the garden from the great hall, her maid trailing behind her. She looked beautiful, almost other-worldly in this light. Part of her hair wound about her head in a plait woven with jewels that winked like the stars above her. The remainder of her tresses flowed unbound in the wind.

To observe protocol, he should murmur a greeting and offer her his arm, but indecision held him fast.

She ran to him on light feet, fetching against him with a gasping laugh.

"It's windy out here!"

He put up a hand and patted hers, resting on his arm. "You should seek shelter. Did you tire of the entertainment?"

She smiled at him, and a dimple curved into her cheek. "Once you left it lost its appeal."

Elcon pulled away from her a little. "I could not linger among a crowd this night. I—I sometimes need solitude."

"I know you grieve."

Her words cut through him. He eased his hands out of fists. "I know you mean well, Arillia, but you cannot drive the pain from me. I will always grieve for Aewen."

Her eyes widened. "I—I'm sorry. I should not have followed you here."

The sorrow in her voice tore at him, and his arms ached to comfort her. He didn't trust himself to respond. In time, the silence told him she'd gone. He turned to call after her. "Wait."

Arillia had already reached her maid, waiting on the path to the great hall. She paused and glanced back to him.

"Come back." His voice croaked as if seldom used. He swallowed against a dry throat. "Please."

She walked back to him, but he could see by the shuttered look on her face, she had withdrawn. That was well, despite the grief it caused him. "Will you forgive me? I should not have been rude to you. It's just that you caught me ill prepared for politeness."

She blinked away tears. "Elcon, really it's all right. I intruded upon the solitude you so love. I—I forgot that we are—we are not as we were once. I am no longer part of the peace you seek."

He wanted to kiss the sorrow from her face. He drew a breath. "You should wed."

She looked down at her clasped her hands. "I shall never wed."

Anger flared white-hot within him. "Have you taken leave of your senses? Of course you shall wed. What of Gaerlic?" He tried to stop himself from saying more. "Don't tell me he doesn't desire you."

Her head came up. "What has my friendship with Gaerlic to do with you?"

"I think he might name your association with him as something other than friendship." He despised the note of jealousy in his voice. "I'm certain he will ask for you."

She flung out an arm. "Since you make my business your own, please know that he has already done so. But I'll not take him, or any other."

He scowled. "What nonsense is this?"

He'd never seen such a passionate look as the one now on her face. "I'll not wed because the man I want loves another and won't have me."

He blinked. Before he could gather himself to respond, she ran from him. The tapping of her feet dwindled, and only windswept solitude remained.

25

Alliance

The gate screeched open and the yawning darkness of the tomb opened before Elcon as musty odors of earth and death wafted to him.

Weilton touched his arm. "Are you certain?"

Elcon felt certain of nothing, except that he would find peace in the tomb of his fathers where Aewen and her child rested. The thought of them trapped here while he enjoyed the comforts of life rent his heart.

Behind Weilton the beauty of a spring morning stood in contrast to the place of death within. Elcon heaved a sigh. "I must go on."

Weilton lifted the lanthorn he held to light the entrance of the tomb. "You need not go alone."

"I must."

Without a word, Weilton passed the lanthorn to him. As the lanthorn swung beneath Elcon's hand, shadows jumped within the tomb. He had to bend his head to enter, but once inside, there was room to stand. Dust stirred underfoot to float upward in motes the frail light caught. A sneeze took Elcon unaware, the sound muffling at once in dead air. The hair on the back of his neck rose, and he could not stop himself from staring into the darkness beyond the circle of light. He lifted the lanthorn high to still his qualms as much as to light his way. The floor was uneven here, its stones shifted by time. Burial chambers fanned on either side in a circular pattern, with the entrance hall behind him. Some of the rooms waited in emptiness. Boulders blocked the doors of crypts, the one containing the remains of his parents among them. He touched a hand to the stone blocking the entrance to Aewen's tomb, where he would one day reside. He did not own the strength or the desire to move the stone.

Elcon leaned his forehead against the stone. "Aewen, forgive me for placing you here." His voice fell without resonance.

A touch he recognized brushed his soul, and peace enveloped him. Somehow Shae reached through time and space to him. Her gentleness strengthened him, and then faded. He was alone again—a half-crazed shraen visiting his own tomb. The cold and damp of rough stone against his hands made him shiver, and he rubbed his palms together. Tears blurred his vision, and he stumbled out of the tomb to gasp draughts of fresh air as sunlight warmed his face.

"Lof Shraen, are you well?"

Elcon opened his mouth to reply to Weilton but then shut it again.

"Have you found what you sought?"

Weilton swung around. "Emmerich! You startled me."

As Emmerich stepped from behind Weilton, Elcon shook his head in response to his question. "Perhaps I never will."

"The dead cannot absolve the living."

"Must you always speak to me of grace?"

Emmerich smiled. "I will speak of it until you understand."

Elcon squinted with the effort of memory. "Let's see... Grace cannot be earned by might, nor can it be won by guile. It must be received in the same way a child takes a crust of bread from a parent's hand."

"You remember my words at least, but you have yet to learn their meaning."

Elcon frowned. "How can you know that?"

"If you understood, you would not seek within a tomb that which you cannot capture or earn."

"Both my wife and child lie dead because of me. I carry a weight of guilt that leaves me no peace."

"You are not responsible for everything that has gone wrong in your life and with your people, but neither are you blameless. The greatest and most noble challenge you face is accepting grace by another's merits and not your own. In that you will find peace."

Elcon shifted, and the sun's rays pierced his eyes, so that he raised a hand to shield them. "If Aewen in death cannot grant me absolution, where can I find it?"

"Lof Yuel's grace sprang fully formed from your sorrow. You have only to accept it and to forgive yourself. For if Lof Yuel forgives you, how can you hold yourself guilty?"

Elcon turned away.

"Consider my words with care, and remember the decision you make affects others."

"What do you mean?"

"Arillia waits to learn if you will allow yourself to live again. She loves you."

Elcon did not ask how Emmerich knew such a thing. He had learned not to question, even when Emmerich asked Elcon to do what seemed too difficult. "I am not certain I can do what you ask this time."

Weilton caught up to Elcon on the path. "Lof

Shraen..."

With a roar, Elcon pushed Weilton away. "Leave...me...alone."

Hurt reflected in Weilton's eyes. "As you say."

Elcon went on alone to the gatehouse, where he climbed the steps to the battlements. He put his hands against the rough stone parapet and squinted into the distance. The landscape beyond the castle and its motte today were bathed in sunlight, but in his mind he still saw fields littered with bodies, sons of Rivenn flung into a mass grave, and pools of blood not yet drunk by thirsty ground.

His selfishness had contributed to the death of many, and he would never forget that. Still, if he did not let go of the grief he'd caused and accept the grace from Lof Yuel that Emmerich described, he would never be able to bring joy and healing to his kingdom.

❧

Arillia walked with her maid beneath twisted strongwoods, their leaves just breaking from pale green buds.

"Arillia," Elcon's low tones must have carried, for she turned back to him. The truth Emmerich had revealed shone from her face. Elcon crossed the distance between them and took her small hands in his. "I've been a fool." She opened her mouth as if to protest, but he squeezed her hands. "Let me have my say, for I find this most difficult."

The corners of Arillia's mouth curved upward in the beginning of a smile but her face held a wary expression. "Speak then, Elcon, and I will listen."

"I regret that I've made you suffer, Arillia. I let

fear blind me to what I should have seen—that you love me still."

Her chin quivered as her eyes shone with tears. "I think you should get to your point, Elcon, if you have one."

"Wait. Arillia, I—I love you, too. Even after all that's happened, will you marry me?"

She laughed even as her tears fell. "I do love you, Elcon, and I want no one else. I'll marry you."

Elcon held her. As Early flowers unfurled and flitlings chattered, they forged an alliance founded on tears and grace.

Author's Note

Consequences follow when we reject God, but He delivers us when we repent and turn to Him. Elcon represents those who fear change and resist following Jesus, despite witnesses to the truth and the pricks of conscience. Elcon loses everything he builds in his own strength, but when he seeks and humbles himself before the DawnKing, he finds deliverance. Aewen stands in allegory as his own plans and desires, which, although appealing, require the compromise of his integrity. Aewen's death represents the natural outcome of our own pursuits outside God's will, with its fruit (her child) falling into the hands of another. It follows, then, that Elcon's marriage to Arillia, symbolizing God's plan for him, can only come after Aewen's death and Elcon's repentance. Elcon says goodbye to Aewen at her tomb in a poignant portrayal of relinquishment. Afterwards, he is able to accept the grace Emmerich offers him. In choosing to live in forgiveness, Elcon frees himself to marry Arillia and embrace life.

Abbey of Westernost—A secluded convent in Westerland

Aeleanor (A-LEE-a-nor)—Queen of Whellein

Aelfred (ALE-fred)—King of Merboth

Aelgarod (ALE-gah-rod)—Healer of Whellein Hold

Aergenwoad (AYR-gen-wode)—Healing herb

Aewen—A princess of the Elder kingdom of Westerland

Allerstaed (ALL-er-stayd)—Place of Prayer

Alliance of Faeraven (FAYR-ay-ven)—High kingdom made up of low kingdoms united under one banner

Anden Raven (AN-den RAY-ven)—Other land from which the Kindren originally entered Elderland

Anders (AN-ders)—Elcon's manservant

Amberoft—Euryon's grandfather, a former king of Westerland

Anemone (Ah-ne-moh-nee)—Low-growing flower with daisy-like petals

Annora—Raelein (queen) of Chaeradon, a Kindren land, and mother of Arillia

Anusian—a high-stepping breed of horse with a flowing mane and tail owned by nobility

Argalent (AR-ja-lent)—Aerlic's silver wingabeast; Kindren for "luster"

Arillia—Raena (princess) of Chaeradon, a Kindren land, who grew up believing she would marry Elcon.

Attarnine (ATT-er-nine)—Rodent poison

Bard—

Baeltor—Weilton's wingabeast

Benisch (BEN-ish)—Steward of Rivenn

Bovine—A ruminant mammal similar to an ox

Braegmet Doreinn (BRAYG-met DOR-ee-in)—Chasm of Confusion

Brael Shadd (BRAYL-shad)—DayStar of Prophecy

Brambleberry—Edible berries that grow in a thorny thicket

Brianda—A kitchen maid within Cobbleford Castle and Maered's mother

Brother Robb—Head priest of Cobbleford Castle who enjoys gardening

Bruin—A bear

Brynn (BRIN)—Heddwyn's red-haired sister

Bursel (BUR-sel)—Dry measurement

Caedmon—Son of Willowa and the huntsman, Camryn, living in Westerland

Caedric (KAY-drik)—Healer within Graelinn Hold

Caerla—A princess of the Elder kingdom of Cobbleford and Aewen's younger sister

Caerric Baest (KAYR-ric BAYST)—Cavern of Wonder

Caerric Daeft (KAYR-ric DAYFT)—Cavern of Death

Catapult—Also known as a stave or staff sling, a length of wood with a sling attached that used lever action to hurl stones and other projectiles in medieval warfare.

Chaeldra (CHALE-dra)—Shae's maid at Torindan

Chrin (KRIN)—Liquid measurement

Circlet of Elder—Crown designating rulership of Rivenn

Clerestory windows—High windows that let in light while preserving privacy and/or security

Chaeradon—Kindren land northeast of Rivenn

Charger—Generic term used to describe a variety of medieval warhorses.

Coast of Bones—Elderland's northeastern coastline

Cobbleford—Rocky location where Cobbleford Castle is built, once a river ford.

Cobbleford Castle—Seat of Westerland and home of Aewen

Cobble River—River that flows past Cobbleford Castle in Westerland

Connor—A prince of the Elder kingdom of Westerland and Aewen's older brother

Coronet of Rivenn—Ceremonial crown worn by the Raelein (Queen) of Rivenn

Counterpane—A quilted coverlet for a bed

Contender—Ancient enemy determined to destroy the Kindren and all Elderland

Craelin (CRAY-lin)—First Guardian of Rivenn

Crobok (CROW- bahk)—Small blue bird

Daelic (DAY-lic)—Healer within Torindan Hold

Daeramor—A northeastern Kindren land

Daevin (DAY-vin)—Prince of Whellein, brother of Kai

Dagger weed—Wild plant with a barbed seedhead growing in open fields in the western part of Elderland

Darbin—One of the gatehouse guards within Cobbleford Castle

Darksea—Coastal Elder kingdom

DawnSinger's Lament—Ancient prophetic song

Demeric—A guardian of Rivenn and wingabeast rider from a noble house within Chaeradon

Destrier—Prized warhorse, usually a powerful stallion raised specifically for war

Destrill—Wingabeast whose name describes the sound of thunder, ridden by Dorann

Devlon—King of Darksea and father of Raefe

Dithmar (DITH-mar)—A guardian of Rivenn

Doctor Jorris—Physician who lives north of Norwood's White Feather Inn

Donia—Caerla's maid

Dorann (DOR-ran)—Tracker for Torindan

Doreinn Ravein (DOR-ree-in RAH-veen)—Canyonlands southeast of Torindan

Draetenn (DRAY-ten)—Tree with spreading branches and fragrant bark

Dragon-tongue fern—Knee-high pale-leaved fern that grow in moist, shady places and are especially common in kaba forests

Dyloc Syldra—Great Eastern Desert

Early flower—A low bush bearing small white flowers in early spring

Eathnor (EETH-nor)—Tracker for Torindan

Ebain (ee-BAIN)—Plain

Eberhardt (EB-er-hart)—Whellein's king

Eberrac—Black bird found in woodlands throughout Elderland

Ederbaer (ED-er-bayr)—Red berry bushes that grow at the edges of meadows and in barren places

Elcon (EL-kon)—High prince of Faeraven; son of Timraen and Maeven

Elder (ELL-der)—Race of humans with darker hair and more rounded eyes; original inhabitants of Elderland

Eldritch (ELL-drich)—Eerie and malevolently strange

Ellendia—A huntress from the Elder land of Sloewood, who married a Kindren from Rivenn and bore half-cast children

Emmerich (EM-mer-ik)—Elder youth

Enric (EN-rik)—Graelin's king and Katera's husband

Erdrich Ceid (ER-drik SEE-id)—Mythical Ice Witch

Erinae (EAR-rin-ay)—Mother of Dorann and Eathnor

Eufemia (YOU-fee-me-uh)—Maeven's serving maid

Euryan (YOU-ry-an)—King of Westerland; an Elder kingdom

Ewaeri (ee-WAHR-ee)—Priests who distribute alms

Feiann (FY-an)—Elusive small folk

Fenning—An Elder kingdom north of Westerland

Ferran—Shraen (king) of Chaeradon, a Kindren land, and father of Arillia

Flaemling (FLAYM-ling)—Tiny bird often kept as pet

Flecht (FLECSHT)—Kai's white wingabeast; Kindren word for "arrow"

Flitling—Small colorful bird found in the western lands, and also Murial's pet name for Aewen

Frael (FRAYL)—Prince

Freaer (FREE-ear)—First Musician of Torindan

Gaerlic—Arillia's admirer and heir to the throne of Daeramor

Garn (GAHRN)—Goblin-like giants

Garreth Shraen of Tallyrand, a Kindren land

Garrison—The troops that defend a castle

Gentian (GEN-ti-an)—Trumpet-shaped flower

Gilead Riann (GILL-ee-ad REE-an)—Gate of Life

Gillyfish—Small white fish found only in western streams and sought after as a delicacy

Gladreinn (GLAD-re-in)—Bride of Rivenn; one of the first Kindren to enter Elderland at the Gate of Life

Glindenn—Southern Kindred land

Glynnda—A dressmaker within Cobbleford Castle

Graelinn—Eastern Kindren land

Graylet (GRAY-let)—Medium-sized bird of prey with speckled gray feathers

Graystone—Sedimentary stone mined in the north of Elderland and used to construct buildings and to pave pathways and floors

Gnarlwood—Giant tree with high branches

Guardians of Rivenn—Highly-trained knights

Guaron (GWAR-ron)—A guardian of Rivenn and keeper of the wingabeasts

Hael—Stableboy at the White Feather Inn in Norwood

Haldrom—A pretender to the throne of Westerland who challenged Amberoft's kingship in the revolt of Lancert

Heddwyn (HEAD-win)—Mistress of White Feather Inn

Herald—An officer who announced news and arranged tournaments and other important events

House of Rivenn—Ruling family of Rivenn; also rule the alliance of Faeraven

Ice Witch—Mythical being inhabiting the Maegrad Ceid (Crystal Mountains) who possesses the power to freeze living creatures through enchantment

Iewald (I-a-wald)—Talan's trusted friend; First Guardian of Pilaer

Iewald's Betrayal—Ancient historical song

Illandel (ILL-an-del) — Glaedreinn's maid

Ilse (ILSS) — Queen of Merboth, sister of Shae and Kai

Inglemarch — An Elder kingdom north of Norwood

Innyde — Queen of Westerland, an Elder kingdom, and mother of Aewen

Ironstone — Ruddy-brown sedimentary rock quarried in Westerland and used to construct buildings, pathways, and floors

Ivan (I-van) — Captain of the Sea Wanderer

Jaenell (JAY-nel) — Grandmother of Dorann and Eathnor

Jaggercat — Predatory wild cat found in the kaba forests

Jost — A weaver whose cottage stands just north of Willowa's farm in Westerland

Kaba — Giant tree that has reddish bark with healing and preservative properties

Kaeroc (KAY-rok) — Lage white bird with long tail feathers that roosts in tall trees and inhabits ruins

Kai (KI) — Guardian of Rivenn and Maeven's personal guard

Katera (Kuh-TEAR-ah) — Shae's twin sister

Keep — Innermost and strongest building or tower within a castle

Keirken (KEER-ken) — Deciduous tree with twisting trunks and spreading branches

Kindren (KIN-dren) — Race of humans with fair hair and slightly elongated eyes who came through the Gate of Life into Elderland from Anden Raven

Krei Doreinn (KRY DOR-ree-in) — Three canyons; a place where two rivers and three canyons meet

Kunrat (KOON-rat) — Descendent of Rivenn

Laesh Ebain (LAYSH e-BAYN)—Lost plains

Lammert—Shraen of Daeramor, a Kindren land, and a childhood friend of Elcon

Lancert—Major city and trade center lying north of Cobbleford in Westerland

Lanthorn (LAN-thorn)—Lantern paned with thin horn instead of glass

Last Battle of Pilaer—Battle that marked the fall of Pilaer to garn invasion

Leisht (LEESHT)—Dagger that breaks enchantments

Lenhardt (LEN-hart)—Morgorad's king

Lof Frael (LOFF FRAYL)—High prince

Lof Raelein (LOFF RAY-leen)—High queen

Lof Raena (LOFF RAY-nah)—High princess

Lof Shraen (LOFF SHRAYN—High king

Lof Yuel (LOFF YOU-el)—High One; God

Lohen Keil (LOH-hen KEEL)—Well of Light

Lute (LOOT)—Guitar-like instrument with ten strings

Lyriss—A watchguard who protects Cobbleford Castle

Lyse (LYSS)—Shae's maid at Whellein Hold

Maeg Streihcan (MAYG STRY-kan)—Broken Mountain; a lone peak rising at the eastern edge of the Plains of Rivenn

Maeg Waer (MAYG WAYR)—Forsaken Mountain; where the Cavern of Death is located

Maegrad Ceid (MAY-grad SEE-id)—Crystal Mountains; Kindren name for the Elder's Ice Mountains

Maegrad Paesad (MAY-grad PAY-sad)—Impenetrable Mountains, located in the north of Whellein

Maegran Syld (MAY-gran SILD)—Forested Hills, Kindren name for the Elder's Hills of Mist

Mael Lido (MAYL LEE-do)—Death song

Maered—A young serving girl within Cobbleford Castle

Maer Ibris (MAYR EE-bris)—Western sea

Maer Lingenn (MAYR LING-gen)—Eastern sea

Maer Syldra (MAYR SIL-dra)—Southern sea

Maer Taerat (MAYR TAY-rat)—Northern sea

Maeric (MAY-rik)—Chief Cook at Whellein Hold

Maeven (MAY-vin)—High queen of Faeraven; queen of Rivenn, Elcon's mother

Merboth—A southern coastal Kindren land

Mercedon—Father of Amberoft and Euryon's great-grandfather

Meriwen (MAIR-ee-win)—Temptress who changed the Kindren's history, mother of the Contender

Morgorad—A southern coastal Kindren land

Muer Maeread (MYOUR MAY-ree-ad)—Coast of Bones; the northwestern shore of Elderland

Murial—Aewen's nurse and maid servant

Mystael (MISS-tayl)—Craelin's silver wingabeast; Kindren for "wild wind"

Norwood (NOHR-wood)—Northerly Elder kingdom

Oalram—A guardian of Rivenn and wingabeast rider from Rivenn

Paiad Burein (PAY-ad BYOUR-ee-in)—Field of blood; a historic battleground

Pawel (PAH-wel)—Son of Daeramor; a kingdom east of Whellein

Pelsney—A guardian of Rivenn and wingabeast rider from Daeramor

Percken (PERK-en)—Rainbow-colored river fish

Perthmon—A prince of the Elder kingdom of Westerland and Aewen's oldest brother

Pilaer Hold (Pil-AYR)—Ancient stronghold of the Kindren; now a ruin

Plains of Rivenn—Grassland in Rivenn

Plaintain (Plane-tane)—Broad-leaved herb growing in most places used for drawing poison from wounds

Psaltery—A stringed instrument much like a zither used widely in the Middle Ages

Praectal (PRAYK-tawl)—Healer

Purr (PUHR)—Trees with thick trunks that grow in the desert oases

Pyrek (PY-rek)—Small, vicious bird of prey

Quinn (QUIN)—Master of White Feather Inn

Raefe—Prince of Darksea betrothed to Aewen

Raegnen (RAYG-nen)—Guaron's blue wingabeast; Kindren word for "summer rain"

Raelein (RAY-leen)—Queen

Raemwold (RAYM-wold)—King of Braeth and Maeven's father

Raena (RAY-nah)—Princess

Raven (RAY-ven)—Kingdom

Reyanna (RAY-yan-na)—Queen of Braeth and Maeven's mother

Revolt of Lancert—A conflict within Westerland that arose over a disagreement among the Elder as to whether to allow the Kindren to move closer to them after they were routed from Pilaer

Rhys—Father of Mercedon and Euryon's great-great-grandfather

Rivenn—A Kindren land lying east of Westerland and south of Chaeradon, seat of the Lof

Saethril — Black wingabeast Elcon rides in battle

Shaycat — Small, ferocious cat inhabiting forested areas throughout Elderland

Shayla — A kitchen maid within Cobbleford Castle

Shraen (High King) of Faeraven.

Siege tower — A tower on wheels with a platform below it that in medieval warfare was rolled by attackers up to a castle wall. Archers in the tower could clear the wall of defenders, and then soldiers waiting on the platform would lower a ramp to invade.

Sloewood — A southern coastal Elder kingdom

Slurry Nuts — Rich nuts from a bush growing in the boggy areas of western Elderland

Surcoat — A tunic-like garment worn over armor and often embroidered with a heraldric device such as a coat of arms

Sylder — Maid who tends Aewen

River voices — Imagined voices caused by the turning of stones in riverbeds

Roaem (ROW-em) — Eathnor's black wingabeast; Kindren for the sound thunder makes

Ruescht (ROOSCHT) — Shae's silver wingabeast; Kindren word for "rushing wind"

Sceptor of Faeraven — Symbolic staff of rulership over the alliance of Faeraven

Seighardt (SIG-hart) — Prince of Braeth and Maeven's brother

Serviceberry — Small tree or large bush with broad leaves and purple berries

Shae (SHAY) — Princess of Whellein

Shaelcon (SHALE-con) — Father of Timraen

Shaenalyn (SHAY-nah-lin) — Shae's full name

Shaenn Raven (SHAYN RAY-ven) — Afterworld

Sharten (SHAR-ten)—Dorann's gray wingabeast; Kindren for "deepening shadow"

Shil shael (SHIL SHAYL)—Hereditary soul touch

Shraen (SHRAYN)—King

Shraen Brael (SHRAYN BRAY-el)—King of the Dawn; DawnKing

Strongwood—Hardwood tree

Sweetberry—Edible berry which grows on brambles

Sword of Rivenn—Sword forged in the flames of virtue for Rivenn and handed down to his descendents

Syllid (SIL-lid)—Wood or forest in Kindren

Syllid Braechnen (SIL-lid BRAYK-nen)—A murky forest

Syllid Mueric (SIL-lid MYOUR-ik)—A beautiful and terrible forest

Taelerat (TAY-le-rat)—Shraen of Selfred

Tahera (Tah-HEAR-uh)—Aeleanor's maid

Talan (TAH-lin)—Early high king of Faeraven who captured and tamed the first wingabeast

Tallyrand—A Kindren land on the northwestern coast of Elderland

Tarrat—A steward of Rivenn

Timbrel—A small medieval hand drum, like a tambourine

Timpani (Tim-PAN-ee)—Kettledrum

Timraen (TIM-rain)—High king of Faeraven; king of Rivenn; Maeven's husband

Triboan (TRI-bone)—Southern land occupied by garns

Trillilium Castle—Seat of Darksea, an Elder kingdom

Turret (TUR-et)—Small projecting tower

Unibeast (UN-i-beest)—Unicorn

Vale of Shadows—Enchanted forest valley wreathed in clinging mists and located in the heart of the kaba forest on the border of Rivenn and Westerland. Forsaken by most wildlife, it swarms with insects. A branch of weild Aenor cuts through the Vale of Shadows.

Vanora—Daughter of Devlon, King of Darksea

Varaedel (Ve-RAY-del)—Glindenn's Shraen

Viadrel (VY-ah-drel)—Flames of Virtue

Waeven (WAY-ven)—Spider-like animal

Walls of Death—Enclosed passageway that could be shut off to capture attackers

Ward—Environ within a castle; also known as a bailey

Watchguard—In Elder kingdoms, members of the garrison assigned to keep watch over the castle walls and gatehouse

Watergate—Gate leading to and from a body of water

Weild (WEELD)—River

Weild Aenar (WEELD AY-e-nar)—Wild River

Weild Rivenn (WEELD RIV-en)—Rivenn's River

Weild Whistan (WEELD WHIS-stan)—White River; Kindren name for the Elder's White Feather River

Weilo (WY-lo)—Tree with weeping branches and long leaves that grows beside a river or in damp places

Weilton (WEEL-ton)—A guardian of Rivenn

Weithein Faen (WY-then FANE)—An estuary

Welke (WELL-key)—Giant creature of prey that is a cross between a dinosaur and a bird

Westerland—Western Elder kingdom

Whellein—Kindren land lying northeast of Rivenn

Whhst—Soothing sound of endearment made by the Elder

Whirlight (WHIR-lite)—Large; ungainly white bird

Whispan (WHIS-span)—Small tree with lacy white foliage

Whistledown—A coastal Elder kingdom

Whyst (WHIST)—A spirit sword, defends both flesh and spirit

Willet—A diminutive owl found in the north lands

Willowa—A huntsman's wife and maker of soap who is the mother of Caedmon, residing in Westerland

Wingabeast (WING-ah-beest)—Winged horses

Wingen (WING-en)—Small, colorful bird

Wreckers—Elder who lure ships to their doom

Yellowroot—Edible tuber

Thank you for purchasing this Harbourlight title. For other inspirational stories, please visit our on-line bookstore at www.pelicanbookgroup.com.

For questions or more information, contact us at customer@pelicanbookgroup.com.

Harbourlight Books
The Beacon in Christian Fiction™
an imprint of Pelican Ventures Book Group
www.pelicanbookgroup.com

May God's glory shine through
this inspirational work of fiction.

AMDG

CPSIA information can be obtained at www.ICGtesting.com
Printed in the USA
BVOW04s1224060214

344021BV00002B/19/P